"I can live without being called 'Mistress,'"

Rachel said with determined composure.

"As you please, Rachel Lindsey." Jamie liked the sound of the name on his tongue. He had guessed she'd be called something more elegant, more exotic, the way she was herself, but now he'd never imagine her as anything other than Rachel. Rachel *Sparhawk* Lindsey. Lord, when was the last time he'd gone moony over a woman's name?

He let his bemusement slide drowsily across his face. "You wanted to trust me when I was dead to the world. But do you trust me now, I wonder?"

She didn't hesitate. "Not in the least."

"Good lass," he murmured. "Not only beautiful, but wise you are, too, Rachel Lindsey. Don't you ever trust me, not for a moment."

Then he smiled, and the sudden, devastating warmth of it was enough to steal Rachel's breath away....

Dear Reader,

Miranda Jarrett's last title, *Sparhawk's Angel*, earned her 5★s from *Affaire de Coeur*, 5♥s from *Booklovers*, and a special mention in Kathe Robin's "Tête à Tête" page in *Romantic Times*. And we are already receiving good reports back about her eagerly awaited new book, this month's *Gift of the Heart*. Be sure to take home this touching story set in the wilds of the New York frontier where a woman, abandoned by her no-good husband, discovers happiness in the arms of a fugitive haunted by his past.

Beauty and the Beast is a new Regency tale by Taylor Ryan, who made her debut during our 1996 March Madness promotion of talented new authors. Don't miss this wonderful story of a troubled nobleman who is badgered into health by an interfering young neighbor.

We are also so pleased to welcome back award-winning author Dallas Schulze with her long-awaited Western, *Short Straw Bride*, the heartwarming tale of a couple who marry for practical reasons, only to fall head over heels in love. As well as Reader's Choice Award winner Laurie Grant with her new medieval novel, *My Lady Midnight*, the intriguing story of a Norman widow who becomes a political pawn when she is forced to go undercover as a governess in the home of the baron she believes responsible for the death of her best friend.

We hope you'll keep a lookout for all four titles wherever Harlequin Historicals are sold.

Sincerely,

Tracy Farrell
Senior Editor

Please address questions and book requests to:
Harlequin Reader Service
U.S.: 3010 Walden Ave., P.O. Box 1325, Buffalo, NY 14269
Canadian: P.O. Box 609, Fort Erie, Ont. L2A 5X3

Miranda Jarrett

Gift of the Heart

Harlequin Books

TORONTO • NEW YORK • LONDON
AMSTERDAM • PARIS • SYDNEY • HAMBURG
STOCKHOLM • ATHENS • TOKYO • MILAN
MADRID • WARSAW • BUDAPEST • AUCKLAND

ISBN 0-373-28941-3

GIFT OF THE HEART

MIRANDA JARRETT

was an award-winning designer and art director before turning to writing full-time, and considers herself sublimely fortunate to have a career that combines history and happy endings, even if it's one that's also made her family regular patrons of the local pizzeria. A descendant of early settlers in New England, she feels a special kinship with her popular fictional family, the Sparhawks of Rhode Island.

Miranda and her husband—a musician and songwriter—live near Philadelphia with their two young children and two old cats. During what passes for spare time she paints watercolor landscapes, bakes French chocolate cakes and whips up the occasional last-minute Halloween costume.

Miranda herself admits that it's hard to keep track of all the Sparhawk family members, and she has prepared a family tree to help, including which characters appear in each book. She loves to hear from readers, and if you write to her and enclose a self-addressed stamped envelope, she'll send you a copy of the family tree along with her reply. Her address: P.O. Box 1102, Paoli, PA 19301-1145.

Prologue

Tryon County, New York
November, 1778

He didn't want to die alone.

Not like this, not hidden beneath the shadows of the tallest trees, unmourned, unburied save for the drifting snow that would cover his body only until the wolves found him. Or the Senecas. Better the wolves.

Jamie forced himself to take another step, and another, the prints left behind in the snow staggered like a drunkard's. If Butler's men were tracking him, they could do it with one eye closed and the other asleep, but Jamie was far past being able to stop them.

The ball from Sergeant Herrick's pistol had gone clear through his left shoulder, and the wound had seemed clean enough. Jamie was a large man, strong, and he'd survived worse. Because he'd been on the trail with the other Rangers, he had plenty of ground meal and dried beef in his hunting pouch, and as long as he stayed within sight of the Mohawk River to the north, he'd keep his bearings, regardless of the snow.

But by the third day the wound had been clearly festering, and the fever had taken him soon after the snow had begun. Now when he looked down at the rifle in his hands, the barrel iced with a fine line of snow, he couldn't tell if his fingers shook from the cold or the ague.

But his mother would know the remedy for that, and how to draw the poison from the gunshot wound, too. He would hold the lantern high for her while she stood on a chair to sort through the bundles of dried herbs and barks that hung from the rafters upstairs, clucking her tongue and frowning a little as her long, graceful fingers sought exactly what she'd need.

Then she'd toss the leaves into the little iron pot with the mended leg and simmer them into a draught, or maybe she'd grind and mix them into a poultice. Whichever it was, he'd submit manfully, sitting in the straight-backed bench near the window in the kitchen without flinching or grimacing as an example to his little brother, Sam. Besides, when his shoulder was finally cleaned and bandaged, his mother would reward him with squash pie, not so much a slice of it as a slab, with sweet thickened cream puddled around golden custard on the red earthenware plate.

Somewhere ahead a branch snapped off beneath the weight of the snow, a loud crack in the white silence, and belatedly Jamie's numbed reflexes took over and he lifted his rifle to his eye. But there was nothing, no Senecas or soldiers or gold squash pie on a red plate, only more bare, black trees against the endless snow.

With a groan of frustration and pain, he once again rubbed his thumb into his eyes. He didn't want to slip into another fever-dream of home. He couldn't afford to. Only dying men thought of their mothers and the places they'd lived as boys. After battles he'd heard too many final, garbled recollections from other soldiers to doubt it. He wasn't going to die, not yet, and he wasn't going to think of his mother, wiping her hands on her green apron before she smoothed his hair back from his forehead and—

Damnation, it was the fever, that was all! That stone house on the hill wasn't theirs anymore and hadn't been for over two years, not since his father had stood up in their Meeting and spoken out against this desolate, destructive war. A Quaker who had counseled peace instead of bloodletting, he had been branded a traitor for his beliefs by the same Congress that promised freedom. The Ryders had lost their house, lost the land that had been in their family for generations. There was no longer an attic filled with pungent, healing herbs, no bench beneath the kitchen window worn smooth by five generations of Ryders, no more of the pie his mother was cutting with the horn-handled knife, the butter crust flaking and crumbling the same way it would on his tongue—*no!*

Jamie shook his head with desperation, the snow dropping in heavy clots from his hat's brim. He guessed it was nearly nightfall, and if he didn't find some sort of shelter, a cave or empty trapper's hut, he wouldn't survive until dawn. He didn't deserve the comfort of memories now. Better to remember why he was running. Better to think of what he'd done and what he hadn't, of why he'd been shot and why he'd be hung if the soldiers caught him. Or the tall Seneca brave with the feathered scalp lock, the one who'd reached the children first. Better to let the grief and horror of all he'd seen eat at his conscience and sharpen his senses to survive.

God preserve him, he didn't want to die alone.

Chapter One

"Hang *on*, Billy!"

Exasperated, Rachel dropped the milking bucket onto the snow-covered path before her and hoisted the giggling toddler higher onto her shoulders. Why did Billy insist on bringing his stuffed calico horse everywhere they went, even the forty feet from the house to the cow shed? Of course, clutching Blackie would seem more important than hanging on to her shoulders, and much funnier, too.

"You're a wriggly little weasel, Billy Lindsey," scolded Rachel good-naturedly as she bent to pick up the buckets again. "Don't you let go again, mind?"

She couldn't really blame Billy for not wanting to ride on her back like a baby anymore. By summer's end he'd been nearly able to outrun her to the orchard, and for his third birthday in October she'd cut and sewn him his first pair of breeches, though he still came to her for help with the buttons. Now with winter here he needed real boots or shoes of his own, the kind she remembered the little boys in Providence and Newport wearing, not the deerskin moccasins he had on his feet now.

Just because they lived so far from town didn't mean he had to grow up wild.

But shoes and boots cost money, more money than she was ever likely to see with William off to war. Not that there'd been much when her husband had still been here on the farm, either. Once they'd left Providence, William had been as chary with money as he was with affection, and far too free with criticism and the back of his hand. With a long sigh she headed off to the barn, her skirts dragging through the new snow and her feet sliding in an old pair of William's boots, the toes stuffed with wool.

She shouldn't complain, not even in her own thoughts. Last winter had been hard because it had been her first here on the farm, and she'd been alone, too, except for Billy. This year would be better. She knew what to expect, and she'd be prepared. She wasn't the same girlish bride she'd been then, full of silly romantic dreams. No, because of William, that part of her was gone forever.

And what of it? she asked herself fiercely. What good came from lamenting what couldn't be changed? If she'd lost her old dreams, she'd found new ones to replace them. She paused long enough to look across the wide sweep of the land, theirs—*hers*—clear to the silver band of the river, feeling the same swell of pride and love she felt when she watched Billy. The sky was so blue it almost hurt to look at it, the new snow white and perfect. How dare she feel sorry for herself on a morning like this? She smiled and bounced Billy to make him laugh as they made their way down the path.

Because she'd taken the time to sweep her front step clear of snow she was late tending to her cow, and as she tugged the door across the little drift of snow Rachel could hear Juno lowing restlessly. At once Billy slid from her back and ran after the rooster and his hens, waving Blackie wildly at the fleeing chickens.

"Good day to you, my lady Juno," said Rachel to the russet cow. "I trust you passed the night tolerably well?"

Yet she frowned as she scratched the cow's velvety nose in greeting, and glanced back uneasily at the planked door. She'd been sure she'd latched that door tightly when she'd finished milking last night, yet this morning the bar had been dangling free. No wonder the animals seemed so skittish. If she wasn't more careful she'd lose her "lady" as well as her poultry to wolves or mountain cats.

"*Mama!*" Billy's frantic, frightened wail drew Rachel at once. She rushed around to the far side of the manger to where he'd chased the chickens, and lifted him into her arms.

"There now, love, all's well," she murmured, stroking his soft gold hair as he burrowed his face into her shoulder. "I wasn't far. You couldn't see me, that was all. I was here the whole time."

But the little boy only wept harder as Rachel strove to comfort him, rocking from side to side. What could have frightened him so badly on such a bright, sun-filled morning? Finally Billy lifted his head with a shuddering sob and dared to peek around Rachel's shoulder. What he saw made him howl again, and cling as tightly as he could to Rachel.

"What could it possibly be, child?" she said as she turned, too. "There's nothing—oh, God in heaven!"

From where she stood the man looked dead, sprawled across the straw where he'd fallen, but still Rachel wished she had her musket with her. The man's own rifle lay beside him where it had slipped free of his hand, and before she could change her mind Rachel put Billy down and darted forward to pick up the gun. Holding it in both hands, she felt better; living alone had given her a greater respect for firearms.

She was sure this stranger was—or had been—some sort of soldier. Though he was dressed like most men who spent their lives in the wilderness—a white blanketlike coat with indigo stripes, deerskin leggings and hunting shirt over another of checked linen, a long knife in a beaded sheath at his waist, a wide-brimmed hat with a turkey feather in the brim, and everything soaked with melted snow—the tomahawk hanging from his belt told another story.

Troubling, too, was the extra powder horn slung around his chest and another bag for shot and wadding, far more ammunition than any common trapper or wanderer would carry. The rifle in her hands was much finer, too, with a cherry-wood barrel inlaid with stars and elegant engraving on the plate. German made, she guessed, or maybe Philadelphia, but too valuable for most of the men in this part of New York.

Still the man didn't move. Carefully she knelt beside him, Billy clinging to her skirts. The shoulder of the stranger's coat was stained dark with dried blood, the ragged hole in the fabric doubtless matching one in him, and sadly she wondered how he'd come to be in such a sorry state.

He was younger than she'd first thought, no more than twenty-five or thirty, his jaw and mouth hidden by a fortnight's growth of beard. His hair was long and untied, the ends curling over his collar, and the rich, burnished color of chestnuts. His features were strong and even, his nose and cheekbones marked with a scattering of freckles nearly lost on his weatherworn skin, freckles too boyish for the hard living that showed in every inch of his face.

A handsome man, admitted Rachel reluctantly, the kind of man who turned ladies' heads with a smile and a wink. But dead or alive, he wouldn't turn hers. She'd had enough of that with William, and she wouldn't make the same mistake again.

"Mama?" asked Billy, all his doubts—and hers, too—clear enough to Rachel in that single word. What *was* she going to do with the man? Much as she wished he hadn't come stumbling into her life, she couldn't very well leave him here. Tentatively she reached out to touch his neck to find his pulse, if one still was there to find. She slipped her fingers inside his collar, his hair curling so familiarly around her wrist that she almost jerked away. Foolish, she chided herself angrily, foolish, *foolish*, to draw away from the meaningless touch of an unconscious man!

His skin was as hot as the snow in the fields was cold, and though she now knew he lived she wondered for how much longer, burning with a fever like this. As her fingers pressed against the side of his neck he groaned, the vibrations of it passing to her fingertips. Billy yelped and retreated behind the manger, and Rachel wished she could, too.

"Hush, Billy, he can't hurt you," she said, reassuring herself as much as the child. She bent over the man, keeping his rifle in her hand just to be sure. "He won't be hurting anyone for a good long time."

She had to get him into the house where the fire would warm him, and where she could tend to his wound. But though she was tall for a woman, he still looked to have half a foot advantage over her, and Lord only knew how much more he weighed. More than she alone could drag along the snowy path to the house, that she knew for sure.

"Sir? Can you hear me, sir?" she asked uncertainly. The man didn't move again. "I want to take you back to the house so I can tend you properly, but you're going to have to help me some."

Suddenly Billy ran forward to the wounded man. With a shriek of bravado and indignation at being ignored by Rachel, he thumped his stuffed horse as hard as he could on the man's chest. The man's eyes flew open and he twisted and gasped with agony, but at the same time his hand groped reflexively for his knife.

"Billy, *no!*" Frantically Rachel pulled the boy away and shoved him behind her as she raised the rifle. Her heart pounding, her gaze met that of the stranger's over the long barrel of the weapon. His eyes were blue, as blue as the sky outside, and filled now with confusion and pain. He blinked twice, his breath coming hard. He opened his shaking fingers and let the knife drop from them into the straw.

"I would not harm the boy," he said slowly, painfully. Despite the cold, his forehead was glazed with sweat. "You must believe me."

"I've no reason to believe anything of the sort." With her toe Rachel kicked the knife across the floor. "I'm willing to help you, but no trickery."

"You are...kind." The man tried to smile, his mouth curving crookedly and with more charm than any man so close to death had a right to. But Rachel didn't lower the rifle. The bluest eyes she'd ever seen and a smile to make angels weep weren't reasons enough for her to trust him.

"And you," he said, every word labored, "you won't kill me with my own gun?"

With a sniff Rachel took the rifle from her shoulder. "Can you stand?"

"If you say I must." With enormous effort and a groan he couldn't suppress, he rolled over onto his knees and stayed there, his breath ragged. Rachel's resolve wavered. Handsome or not, the man was weak from pain and lost blood, and he deserved her help.

Sighing, she leaned his rifle against the wall, opened the barn door and bent to slide her arm around his waist. Gratefully he put his arm across her shoulder and with a grunt managed to stand upright. Together they swayed unsteadily, the man's weight almost too much for Rachel to manage. Having Billy clinging jealously to one of her knees didn't help her balance one bit, either.

"Where's your man?" the stranger asked when they'd managed to hobble to the wall for him to rest.

Rachel chewed on her lower lip, considering how best to answer. Most likely the man wanted to know if there was someone larger and more able to help him, but even weak as he was, she didn't want him knowing exactly how alone she and Billy were.

"My husband's not here at present," she answered stiffly. With her arm around his waist, she was acutely aware of the man's size, how he seemed all lean muscle and bone and sinew. Seventeen months had passed since William had left, seventeen months without feeling a man's body pressed this closely to hers. "But I expect him back directly."

The man glanced down at her beneath his long lashes. "Which army is he with?"

"American, of course, though—" She broke off, shamed by how easily he'd discovered the truth. "You're a soldier, too, aren't you? Is that how you were wounded, in a battle?"

"Aye, in a battle." His voice was flat, so unemotional that Rachel guessed he had secrets of his own to hide. So be it; she'd respect that. But she couldn't deny that she was curious about who he was and where he'd come from, why he hadn't told her his name or asked hers either, and if the battle he'd fought would draw the war closer to her home. She'd simply have to wait until he told her himself, that was all. If he was like William, the next words from his mouth would be bragging and boasting about himself.

But somehow already she knew this man wasn't at all like her husband.

"You go." Billy looked suspiciously up the man's long legs to his face. "You leave Mama alone an' *go.*"

The man smiled again. "I'm trying my best, lad." He pushed away from the wall with a grunt, leaning heavily on Rachel. "If you can spare something warm—broth or cider—I'd be obliged, and then I won't trouble you further. I've tarried here long enough."

"All the hot cider in this county couldn't make you fit to travel," scoffed Rachel. "You'll stay here until you're able to move on."

He looked at her warily, in a way that reminded Rachel of how he'd evaded her question about the army. "Nay, you are kind, but I can't ask you to shelter me."

"You didn't ask. I offered." And only common hospitality made her offer, she reassured herself. Blue eyes and the neat way her body fit next to his had nothing to do with it. "There's precious few white folks in these lands, and we all do for each other. I wouldn't want to think of you perishing by yourself in the woods."

"So I won't be alone after all, will I?" He might have laughed; the sound was so hollow that Rachel couldn't tell. "How far to your house?"

"Not far." Not far to her, thought Rachel grimly, but for him the short path would seem like forty miles instead of forty feet. She could feel the heat of the fever burning through his heavy clothing, and she suspected he was a great deal sicker than he wanted her to know. "Not far at all."

The man nodded. "What's the horse's name?"

"Horse?" repeated Rachel, mystified. When William had left, he'd taken the one horse they'd owned.

"Aye, the lad's."

"Oh, Blackie." Realizing belatedly that the man meant the stuffed horse that Billy was swinging purposefully in his hand only made her wonder more. Why under the circumstances should any man ask about a child's toy?

"Blackie's my horse an' she's my Mama." His jaw set stubbornly and his small fist balled possessively in Rachel's skirts, Billy glared up at the man who was claiming far too much of Rachel's attention. "Now you *go!*"

"Your Blackie's a fine horse, lad," answered the man with a seriousness neither Billy nor Rachel expected. "'Tis shameful to see him bound up in here with the cows. You'd best take him outside. Go on, lad. Show me how fast you and your horse can run!"

For a moment Billy looked at Rachel, clearly amazed by the freedom he'd just been given, and then he was gone, off through the open door as fast as his short legs, and Blackie, would carry him.

Trapped beneath the stranger's arm, Rachel was powerless to stop him. "You've no right to do that! He's scarce more than a babe!"

"He'll be well enough, and you know it." Resolutely the man took a tentative step, swayed unsteadily and grimaced with the pain. "Better than I will, anyways."

He was right. By the time he and Rachel finally reached the little log house, the man's face was white as the snow, his shirts soaked through with sweat, and he'd long ago stopped trying to talk. Rachel steered him toward the bed she'd shared with William in the house's single room, and the man collapsed on it without a word, already past consciousness.

Quickly Rachel stripped away his damp clothing, striving to be briskly efficient and feel nothing else. Until she knew for certain that William was dead, she was still his wife, and she'd no business beyond compassion touching another man's body.

And he would need all the compassion she could give, for the man had already slipped beyond the limits of her healing skills. As soon as she cut away his shirt she saw that the wound in his shoulder was worse than she'd feared, the skin around it purple and angry with infection. While Billy watched, she tended the man as best she could and covered him with three coverlets to keep him warm and help break the fever.

"He's hurt," said Billy sadly, his small face serious with concern and his jealousy forgotten after the euphoria of running free through the snow to the house.

"I'm afraid he is, Billy," said Rachel softly. She lifted the boy into her arms and hugged him, the feel of his warm little body in her arms comforting to her as she held him close. "He's hurt and very, very sick, and your mama can't do anything more but hope and pray that he'll get better."

Through the rest of the day she stayed close to the man's bedside, hoping he'd wake and speak to her again, or at least take some of the soup she made to help him build back his strength. Past sundown, after she'd put Billy to bed, the man stirred restlessly, and she flew to kneel on the floor beside the bed. He muttered odd fragments that made no sense to her, speaking of his mother and someone named Sam and then, though Rachel wasn't sure, asking for a piece of pie. Yet too

soon he stilled again, moving deeper into unconscious-
ness, and as she listened to his labored breathing
through the long night, Rachel knew to her sorrow he'd
likely be dead before morning.

She didn't know when she fell asleep in the spindle-
back chair by the fire. She dreamed that winter was over
and spring had come, the apple trees in the orchard a
mass of pink and white flowers and the warm air fragrant with their scent. She was sitting on a coverlet with
the stranger on the grass, laughing merrily.

Because it was a dream, she didn't wonder that the
man was strong and healthy again, his blue eyes bright
and teasing, or that she was wearing her favorite gown
from when she'd been Miss Rachel Sparhawk of Providence Plantations, the rose-colored silk lutestring that
had no place on a farm. Still laughing, the man reached
out to smooth back her black hair and tuck a sprig of
apple blossoms behind her ear. With his hand still gently
beneath her chin, he drew her face close to his and
kissed her.

Abruptly Rachel awakened. The hearth fire had
burned low, and the house was cold, the sick man's
ragged breathing still echoing in the little house. Shivering, she put another log on the fire and fanned it
bright, then turned to look first at the sleeping boy on
the trundle, curled safely in the little nest of his quilt,
and then at the man in her bed.

Gently she swept the fever-damp hair back from his
forehead, her smile tight. Sometime while she'd slept,
Billy had come and placed Blackie on the pillow beside
the man's head.

Tears blurred her eyes, tears she had no right to shed. To be alone on the farm held no fears for her now; she'd welcomed the solitude when William had left. But why had it taken this stranger to remind her again that the price of being alone was loneliness?

Chapter Two

Jamie was weak, Lord help him, he was so weak and
wasted that to raise his heavy eyelids even this much was
more than he thought possible. But if he did, he could
see the woman kneading the bread dough on the long
wooden table, her hands and forearms white with flour,
and for one glimpse of that he would have dragged
himself through the snow to Albany and back.

She was so beautiful that at first he'd wondered if she
was real or only one more groundless fever-dream. She
was tall and graceful as she went about her tasks in the
little cabin, her figure rounded but neat, the bow of her
apron emphasizing the narrow span of her waist.
Strange how often he'd focused on that bow when the
pain had burned him the worst, struggling to concentrate on something, anything, but his own tortured
body.

And damnation, she had made it almost easy. On the
first night he remembered her coming to him by light of
the fire alone, bending over him so her unbound hair,
black as a moonless night, had rippled over her shoulders. Her fingertips had been cool as she'd gently, so

gently, stroked his cheek above his beard. Then he had seen the color of her eyes in the firelight, the same bright green as young maples in the spring, and with feverish fascination he had watched as the little gold hoops with carnelian drops that she wore in her ears swung gently against the full curve of her cheek.

She'd saved his life, he knew that, but his pleasure in her company ran deeper than that alone. After all the ugliness and suffering he'd seen in these past two years since the war had become his life, her beauty was a balm to his soul, healing and easing him as much as the broth and herb possets she'd spooned between his parched lips.

Not that he'd a right to it, not for a moment. He knew that, too. After what he'd done, he deserved no beauty, no sweetness, no comfort at all.

Fiercely he reminded himself that he knew nothing of the woman's allegiances, nor those of her husband's. She was kind, she was beautiful, but he'd seen before how hatred could make other kind, beautiful women turn on their enemies. For all he knew she'd kept him alive only to be able to claim the bounty Butler offered for his capture.

"More milk, Mama," said the little boy, waving his battered pewter mug imperiously as he tugged on his mother's skirts for her attention. She turned and glanced so meaningfully at the cup that, mystified, he looked inside before he realized what she intended. Then he grinned, and held the empty cup out again. "More, *please*, Mama!"

Jamie watched as the woman smiled and bent to wipe the smudged jam from the boy's mouth, and a fresh wave of guilt and sorrow swept over his soul as he thought of another boy, one who would never again be treated to blackberry jam and corn bread or a mother's kiss to his sticky cheek. He closed his eyes again, desperately wishing it was as easy to shut out the memory of the past.

He would leave now, today. There was no other way.

Through sheer will he raised himself up on his uninjured arm. "Friend," he began, his voice croaking from disuse, "I must thank you."

With a startled gasp she turned toward him, her green eyes turning wary as she shoved the child behind the shelter of her skirts.

"You're awake." She brushed away a strand of hair from her forehead with the heel of her hand, forgetting the flour that left a powdery streak against the black waves. "Heaven help me, I knew this would happen when your fever broke yesterday."

"Don't rejoice too much," said Jamie dryly, wincing as he shifted higher against the pillows. "Given a choice, I'd rather I'd waked than not."

"I didn't mean it like that," said Rachel quickly. Though it had made more work for her when he'd been ill, she was doubly glad now that she'd put him to bed in his breeches and shirt. "I wouldn't have tended to you at all if I didn't wish you to live."

"Or given me your bed?"

Rachel drew back sharply, her face turning hot at what he implied. How much did he remember of what she'd murmured to him as he'd tossed with fever and pain? Unconscious, he had been only a lost, wounded man who would most likely die despite her efforts, and in her loneliness she had caught herself pouring out her heart into his unhearing ears. At least, then she'd believed he hadn't heard. But now, under the keen, unsettling gaze of his blue eyes, she wasn't certain of anything.

"This isn't an inn with a bed to suit every traveler," she said defensively. "You were too ill to sleep on the floor, and too large for the trundle."

"The floor would have suited me well enough," he said gruffly, wondering what devil had made him mention the bed at all. He'd meant to thank her, not insult her. "I didn't ask for your man's place."

"What makes you think you have it now?" Lord help her, why hadn't she kept her mouth shut? Furiously she began wiping the flour from her hands onto her apron. No man could ever fill the empty place William had ripped in her heart, nor would she let another come close enough to try. She'd no intention of making a mistake like that again. "A husband's considerably more than a valley worn deep in a feather bed."

"I never said otherwise," replied Jamie softly, responding more to the unmistakable pain in her eyes than to her words. "So you miss him that much, then?"

But even as Rachel opened her mouth to correct the stranger, she realized the folly of telling the truth. Hadn't she said enough already? She knew nothing for certain of this man, not even his name. She was miles from any neighbor or friend, doubly bound in by the snow. Better to let him believe that she loved William fervently, better still to hint that he was expected home again at any time.

"Of course I miss him," she said carefully. "He's my husband, and this is his home. I pray for his safe return soon, before Christmas and the worst snows."

"Then he's a fortunate man, your husband," said Jamie with a heartiness he didn't feel.

"He is." Rachel nodded, a single swift motion of her chin to mask her bitterness. William *was* lucky, barbarously lucky; she was the one that fortune had frowned upon. "He always has been."

"Luck of any kind is a great gift in this war." Jamie sighed, trying to remember what else, if anything, she'd told him about her husband beyond that he was away with the rebel army. Not that it mattered. He meant to be gone long before the most fortunate husband returned.

She was watching him warily, stroking the little boy's flaxen hair over and over with the palm of her hand, more to calm herself than the child. By the firelight her eyes were as green as he remembered, and unconsciously she swallowed and ran her tongue around her lips to moisten them.

Oh, aye, her husband was a fortunate man. Afraid that his expression would betray his own despondency, Jamie looked away from her face to the boy at her side and smiled. The child reminded him of his brother, Sam, his cheeks rosy and plump and his little chin marked with the same resolute stubbornness.

Like Sam, and not like the boy he'd abandoned in Cherry Valley....

"How's the horse, lad?" he asked, jerking himself back to the present. "How's Blackie?"

The boy's eyes lit with excitement. "Blackie's a good horse!" he declared eagerly, wiggling free of his mother's hand and the safety of her skirts so he could stare more openly at this fascinating stranger who was finally awake. "Blackie's my horse, and he's very, very fast!"

Jamie nodded sagely. "Fast as lightning, too, I recall. But mind, now, Billy, that you keep Blackie—"

"*No.*" Swiftly Rachel caught Billy by the shoulders and pulled him back. "I won't have you hurt him."

"I meant the lad no harm—"

"But you *will* hurt him with your careless kindness, as surely as if you used your knife!" With a fierce possessiveness she held Billy close, smoothing her fingers over the fine, babyish ringlets that she couldn't bear to cut. "The child's too young to remember his own father, and weeks pass when he sees no one but me. Then you appear, smiling and asking questions about his horse as if you *care.* Little enough it means to you, but what will he think when you vanish from his life as suddenly as you came?"

"You coddle the lad too much," he said, more sharply than he'd intended, but her vehemence stung. He'd never meant to hurt her boy; he'd never meant to hurt any child. "But it's of no matter. I'll be gone before it is."

Impatiently he shifted toward the nearest narrow window, the only one with the shutter drawn for light. By the height of the sun he guessed it was midmorning, later than he wished, but there would still be enough daylight hours left to make a start. He touched his shoulder, lightly prodding the bandage over the wound, and sucked in his breath as the dull ache changed abruptly to a raw stab of pain.

The woman clucked her tongue with disapproval. "There, now, see for yourself how badly you're hurt. You can bluster all you wish, but you won't be leaving until that's healed. Another week at least."

Jamie scowled, striving to hide the pain that was finally receding. "Don't you think I'll be the better judge of that?"

For the first time she dared to square her gaze to meet his eyes. But was she daring him, wondered Jamie, or herself?

"You're a man," she declared, "which is as much to say that you haven't a blessed trace of sense where your own weakness is concerned. So, no, I don't think you're a good judge at all. Why, I doubt you could even lift that fancy rifle of yours this morning, let alone hold it steady enough to fire."

He wasn't about to admit she was right. "There's more to that rifle than looks alone. With it I can shoot the seeds from an apple at a hundred paces."

"I don't doubt that you can," she said. "But you can't do it now, and you won't ever do it again unless—"

"Someone's here." Jamie jerked his hand up to silence her as he strained his ears to listen. "One horse, one rider. Where's my gun?"

Rachel rushed to the window, anxiously wiping away a corner of the frost with the hem of her apron to peer outside. What she saw made her mutter one of her seafaring father's favorite imprecations under her breath as her whole face tightened.

"What's amiss? Where's my rifle?" demanded Jamie, struggling to shove himself free of the coverlet. "If you think I'm going to lie here like a trussed turkey-cock while you—"

"Hush, now, you won't be needing your gun just yet." She smiled grimly as she reached for her cloak from the peg on the back of the door. "'Tis only my husband's brother, and if anyone's going to pepper Alec's backside, I plan to be first. But you needn't worry. I'll send him on his way soon enough."

She swung the cloak over her shoulders, trying to decide whether to bring Billy with her or not. There was an even chance that he'd babble to Alec about the stranger, but she wasn't sure she wanted to risk leaving him behind in the house, either. With a sigh she reached down and yanked the quilt from the trundle bed, wrapped it around Billy and scooped him, wriggling, onto the curve of her hip. Finally, with her free hand, she took one of the pair of long-barreled muskets that hung, loaded and ready, beside the door.

A new layer of snow had fallen in the night, not more than an inch or two on what already lay on the ground, but enough to soften the edges of the paths Rachel had shoveled and swept from the house to the barn. She walked forward only a dozen paces from the house, unwilling to go any farther to greet or encourage Alec, and set Billy down at her feet.

"Listen to me, Billy," she whispered, bending to the height of the child's ear. "This is important. We must not say a word about the poor man inside, or Uncle Alec may try to hurt him more. Not a single word, love, not even a peep like a baby chick's. Do you understand? Shush!''

She laid her forefinger first across her lips and then across Billy's, miming the silence she prayed he would keep.

"Shush, Mama," he whispered back solemnly, hunching his shoulders beneath the quilt as he pressed his own finger across his lips. "I'm *quiet!*"

"Thank you, love, that's all I ask," she whispered as she gave him a little squeeze. "You're Mama's good boy."

She knew her request wouldn't be a hard one for Billy to obey. At best Alec had treated his nephew as an inconvenient nuisance, and even as a baby Billy had wisely learned to keep from his uncle's path.

She straightened, lifting the musket to her shoulder. Long ago her father had insisted that she and her sisters learn how to load and fire a gun, but it was only since she'd come here as William's wife that she'd been forced to put her skills to the test.

Not that Alec would be any kind of test; his visits were more of a trial that sent her heart to pounding with dread. She hadn't expected him to come again until spring, when the snow was gone and the journey from his own cabin could be made in two hours instead of four. Carefully she kept her face impassive as he labored up the hill toward her, digging his bootheels into the sides of his weary horse. Most men would have dismounted and led the animal through the drifted snow, or at least found an easier path, but the only other man that Alec Lindsey resembled was his brother—and her husband—William.

And the resemblance was disturbingly strong. The same pale gold hair above arched brows, the same squared jaw turning soft from drink and the same slightly bored expression to his gentlemanly features that could so easily turn to sullenness, the fashionably cut coat of imported broadcloth beneath the heavy overcoat—all of it nearly a mirror to William.

Once Rachel had congratulated herself on marrying into a family with such handsome, charming men, but that was when she'd believed as well in the elegant country seat that the Lindsey brothers promised was the centerpiece of their vast estates here to the west of the Hudson, and well before she'd learned that the only thing vast about the Lindseys were the lies that slipped so easily from their lips.

She took a deep breath to calm herself, and flexed her fingers against the icy metal of the flintlock. "You can just turn yourself directly about, Alec," she shouted when she was certain he was near enough to hear. "I told you before you weren't welcome here any longer."

"And a good day to you, sister!" Alec raised his beaver tricorn, dusted with snow, and gallantly swept it across his breast. "But pray put aside the musket, my lady. It's not a greeting I particularly fancy."

"The musket stays, Alec, for I intend neither to greet you nor to tease your fancy," she called back. "Now, away with you, and off my land before I'm tempted to try my marksmanship."

"The only thing you're trying, Rachel, is my patience." With a grunt he swung his leg over the saddle and dropped heavily to the snowy ground. "You'll thank me when you learn why I've come."

"If it's more of your self-styled help, Alec, I want none of it." Though she didn't dare look away from her brother-in-law, she could feel how Billy shrank uneasily against her leg.

"You wanted it readily enough last year," said Alec, his breath coming in great gusts in the icy air as he trudged through the snow. "And this past autumn, too. Who saw to it that you'd firewood to last through the snows, eh?"

"Only half of what you promised," she declared, but grudgingly she rehooked the catch on the flintlock and lowered the gun. Though she hated to admit it, she wouldn't have survived last winter without his assistance. It was what he'd expected in return that had made his charity so loathsome, and her position so complicated now. "What is it this time Alec?"

He stopped a half-dozen paces away and smiled with the full force of his considerable charm. "A chance to gild our pockets, Rachel. Twenty dollars, all going begging. You won't say nay to that when times are so hard now, will you, sister?"

"No one lets gold go begging, hard times or not," answered Rachel suspiciously. "Especially not you. The truth, Alec, plain and simple."

Seeing how little charm was getting him, Alec jammed his hat squarely on his head and spat into the snow. "The truth, Rachel, is that one of those bloody Tory Rangers lost his head in the middle of a battle, quarreling over a woman or some other plunder. Shot an officer dead without so much as a by-your-leave. At least, that's what they're saying at Volk's."

"Oh, my, what's said at Volk's," she scoffed. "Why do you think I'd care about your tavern tattle?" But despite the scorn she poured on his words, she did care. She cared very much, more with every second as she waited with dread for what Alec would inevitably say next.

"Because Colonel Butler himself's put a price on the poor bastard's life," said Alec with obvious satisfaction.

The chill that swept through Rachel had nothing to do with the snow. As isolated as she was from the war, she still had heard of Walter Butler and the hellish pact he'd made with Joseph Brant, the chief of the Mohawk nation. Together Butler's Rangers and Brant's braves had cut a ruthless, bloody swath through to the east in the name of the king.

But, God help her, how could the man with the summer blue eyes, the man whose smile had haunted her loneliness as she'd drawn him back from death—how could this same man be so heartlessly cruel?

"They're offering twenty dollars," continued Alec. "Double the usual rate for a white man's scalp. Of course, Butler'd rather have the man alive to deal with properly, but Brant and the rest of his savages aren't inclined to be overnice with traitors."

Rachel swallowed her revulsion, imagining all too vividly the stranger's long, chestnut hair trailing from the belt of some Seneca brave. "I still don't see what this has to do with me. This land here belongs to the Americans, not the British."

"Only this, you foolish chit. Butler swears the man was shot before he fled, and in this weather he wouldn't go far. If you find him on your land before the wolves do—or even after they have, as long as you can take his scalp—then we can claim the reward.''

Appalled both by his suggestion and that he'd make it before Billy, Rachel stared at him. "What kind of woman do you think I am, that I would use some wounded stranger so cruelly?"

"Oh, I think you're a decent, loyal woman who loves her country and the sweet cause of liberty," said Alec, his sarcasm unmistakable. "You wouldn't want people thinking otherwise of you, would you? Whispering that you've forgotten your husband and gone over to the king? You'd learn soon enough how short tempers are in this county, Rachel, you and the boy both."

"But I couldn't—"

"You can do anything if your life depends on it," said Alec firmly. "You've skinned game. Taking a scalp's not much different. A tall man, they're saying, name of Ryder, with coppery hair and a bullet in his shoulder. Shouldn't be too hard to mistake, eh, sister?"

But to her dismay she felt Billy begin to shuffle and tug at her skirt. "Mama?" he began, unable to contain himself any longer, "Mama, why—"

Instantly she crouched down to the child's level, praying that her voice alone could silence the damning question. "Hush, now, Billy," she said urgently, resting the musket in the crook of her arm as she brushed her fingers across his cheek. "Mama's talking with Uncle Alec."

"And she's not done talking to me yet."

Before she realized it Alec was beside her, seizing her arm and dragging her to her feet so roughly that the musket slipped free and fell with a soft *swoosh* into the snow. She gasped with surprise, but didn't fight him or struggle to free herself, instead going perfectly still. She wouldn't give Alec that satisfaction, nor did she wish to frighten Billy any more than he already was, his fists locked tight around her knee.

"What in God's name do you think you're doing, Alec?" she said as evenly as she could. Lord, how had she let herself be so careless? "This is ridiculous!"

"Not as ridiculous as you pointing that damnable musket at me," he said, his face near enough to hers that she could smell the rum and stale tobacco on his breath. "Perhaps next time you'll remember that I don't like to be kept out in the snow at gunpoint like some gypsy tinker."

"There won't be a next time, not if I can help it!"

"But there will, Rachel." For a moment that was endless to her, Alec's grasp seemed to turn into a caress that burned through her sleeve before his fingers tightened once again. "I swore to William I'd look after his pretty little wife, and look after you I shall."

"I never asked you for that!"

"You took my food and my firewood when I offered it, didn't you?"

"Because you were my husband's brother!" she cried, her bitter anguish still fresh after so many months. "You were all the family I had for hundreds of miles, and I trusted you!"

"Then I've every right to be here, haven't I? You can't order me away, Rachel, not for wanting to offer you advice and comfort." He let his gaze slide boldly down her throat to her bodice, and chuckled as Rachel self-consciously clutched the front of her cloak together. "The whole county knows what I've done for you and the boy. I've made quite certain of that. And if in return I ask some small favors, some little indulgences, why, there's none but you who'd begrudge me that."

"'Small favors'!" Unable to bear his touch any longer, Rachel finally jerked her arm free, rubbing furiously at her forearm as if to wipe clean some invisible stain. "What you ask, Alec, what you expect—William would kill you if he knew!"

"We're discussing my brother, Rachel," he said with insolent confidence, "and I'm not so convinced that he'd mind at all."

And neither, thought Rachel miserably, was she. With William, she never did know for certain. In humiliated silence she watched as Alec fished her musket from the snow where she'd dropped it. Slowly he brushed off the snow that clung to the stock before he held the gun out for her to take.

"I'll be back, Rachel," he said softly. "Be sure of that. And mind you keep your eyes open for Ryder. I wouldn't want the talk to start about my brother's wife."

Rachel snatched the gun away from him, her eyes blazing with shame and anger. "Just leave, Alec," she said. "Leave *now*."

He laughed and lifted his hat again with mocking gallantry, then turned away to retrieve his horse, his boots crunching heavily through the snow. Rachel wasn't sure which hurt her more: that parting laugh, or the way he was so infuriatingly confident that she wouldn't shoot him in the back.

She felt Billy's grip on her leg beginning to relax as he peeked around her to see if his uncle had left. She pulled him up onto her hip and with a trusting little sigh he snuggled against her body for warmth and reassurance.

"I hate Uncle Alec," he muttered into her cloak. "He's bad."

"I don't much care for him, either, love," she confessed, pressing her cheek against the little boy's soft curls. When she held him like this, wrapped up in the quilt with his hands curled against her breast, she could imagine he was a baby again, when she was all of the world he knew or needed. But sorrowfully she knew in her heart that that time had already come to an end. Now it would take more than a hug and a kiss and a spoonful of strawberry jam on a biscuit to make things right in a world that included both Alec Lindsey and a violent war that had suddenly come to their doorstep.

She watched Alec's horse pick his way through the snow, her brother-in-law's red scarf the single patch of color in the monochrome landscape. Without mittens, her fingers were growing stiff and numb from the cold, and she shouldn't keep Billy outside any longer.

Ryder, that was the name Alec had mentioned, and she sighed unhappily. That was the name—J. Ryder—elaborately engraved on the brass plate of the stranger's rifle, and the hem of his checked shirt had been marked with the same initials in tiny, flawless cross-stitches. She had tried so much to distance herself from the stranger, to keep herself apart from whatever had brought him here. She hadn't wanted to know his secrets any more than she wished to share her own. Now he had a name, a past and a price of twenty dollars on his head, while she'd lost every notion of what she'd do next.

"I'm cold, Mama," said Billy plaintively, "an' I want t'go inside."

That at least would be a start, and with another sigh she wearily headed back to the house, the musket tipped back over her shoulder. She pushed open the door, already framing what she'd say to the wounded man waiting in the bed.

Except that now the bed was empty.

Frantically her gaze swept around the house's large single room, from the bed with the tangled sheets past the stone hearth and the flour-covered table and Billy's blocks and the tall mahogany chest with the shell-front drawers that had come with her from Providence. There was no other doorway but the one she stood in, and the ladder to the loft was still neatly hooked on its pegs. But how could a man of his size disappear?

"Mr. Ryder?" She set Billy down but kept the musket. "Mr. Ryder, are you here?"

She swung the door shut, and gasped when she found him there on the other side, braced against the window's frame. He was sickly pale and his face glistened with sweat, but the rifle in his hands never wavered as he kept it trained on the last dark speck that was Alec's retreating figure.

"I would not have let him hurt you," he said softly when he looked at her at last. "Not you, not the boy. Not for all the world."

Chapter Three

"That—that would not have been necessary," stammered Rachel, her heart thumping almost painfully within her breast. She didn't doubt for an instant that he would have killed Alec if she'd struggled or screamed for help, and it terrified her to think of how unwittingly she'd risked Alec's life. "My husband's brother can be a bully, true, but nothing more."

"Nothing?" Slowly the man lowered the rifle, his unflinching gaze never breaking with Rachel's. "That wasn't how it appeared to me."

"Appearances aren't always what they seem," she said quickly, too quickly. In all the foolish fantasies she'd woven about this man to pass the hours at his bedside, she'd never imagined him with this kind of deadly, intense calm that came from deep within. "I don't believe Alec would ever do either Billy or me any real harm."

"No, Mama, he *would* hurt us! You said!" piped up Billy indignantly. "Uncle Alec'd hurt you an' me an'— an' *him!* You *said!*"

"Hush, Billy, no one's going to hurt anybody," scolded Rachel, secretly thankful to have a reason to look away from the man near the window. Now, she thought with dismay, if she could only find one for Billy, as well; she'd never seen his face shine with such endless admiration and awe as it did now for this wonderful new champion. She hung the musket back on its pegs and pulled down the narrow ladder to the loft. "You've had adventure enough for one day. Now please take Blackie upstairs and play there until supper."

Billy ducked his chin stubbornly. "Don't have stairs."

Rachel sighed with exasperation. "Oh, I know, it's only a ladder, not a staircase, but regardless I want you up there directly."

The boy's chin sank lower, into open rebellion. "Don't wanna go. Wanna stay here." He pointed at the man near the window. "With *him.*"

"Billy," said Rachel sternly, desperate to forestall the tantrum she felt sure was brewing. "Please go to the loft so I can speak to Mr. Ryder."

"Don't wanna go, Mama!" The little boy's voice shrilled higher, almost to a wail. "Don't *wanna!*"

"Of course you don't, lad," said the man softly, so softly that Billy immediately stopped arguing so he could hear. "Why should you want to go up there when everything that's interesting is down here?"

Billy's brow stayed furrowed, unconvinced, and for extra emphasis he stamped his moccasined foot. "Don't *wanna.*"

"Billy Lindsey!" Mortified by the child's behavior, Rachel took a step forward to haul him bodily up the ladder before he did anything worse.

But before she could the man bent down on one knee, leaning heavily on the rifle, to be closer to Billy's level. "You don't want to go, Billy, and I can't say I blame you. Well and good. But there's plenty of things in this life that we must do that we don't want to. While your pa's away, you're the man here, aren't you?"

Miraculously the stubbornness vanished from Billy's face, replaced by the same unabashed worship that Rachel had noticed earlier. "I'm a big boy," he announced proudly. "I'm Mama's best boy, an' I help her!"

"I reckoned you are," said the man, nodding wisely as if he'd expected nothing less. "That's why you won't want to hurt her the way your uncle Alec tried to."

"Not Mama!" Anxiously Billy glanced at Rachel. "I'll never hurt her!"

"You're hurting her now," said the man mildly. "Hurting her by being so thickheaded about going to the loft the way she asked. She wants to be proud of you, but instead you're making her sad and shamed."

Without stopping to answer, Billy raced to the table to grab his toy horse, threw his arms around Rachel's knees for a moment of reassurance and apology, then clambered up the ladder to the loft overhead, disappearing with one final grin over his shoulder for the man who'd explained everything so neatly.

"You have a way with him, Mr. Ryder," said Rachel grudgingly, her arms folded tightly over her chest. She told herself again that she didn't wish to see Billy become too attached to his new hero, especially since he had a price on his head. But if she was honest with herself she knew she was also a bit jealous of how swiftly

Billy had listened to someone other than her. "Though as I told you before, I'd rather you had as little to do with Billy as you can."

He sighed, glancing up the ladder to where the boy had disappeared. "By my lights, you needed a bit of help."

Rachel bristled. "I assure you Billy's not usually so ill-mannered."

"Ill-mannered or high-spirited, it's all the same to mamas, isn't it?" he said. "I was a boy once myself, and it doesn't take too much to remember how it was."

He was still leaning on his rifle, kneeling at her feet in a way that she found oddly unsettling. Because she had taken his own shirt to clean and mend, he was wearing an old shirt of William's, the too-short sleeves turned up over his thick-boned wrists, and that disconcerted her, too. The shirt belonged to her *husband*, she reminded herself fiercely, yet still she noticed how the worn cambric strained to cover the unfamiliar shoulders beneath it, and tried not to look at the triangle of dark, curling hair framed by the shirt's open throat.

"You haven't been a boy for a good long time," she said, and immediately flushed guiltily, realizing too late how she'd as much as confessed her indecent observations. Lord, how bold would the man think she was? "That is, Mr. Ryder, I meant there's a world of difference between you and Billy."

He nodded, saying nothing more. Beneath the ragged growth of beard he might have been smiling up at her, and at her expense, too.

"You don't have to stay there on the floor, you know," she said stiffly, her cheeks still on fire. "You can stand now."

"I'm not sure I can." What she'd feared was a smile turned into more of a grimace as he tried to push himself back up to his feet. "Seems I'm fit for little more than impressing boys."

"Oh—*oh!*" Rachel hurried to his side, slipping her shoulder beneath his arm to help guide him across the room to the bed, then darted back to bring him a cup of water.

"How thoughtless I've been!" she said contritely as she watched him drink. "You must forgive me, please, for—"

"Ask yourself for forgiveness, not me," he said sharply, his eyes suddenly snapping despite the pallor of his face. "Consider what your brother-in-law must have told you about me. Your sympathy could have cost you your life, coming so close to me like that. You should have kept your musket until I'd given up my rifle."

"Oh, bother and fuss! As if I put any stock in what Alec tells me!" Rachel tossed her head indignantly. "I decide my own mind. You'd never have walked two steps without my help."

"And that's two times this day alone that your deciding's made you careless," he said relentlessly. "If you want to go on living by yourself out here, you'll have to do better."

"While you, sir, would do better to learn gratitude to those who help you." With an angry flurry of her skirts, Rachel turned her back to him and returned to her neglected baking. Left so long, the dough on the table had begun to rise into a lopsided lump toward the warmth of the open hearth, and with her fist she smacked it down.

Watching her, Jamie swore softly and leaned back against the headboard. He hadn't meant to be so hard on her like that, but she had been dangerously trusting, both with him and the man she said was her husband's brother. He'd rather make her angry than keep silent.

Absently he ran his fingers back and forth along the rifle's barrel. He wondered how she'd come to this little log house, where she was as out of place as the gilded bull's-eye mirror hanging over the crude stone fireplace. Her speech, her self-assurance, even her cheerfully ignorant trust, belonged in some elegant city parlor, not here. He remembered the wealthy daughters and wives of merchants he'd seen riding in their carriages through the Philadelphia streets—beautiful, expensive women in rich imported silk and kerseymere. She'd been born one of them; even the rough linsey-woolsey skirts she wore now couldn't hide that. But what kind of fool of a husband would bring a gently bred lady like her to the wilderness?

She was putting her whole body—and her anger—into thumping the dough, bending over the table far enough to give him a clear view of her ankles, neat and trim even in woolen stockings. Humiliating though it had been to ask for her help, he'd learned again how softly curved her body felt against his, how readily she fit against him, and he'd learned that she found him attractive, too. He'd seen that shy but eager interest in the eyes of women enough times before to recognize it, though the devil only knew how she'd feel that way when he must look like a scarecrow complete with a mouth full of straw. Perhaps, he thought wryly, she *had* been alone too long.

But was that reason enough for her to have shielded him from her husband's brother the way she had?

"How much did your brother-in-law tell you?" he asked softly.

Her back stiffened, but she didn't turn to face him. "I told you already that I don't heed what Alec says."

"I didn't ask you what you believed. I asked how much he told you."

She swung around, her black brows drawing downward at being challenged. "He told me, Mr. Ryder, that you are one of the Tory Rangers serving under Colonel Walter Butler."

His expression didn't change. "As I recall, your husband fights with the rebel army. I'll warrant that makes me your enemy as well as his."

She raised her chin with the same stubbornness he'd seen in the boy. "At present you are a man who needed my assistance. You've trouble enough without me turning you away into the snow on account of your politics."

"I'm caught in my enemy's territory with the wind whistling through the hole in my shoulder." His mouth twisted bleakly. "Oh, aye, that's trouble enough."

"Not quite." Rachel leaned closer, lowering her voice so Billy, doubtless eavesdropping overhead, wouldn't hear. "It's worse than that. Somehow you've managed to cross your Colonel Butler badly enough that he's offering a bounty on your scalp. Twenty dollars, according to Alec."

"Twenty dollars?" Jamie's heart plummeted. He'd never dreamed Butler would offer such a reward. Twenty dollars would set every penniless rogue in the land on his trail.

Rachel nodded. "Twenty it was. Where money's concerned, I've never had reason to doubt Alec."

"But you doubt the rest?"

"I make my own decisions. I told you that already, too." She noticed how he'd neither denied nor confirmed Alec's story, and she wondered uneasily whether she'd been wrong to trust him as much as she had. As he'd told her himself, he was her enemy. "Whether it's twenty dollars or forty pieces of silver, Mr. Ryder, I'm not in the habit of putting a price on any man's life."

"Thank you." It didn't seem enough for what she'd done, but he was afraid that anything more would sound false. "And the name's Jamie Ryder, without the trappings. You can save the 'sirs' and 'misters' for the next gentleman who wanders into your barn."

But Rachel didn't smile, considering instead the easy familiarity he was proposing as she turned back toward her work table. There were already too few barriers between them, crowded together like this in her home's single room, and she wasn't sure she wanted to give up the fragile formality of that "mister."

He waited, puzzled by her silence. "There, now," he said gruffly. "I've handed you leave to call me by my given name, but it seems instead I've offered you some sort of offense."

"Oh, no, it's not that," said Rachel hastily as she moved to the hearth to lift the iron pot with their supper closer to the coals. She lifted the lid of the pot to stir the contents while she thought, brushing her hand briskly before her face against the rush of fragrant steam. His insistence on no formal title might have another, very different explanation. She could know for certain, if she dared risk making a fool of herself.

And it was, she decided, a risk worth taking. With a brief, nervous smile, she glanced back at him over her shoulder.

"Does thee believe that thy appetite could be tempted by a plate of stew?" she asked as cheerfully as she could. "To me thee seems well enough for heartier fare."

He relaxed and set the rifle in his lap to one side, his mouth watering already from the smell alone. "Thee couldn't keep me from thy table now, as thee knows perfectly—"

He broke off, realizing too late how neatly she'd tricked him. Butler must have described him in every detail when he'd posted his blasted reward.

"Thee's a clever woman," he said dryly. "Thee knew to use stewed rabbit and onions as bait to catch a poor feeble invalid weary of gruel."

"There's nothing feeble about you that time and stew won't cure." She concentrated on spooning the hot stew into a pewter bowl, avoiding the reproach that she knew would be on his face. She *had* tricked him, true enough, but now she had her answer, too.

Carefully she wrapped a cloth around the bowl to hold in the heat, and brought it to him in the bed.

"Don't eat so fast that you burn yourself," she cautioned. "And mind you don't spill. I don't want to consider what sort of hideous mess that would make on the coverlet."

"My, my, but your concern's alarming," he said as he took the bowl and balanced it on his knees. "I think I liked the plain speech better."

She dragged a chair closer to sit at his bedside to keep him company while he ate. "My grandmother was a Friend, and I always liked to listen to her talk. She could make even a scolding sound special. While you were ill, you often spoke that way, too."

He stared at her, mute with horror, while the stew turned tasteless in his mouth.

God preserve him, what else had he babbled to her? Had he told her of the dull whistle that a tomahawk makes as it whips through the air, the sickening thud when it buries deep in its mark? In the grip of the fever had he raved about the smoke from the burning houses, the screams of the dying or the last frantic wails for mercy that had filled the early-morning air? Had he confessed to her what he'd seen, what he'd done in the empty name of his king, and failed to do for his own conscience?

To Rachel it seemed his face shuttered in an instant, closing her out as his eyes turned cold and empty. Her curiosity had done this, she thought with an inward shiver, her infernal curiosity had driven away the man who'd so gently teased Billy, and left her instead with another whose face was as hard as if carved from the same granite as the cliffs in the valley.

A face that belonged to one of Butler's Rangers, to one of her enemy, to a man who, weak though he was, could still load and aim a rifle with terrifying accuracy.

"It wasn't what you said, but how," she said, struggling to explain herself. "I didn't mean it as an insult, you know. In this part of New York, there are so few Friends that I found your words remarkable."

"And you thought I might have a Quaker grandmother, too?" He forced himself to make his manner light, to lift the carved horn spoon dripping with gravy again and again to his lips as if nothing had changed.

If she knew the truth, she could not sit here with him, not this close. No decent woman could. Butler's reward would be nothing compared to her horror if she knew the truth. With luck, she never would, at least not until he was gone from her life.

She shook her head, her carnelian earbobs swinging. "I thought you were a Friend yourself," she said, almost wistfully. "Even with you dressed as you were, and carrying the rifle and a knife."

"You're right enough there," he said wearily. "No decent, godly Friend would carry a weapon of any sort to be used against another man."

"My grandmother wouldn't allow guns anywhere in her house, not even for hunting game. Not that there was much to shoot on an island, anyway." She tried to smile in the face of his still-grim expression. "So I misjudged thee, and thee has no Quaker grandmother after all?"

"Nay, she's there in my past. Grandmother and grandfather, father and mother, and all manner of cousins." He stared down at the bowl in his hands, sorrowfully remembering too much of a life that was forever gone. "Because my whole family belonged to the Society of Friends, I was a birthright member of our Meeting, too. But—now I'm not much of anything."

"Ah." Solemnly she nodded again, and with her fingertips smoothed her hair around her ears. She could understand that. There were days—too many days, and nights—when she believed she wasn't much of anything, either. "I suppose I believed you were a Friend because I wanted you to be. It made you easier to help if you didn't belong to either side. Not that it matters now, of course."

He shrugged his uninjured shoulder, volunteering nothing more. Though she could understand his reticence, she wasn't used to it in men, especially not after William, and it made her uncomfortable.

"My grandmother was turned out of her Meeting," she said, determined to fill in the silence. "For marrying a man who wasn't a Friend. It was quite a scandal at the time, mostly because she wasn't the least bit contrite."

"If she was anything like you, then I'm not surprised she was turned out of her Meeting."

Rachel looked up sharply, so ready to defend herself that Jamie very nearly laughed.

"I didn't intend that as an insult, either," he said softly. And he didn't. He remembered the girls in Meeting as dutifully demure, shrouded in sober gowns with their eyes downcast beneath their bonnets. This one, with her vivid coloring and green eyes and swinging black hair, would have shone like an irresistible beacon in their midst, and he would have followed.

He'd always had a fondness—a weakness, according to his father—for worldly women; it had brought him no end of trouble when he'd been younger, before the war, and he didn't want to consider what could happen now if he wasn't careful.

"I didn't take your words as an insult," she said quickly.

"No?"

"No." She shook her head again for extra emphasis, loose strands of her black hair drifting about her face. "How could I? My grandmother was a very fine, gracious woman."

"Then I'm honored that you imagined I'd be like her," he said with the perfect degree of bland politeness.

"I did?" she asked, baffled. This man with the rifle cradled beside him on the bed had precious little in common with her peaceable, silver-haired grandmother.

"Aye, me. If you imagined I was a Friend, and the only one of the lot you seem to know well was your paragon of a grandmother, then it stands to reason that you believed that I was a paragon, too. At least, you did until I opened my eyes and my mouth." It had been a long, long time since he'd teased anyone like this, especially a girl this pretty, and he surprised himself by doing it now. "Mightily flattering, that."

"I suppose it is," said Rachel faintly, not quite sure what had just happened. She'd rather thought he was flattering her, not the other way around, and the extra spark in those blue eyes wasn't at all reassuring.

Jamie took another bite of the stew while he collected his wayward thoughts. What the devil was he doing, anyway? Was it some lingering fever from his wound, or the warm food in his belly, or the hot flush on her cheeks? He was endlessly grateful she couldn't read his mind, or she'd realize how wrong she'd been to judge him safe simply because of that grandmother of hers. Himself, he'd been born a Friend, but hardly a saint.

He fiddled with the spoon between his fingers. "Though you flatter me, aye, you keep the advantage. You know my name, but you haven't told me yours."

Rachel's cheeks grew hot. "It's Rachel. Rachel Sparhawk Lindsey."

He liked to see her blush, especially over something as foolish as her name, and though he knew he'd no right to do it, he held his silence a moment longer to savor her discomfiture. Strange how she clung to her maiden name, and stranger still that her husband permitted such a thing.

"Well, then, Mistress Lindsey," he said at last, "a fine good morning to you, and pleased I am to make your acquaintance."

Her cheeks grew warmer still. He might not say much, but what he did say seemed to disconcert her more than all of William's grand speeches put together. Not that she intended to let him get the better of her. She couldn't afford to do that, not for her sake or for Billy's.

"If you wish no titles for yourself, Jamie Ryder," she said with determined composure, "then I can live without being called 'Mistress.'"

"As you please, Rachel Lindsey." He liked the sound of the name on his tongue, just as he'd liked hearing his on her lips. He had guessed she'd be called something more elegant, more exotic, the way she was herself, but now he'd never imagine her as anything other than Rachel. Rachel, Rachel Lindsey. Rachel *Sparhawk* Lindsey. Lord, when was the last time he'd gone moony over a woman's name?

"Rachel Lindsey, Rachel Lindsey," he said again as he let his bemusement slide drowsily across his face. "You wanted to trust me when I was dead to the world. But do you trust me now, I wonder?"

She didn't hesitate at all. "Not in the least."

"Good lass," he murmured. "Not only beautiful, but wise you are, too, Rachel Lindsey. Don't you ever trust me, not for a moment."

Then he smiled, his whole face lightening, and the sudden, devastating warmth of it was enough to steal Rachel's breath away and her wits, as well. Oh, she was right not to trust him, and it had nothing to do with wars or Tories or long-barreled rifles. If he could do this to her when he was weak and ill, what havoc could he bring when he'd recovered?

Swiftly she stood and reached to take the empty bowl from him, being sure that their fingers didn't touch.

"You will understand, then," she said as she briskly carried the bowl back to the table and away from the tempting power of that smile, "that while you're welcome to stay as long as you need to recover, I also expect you to leave when you're well. If Alec guesses you were here, he may be back, and I daresay others will come, too, once they've heard of the reward. Hard money's scarce in this county, especially twenty dollars."

She swallowed hard, longing for him to say something in return. "I have to think of Billy," she said, hoping she sounded firm, not strident. "With William away, life is difficult enough for us as it is. Surely you must understand that."

Still he didn't answer. Impatiently she wiped her palms on her apron and turned to face him again. "Surely you must see my—"

But he wasn't going to see anything. His eyes were closed, and he was fast asleep, the hint of his smile still lingering on his lips.

With an exasperated sigh, Rachel collected his powder horn and bullet pouch where he'd left them beside the window and set them beside the bed. Gingerly she eased the rifle away from him and laid it, too, on the floorboards. Perhaps letting him keep the gun was not the wisest thing she'd done, but still she sensed it was in her favor. She would put off changing the dressing until morning. Sleep now would be the best thing for him. At last she drew the coverlet over his shoulders, tucking it protectively around him the same way she had when he'd been so sick.

The same, yet different, the way everything between them had changed in little more than an hour's time. There wasn't any "same" left now, and the Lord only knew what would happen next.

"Oh, Mama, is he asleep *again?*" asked Billy mournfully as he leaned over the edge of the loft.

"Rest's the one thing now that will help make him well." She glanced upward, wondering if the boy had been there all along as she'd suspected. "Come down and wash up for supper."

But now that Billy had her attention, he was in no hurry to move, instead leaning on his elbows as he stared down at the sleeping man. "You said he had to go, Mama," he said accusingly. "You said he couldn't stay."

"Oh, Billy, sweetheart, it's not up to me," she said unhappily. "I know he's been very kind to you, but he doesn't belong here. Once he's better, he must return to his own family and friends. I'm sure they miss him very much, and they'll be glad to see he's well again."

"Don't want him to go," said Billy, more wistful than stubborn. He hugged Blackie closer, resting his chin on the horse's worn back. "He made Uncle Alec go away."

"Not really, love. Mr. Ryder was watching, but that was all. Uncle Alec left on his own."

"Not 'Mr. Ryder,' Mama," corrected Billy patiently. "It's *Jamie*. An' Jamie made Uncle Alec go away."

"Well, then, *Jamie* didn't make your uncle go home. Uncle Alec didn't even know anyone else was in our house."

Unconvinced, Billy shook his head, and Rachel knew exactly what he meant. She might not trust Jamie Ryder, but she had believed him when he said he'd do all he could to keep her and Billy from harm. Why else would she have put his rifle where he'd find it as soon as he woke?

"Uncle Alec's bad," continued Billy steadfastly, "an' Jamie's good, an' I like him, Mama, an' I want him to stay *here*."

"Oh, Billy, that's simply not possible, you see, because he—because we—" She broke off, searching vainly for the words to explain her reasons to a child. She looked back at the man in her bed, his face relaxed and boyish in sleep. How could she hope to explain how she felt about Jamie to Billy when she couldn't explain it to herself?

"It's simply not possible, Billy," she said wistfully. "Jamie must leave as soon as he can. But I like him, too, Billy. I like him just fine."

Chapter Four

Rachel hurried down the path to the barn, her feet slipping here and there across the packed snow she'd worn slick to ice. With little clumps of ice clinging to the hem of her skirts, she balanced the lantern in one hand and the empty milk bucket in the other, the musket slung on a strap over her shoulders banging against her back. Only the scent and feel of more snow in the icy air, the threat of a new storm, could have brought her out this early at all.

She hated the dark that closed in around her, the black shadows that swallowed up the feeble light her lantern cast over the snow. This darkness that came when the moon had set and before the sun rose, the darkness of the deepest winter morning, made her heart pound and her imagination race to picture all that could be hiding in the murkiness around her.

Fiercely she tried to remind herself this was *her* land, *her* home. Nothing could harm her here. She knew every inch of this path, just as she knew exactly how many paces lay between her house and her barn. But all the fierce reminders in the world couldn't brighten this darkness, and by the time she reached the barn she was almost running, the lantern's light bobbing wildly and the empty bucket thumping against her thigh. With fingers clumsy from the cold, she tore at the latch, flung back the door and slammed it shut after her as if the devil himself were at her heels.

As crazy shadows from the swinging lantern danced across the walls, the hens flew squawking from their roost, flapping furiously in the air, and the cow lowed and thumped uneasily against the sides of her stall.

"Hush, now, hush, all of you!" called Rachel, her voice shaking for all she tried to hold it steady. "It's only me, and I swear there's nothing to be frightened of!"

Brave words, those, she thought as she hurriedly hung the lantern from a beam. How could she scold the poor hens for skittering and squawking when she'd been the one seeing demons in the dark? She sighed with exasperation at her own foolishness and tried to calm the frightened animals, murmuring nonsense to the cow, Juno, as she broke the ice in the water trough and replaced the winter straw in the manger.

She set the bucket on the floor and ran her fingers through the bristly hair between the cow's ears. This was all Jamie Ryder's fault, filling her head full of grim warnings and cautions, and Alec's, too, with all his tales of Tory and Indian raids. Indians, pooh. In the eighteen months since she'd come here she'd seen only two Indians, a pair of Mahicans traveling north with an English trapper.

And as wild as it had once seemed to her, this land so close to the river was downright civilized. On clear days she could easily make out the smoke from her nearest neighbors' chimney, and though the journey to Ethan and Mary Bowman's house took more than an hour through the forest, by the standards of this part of New York that was only as far as the house next door was in Providence. The war that was tearing apart so much of the country was so far away as to seem unreal to her, one more thing she'd left behind in Rhode Island. She was likely safer here than anywhere else in the state.

Besides, the sun itself would rise in an hour, and banish the dark and the shadows for another day. So why, then, was her heart still pounding, her breathing still as ragged as if she'd run four hundred paces instead of forty?

Though the rooster and his hens had settled once again with only a few lingering, irritated clucks among them, Juno had not, shifting uneasily in her stall with her eyes white-rimmed.

"Hush now, my lady," said Rachel, her own voice finally settling down. "Hush now, you silly old madame cow."

Yet still Juno tossed her head, the most defiance a cow can show, and enough to make Rachel wish she could postpone the milking. Once she'd made the mistake of continuing when Juno was feeling out of sorts, and learned the hard way how quickly a cow can kick. She'd had the bruise for a fortnight.

Instead she pulled the three-legged milking stool back and dropped down onto it with a sigh. She couldn't wait forever; not only was Juno's bag heavy with milk, but Rachel herself had to be back in the house before Billy woke and missed her. And Jamie Ryder, too. When she'd left he'd been sleeping soundly enough, but she didn't want to give him any more time than she had to alone in her home, or alone with Billy, either. Lord, how everything changed with him here!

She pressed her forehead against the cow's side and softly began to sing, hoping that would cure Juno's restlessness. It usually did. The more morose the song, the better, as far as the cow was concerned, and she was particularly partial to the sailors' laments Rachel had learned long ago from her brothers.

He has crost the raging seas his Molly for to tease
And that is the cause of my grief,
I sigh, lament and mourn waiting for my love's re-
turn,
Of whom shall I seek—

Abruptly Rachel broke off, listening. She thought she'd heard a scuffling sound, almost scratching, but as soon as she fell quiet it stopped. Daft, she thought with disgust, she'd gone daft and soft brained as an old rotten log.

So farewell, my dearest Dear, until another year
Then the sweet Spring I hope for to—

There, she'd heard it again. Swiftly she moved the milk bucket aside and caught up the lantern. She smacked Juno's angular hip to make her move away from the wall, and then knelt in the straw with the lantern held low. The scuffling sound was definitely there now, like something digging against the wooden wall, searching for a loose deal. Rats or squirrels, most likely, starving from the snow cover and desperate for the grain in the barn.

Scowling, Rachel rose and grabbed her musket. She'd had to pay dearly for that grain from Alec, too dearly to let it be nibbled away by rats. She stormed out the door with her skirts flying, ready to teach the thieves a lesson.

She slipped once on the ice and swore impatiently. She'd left the lantern inside, but with the door ajar a narrow beam of light slid across the snow. She peered into the shadows where the scratching sound had come from, trying to see as her eyes adjusted to the lack of light. Something moved, something low and dark, and she kicked the door open a little farther.

The pale light washed farther over the snow, down to the corner of the barn and the stone wall beyond. The low, dark shadow rose up from the snow, startled by the light, growing larger by the second. A long tail, the sharp triangles of ears and yellow eyes glowing in the lantern's light. No scratching now, no digging, only the deep rumbling growl as the wolf drew back on its haunches to face her.

There *had* been something in the dark. She hadn't been imagining things. But a wolf, God help her. Not a rat after corn, but a *wolf*.

He crouched there in the snow, cornered between the barn and the wall, his lips curled from his teeth and the hair bristling on the back of his neck like some mongrel guarding a stolen bone. But the wolf was bigger than any dog she'd ever seen, and she didn't think he was going to run off if she stamped her foot and shook her apron.

Slowly, so slowly, she raised the musket to her eye and released the lock. Her hands were shaking, making the sight tremble, and she took a deep breath to steady herself. She had to make this single shot count; it could take her a full minute, sixty seconds at least, to reload the musket, and she wasn't sure she'd have that time.

The wolf angled sideways, closer, testing her, the yellow eyes bright and hard.

She had to do this, shoot him *now,* before he came any closer. She told herself she couldn't miss at this range. She couldn't afford to, anyway. She swallowed hard, whispered a terse little prayer and squeezed the trigger.

She heard the hammer click, the little sizzle of the pan and the bright flash, she smelled the familiar acrid puff of gunpowder, and then—

And then nothing.

No thump as the butt kicked back against her shoulder, no *crack* from the ball flying from the barrel. Only the flat, worthless silence of a gun that had misfired.

Somehow the animal seemed to know Rachel had lost her advantage and began inching closer. His nails clicked softly with each footfall on the frozen snow, his breath gathering in white puffs around his bared teeth.

With a muffled cry of dismay and fear Rachel dropped the musket from her shoulder, her forefinger tangling clumsily with the trigger as she fought her panic. Eight feet away, maybe six. There was no time to clear the fouled gun, no time to reload, not even time to run back into the barn, not now that the wolf was closer than she to the open door. If she turned and tried to run for the house, the wolf would surely head for the open barn and poor Juno.

Or he could choose instead to chase after her. Forty paces uphill, across a frozen path in the dark where the animal could see so much better than she, chasing after her to seize her ice-heavy skirts in his jaws and drag her down, down.

Suddenly the wolf lunged across the snow and Rachel staggered back, barely keeping from the animal's reach. Gasping, she slid her hands down the musket to the end of the barrel and swung it as hard as she could. She felt the impact of the butt striking the wolf, and heard the startled yelp of pain. But the same sweep of the musket through the air threw her off-balance, her feet sliding out from under her on the ice, and she pitched forward hard, the musket flying from her hands to spin across the crusted snow.

"No," she gasped as she tried to scramble away on her hands and knees. "Dear God, *no!*"

She saw the white fur of the wolf's underbelly as he whirled through the air, a blur as white against the black sky as the snow she lay upon. The scream she knew was her own, shrill with fear. But the sharp crack of the rifle's shot made no sense, not even when the wolf dropped lifeless to the snow before her. No sense, she thought, her heart pounding wildly as she crouched on the snow, it made no sense at all.

"Are you hurt, Rachel?" Jamie pulled her to her feet, his voice harsh from concern and strain. "Look at me, lass. Are you hurt?"

She stared at him, uncomprehending, her eyes still wide with terror and her breath coming in short little gasps. Her braid had come unraveled, her hair hanging half-loose around her face, and when she lifted her hand to brush it back he saw the raw scrape across her knuckles where she'd fallen on the ice. But nothing worse, thank God.

He glanced again at the lifeless body of the wolf, then slung his rifle on its strap across his back and set his hands gently on her shoulders. "You'll be fine, Rachel," he said, forcing her to look at him and listen. "The animal's dead, and can't harm you."

"Yes," she said hoarsely, nodding her head even as she searched his face for reassurance. "Yes, I'm quite fine. Quite."

It was Jamie Ryder, of course, Jamie who had saved her. With the light from the open door behind him, his face was dark in shadow, but she would have recognized his voice anywhere. And who else, really, could it have been?

Yet even as she realized what he'd done, she wished it hadn't been so. She wanted to be like all the other women in her family, her grandmother and her mother and her older sisters. She wanted to be strong, independent, able to take care of herself and Billy, and this winter, before this man had come, she'd thought she was. But then she remembered how the wolf had sprung toward her, and she didn't feel very strong or brave at all. What she felt was weak and weepy, and if he said one more kind word to her she knew she'd shatter at his feet.

Instead she drew away from him, smoothing her hair from her face as if her fingers still did not shake, and bent to pick up her musket.

"It misfired, you know," she explained, almost grudgingly, as she peered at the flintlock, poking the bits of snow away from it. "Else I would have made the shot myself."

"True enough. But 'twas a good thing my rifle didn't suffer the same ill."

Frowning, she glanced up at him without raising her chin. "How far were you from—from me?"

"Not far." He shrugged carelessly, but Rachel saw how he favored the wounded shoulder. "I'd just stepped outside the house."

"That's forty paces, and in the dark, too." She was impressed, as much by his modesty as by what he'd done. She'd never known another man who'd have been able to resist such an opportunity to boast. "You said you could shoot the seeds from an apple, and you weren't bragging."

She heard his smile without seeing it. "That old wolf's a sight bigger than an apple."

For the first time Rachel forced herself to look at the dead animal. The sky was beginning to pale with dawn, and the gray shape of the wolf was clear against the snow, framed by the darker puddle of its own blood. Only luck and Jamie had saved her from lying there instead, stiffening on the snow, in the blood. She looked, and could not look away, any more than she could stop the trembling that suddenly racked her or the tears that blurred her eyes, and this time when Jamie reached for her, she crumpled against him, her musket slipping forgotten from her hand.

"There now, lass, I told you you'd be fine," he murmured as he folded his arms around her. "I'll grant you it was a close thing, but you'll be fine."

And she *was* fine, thought Jamie, fine and soft to hold against his chest, the way he'd known she would be. Her hair slid like silk across his wrists as she pressed her cheek against the fringed yoke of his linen Ranger's shirt, her hands curled loosely together like a child's. He'd heard once that the fringe was meant to draw rain away from a man's shoulders, to scatter the drops where they'd shake away. Would they work the same way now, he wondered, to draw away a woman's tears?

Instinctively he tightened his arms around her and she burrowed closer. The image of her bravely swinging the musket at the wolf was burned forever in his consciousness, along with the sickening lurch he'd felt deep inside when he'd realized what it would take to save her. And he'd done it; he hadn't failed her. But he couldn't remember the last time a woman had turned to him like this, and he longed to give her the comfort she needed. Aye, that was all, comfort, to ease her fears like a brother or a friend.

Like hell that was all, he thought wretchedly, as if he could ignore her womanly scent or the soft warmth of her breasts pressed against him. Like hell was exactly *what* it was. He'd warned her not to trust him. Why the devil hadn't she listened?

"I thought—thought I was going to die," said Rachel raggedly, hiccuping with her sobs. "I thought ev-

erything was—was going to end, and I was so scared,
and—and oh, I'm such—such a silly *coward!*''

He smiled in spite of himself. "Oh, hush, that's nonsense. Whatever else you are, Rachel Lindsey, you're no
coward."

"No?" Her voice squeaked upward, and she pulled
back to look at him, but not so far that she'd be free of
his embrace. Furiously she dashed at her tears with the
back of her fist. "Then why—why else am I crying so?"

"Because you're wise enough to know you're mor-
tal," he said as he gently traced his fingers along her
cheek, her face so close to his. "Frightening thought,
that. Because you know how sweet life can be."

He kissed her then, and she didn't stop him. The
wolf, and the gun misfiring, and now Jamie's lips on
hers—none of it was real. Swiftly she parted her lips for
his, swaying into him as she let herself become lost in his
kiss. This was the sweetness he'd spoken of, the dizzying richness of pleasure and life that she hadn't wanted
to abandon.

Her palms flattened against his chest, pressing against
his shirt to feel the steady beating of his heart. She was
glad his was steady, for her own was racing like a rabbit across a meadow. The taste of him, the maleness of
his desire, stole her breath away and made her limbs
turn to butter. His hands slid lower, following the curve
from her waist to her hips, and she shuddered as he
pulled her closer against his long, hard body.

Yet she wanted this; no, she *needed* it, more than
she'd realized was possible. This fire of a man's kiss on
an icy morning and the heady security of his arms

around her proved that she wasn't alone, that someone cared whether she died or lived.

The same pleasures she'd once believed she'd find with William. With her *husband*.

With a shudder she shoved herself back, tucking her wayward hands beneath her arms. "I didn't mean anything by that," she said with a swift, ragged urgency. "Nothing, you understand?"

He didn't move to reclaim her again, instead standing impossibly still before her. "Nothing at all?"

"Nothing," she declared, the lie so great she nearly winced.

"Then that's a great pity," he said softly. "Because I did."

She prayed the same half-light that masked his expression would hide her own guilty flush, as well. "That's—that's not possible."

"Aye, it is." He turned away and went to prod the dead wolf with his toe. "Kissing you could never be meaningless, Rachel Lindsey. I wouldn't have done it otherwise. Nor, I think, would you."

Some place near her heart tightened in her breast. "You must not say such things."

"Even if they're true?"

"They can't be," she said, bowing her head beneath the weight of her shame. "You forget that I'm married."

"True enough. I kissed the woman, not the wife." He sighed deeply, staring down at the dead wolf instead of her. "But if it displeased you, I'll try not to do it again. I can't swear an oath to it—I've kept that much of my father's beliefs—but I will give you my word. That should be enough.''

The tears smarting behind her eyes were dangerously close to spilling over. What else had she expected from him? That the foolish dreams she'd whispered to him when he'd been delirious would turn real?

He'd saved her life just as she'd saved his, with the same justice and decency that ruled the frontier. She was the one who'd erred by falling into his arms, and he could hardly be faulted for expecting more. Men always did. Hadn't she learned anything from William and Alec? At least Jamie Ryder was simply doing what she'd claimed she wanted, to be left alone as any decent married woman would wish.

Kissing you could never be meaningless, Rachel....

Fiercely she rubbed her sleeve across her eyes. If he could be so unbearably calm about this, then she could, too. She'd just survived being attacked by a wolf. She wasn't going to let herself be felled by her own misplaced emotions and a handful of empty compliments.

''Billy must be stirring by now,'' she announced in a voice as loud and stilted as a town crier's. ''He'll be wanting breakfast. I'd best go.''

''Not until you tend to your stock, you shouldn't,'' said Jamie. ''That's the whole reason you came out here, isn't it?''

''But Billy—''

''When I left Billy he was sleeping as deep as a boy can, and I'd wager he is still.'' He bent to slide his fingers along the weathered gray deals of the barn, seeking and finding the loose board that the wolf had been digging at. "You look after your milking, and I'll mend this."

Silently Jamie counted to three, then ten, putting off the inevitable moment when he had to turn and face her. He had no choice, not with her standing between him and the barn door, but he still wasn't sure he could do it. Once he'd had her in his arms, he'd forgotten every vow he'd sworn to himself.

A woman as good and honorable as Rachel Lindsey didn't deserve to be handled like some backwoods strumpet. It shouldn't have mattered one whit that she was also one of the loveliest creatures he'd ever seen. She had trusted him and he'd taken advantage of that trust until she'd been forced to remind him she was married, and even then she hadn't berated him the way he'd deserved.

But what was worse, what disgusted him more, was that he knew he'd kiss her again in a moment. Even now he could feel his body grow hard at the memory of how her soft lips had parted for him, innocently welcoming his intrusion just as she'd welcomed him into her home.

But no more. If he'd a mite of decency left in his weary soul, he'd never touch her again. Swearing to himself, he gave one final desultory kick to the loose deal on the barn with his moccasin and slowly walked toward her.

"Come along, now," he said as he tried to smile. "I've no mind to cross Billy if he's expecting a cupful of that milk when he wakes."

How it pained him to see the way she stepped back, away from him!

"You've shaved," she said, her voice oddly breathy.

"Aye, this morning." He held the barn door open for her to slip inside. "I didn't know when I'd next see a mirror or hot water, so I took advantage of the kettle on your hearth while I had the chance."

Her eyes were round, her tongue clearly speechless, so much so that his smile turned lopsided from uncertainty. "I hope the results aren't too dreadful."

"Not—not at all," stammered Rachel as she reached for the milking bucket to hide her confusion. "I just hadn't expected the change."

Swiftly she retreated around to Juno's far side, away from Jamie. *Dreadful?* How could the man look in a mirror and consider himself dreadful? The sorry truth of it was that the razor had finished what the rabbit stew and the sleep had begun. Hidden beneath the unkempt beard and the pallor of illness had been a jewel of a man, with a square-cut jaw and firm, full lips that combined with those blue eyes of his to make him every bit as devastating as she'd feared. And she'd gone and kissed those lips. Lord, how stupidly besotted she must be not to have noticed then that the man was clean shaven!

She pressed her cheek against Juno's warm, rough side and once again began to sing the sailor's lament for his lost sweetheart Molly, trying hard to concentrate on holding the tune instead of Jamie Ryder. But her singing couldn't drown out the sounds of him working on the wall, driving the pegs he'd deftly whittled through the deal and into the post with the single battered mallet William owned. She listened, imagining each step of what he was doing until her singing faltered and stopped. Not that Juno cared; she'd craned her red neck to watch the man work, too.

"There, now, that should hold," he said with satisfaction almost exactly as she finished her milking. "You can remember me with kindness each time you pass this wall."

She glanced at him suspiciously, wondering again if he was teasing or not as she laid a checkered cloth over the fresh, steaming milk. "Why should I need an old gray plank as a reminder?"

"Because I'm leaving," he said, and to her surprise that flawless grin wobbled again. "This morning. I thought I'd wait to bid farewell to Billy, and then be gone."

"Then you're a greater fool than ever I credited you." Briskly she slung the musket over her shoulders and picked up the bucket of milk, holding it out to him. "Would you please carry this back to the house for me?"

He didn't miss how neatly she avoided letting even her fingers touch his as he took the bucket from her. "I know I owe you a debt I'll never be able to repay—"

"You already have," she said as she took a thick coil of rope from a hook on a beam. "You killed the wolf, and thereby saved my life just as I likely saved yours. I'd say that debt is as squared as ever it will be."

"Then square it is. But I am leaving, Rachel, leaving this morning after I've said goodbye to Billy, and if that makes me a fool in your eyes, then so be it."

"So be it indeed." She jerked the barn door open and stepped outside, not looking to see if he followed. Making a loop in one end of the rope, she slipped it over a peg placed shoulder high beside the door and tugged the rope taut. Then she began to back slowly toward the house, feeding the coiled rope out behind her.

Left holding the milk, Jamie scowled. He had the distinct impression that he'd just been dismissed, and he didn't care for it. "What the devil do you think you're doing with that rope?"

Rachel paused and looked at him exactly long enough for him to feel every bit the fool she'd called him. "I'm rigging a lifeline," she explained patiently. "To keep me on course. The distance from the house may seem short, but in the middle of a blizzard it would be easy enough to lose my way."

Though she smiled sweetly, Rachel spoke from terrifying experience. Last winter she'd lost her way and all sense of direction in the swirling snow and wind, her own footsteps swept clean from the snow behind her, and only blind luck had let her finally stumble against the end of the barnyard's stone wall. "It's an old mariner's trick, you know, to keep from being washed over the side in a gale. My father spoke of it often."

Forgetting his own disgruntlement, Jamie looked at her with new appreciation for her cleverness. "Your father's a sailor?"

"Oh, my, yes," she said with obvious pride. "My father and my grandfather and my brothers and goodness knows how many cousins and uncles. Masters all, too. There was a time before the war when nearly a quarter of the vessels clearing Newport had a Sparhawk captain at the helm or registered as the owner."

So he'd guessed right: she did come from money, and a great deal of it, too, if her father was a Newport captain and shipowner. He'd never been to the city himself, but he'd heard tales of the richness and elegance of the place, enough to rival London. "How did a Newport captain's daughter come to cabin in Tryon County?"

"The usual way for a woman." The pride slipped from her eyes, replaced by a kind of determined bitterness. "This was—is—my husband's home. When I wed, it became my home, as well. I didn't—"

She broke off suddenly, staring past him. "The wolf," she gasped. "The wolf is gone!"

Automatically Jamie swung his rifle to his shoulder again, the hastily dropped bucket sloshing warm milk over his foot. The wolf's body had vanished. All that remained was the dark red stain on the white snow and a flurry of footprints around it, and swiftly Jamie's gaze swept across the empty landscape.

Uneasily Rachel, too, now held her musket ready, though the way her fingers trembled she doubted she could have hit the barn door. "Where could it have gone, Jamie? I know it was dead. It couldn't have crawled off by itself." She glanced at him uncertainly. "Could it?"

"Hush, now, of course it couldn't," he said. "But the Abenaki swear that wolves can't tolerate the shameful death of one of their kin, and so will always come back to claim the bodies of their brethren."

"More wolves? *Here?*"

"Aye." Jamie went to where the wolf's body had been, crouching only long enough to brush his fingers lightly across the prints. "A good half dozen at least, from the look of it. The winter makes them hungry, and bold.''

"I see," said Rachel faintly. She'd never seen a wolf on her land before this morning, and now it seemed there were six. *Six,* for all love, and she shuddered as she remembered the yellow eyes and bared teeth ready to rip into her.

Jamie rose, dusting the snow from his fingers. "It's just as well I mended that deal for you. Not that I expect this pack to return. They're clever enough creatures not to come back to the place where one has met his end. But mind to be sure you keep the door barred, and watch yourself and the boy."

Rachel nodded, and swallowed hard. She'd known from the moment she'd found Jamie Ryder in her barn that he would leave. He had no single reason to remain, and a score of them for going. Though he was still too thin and his shoulder wasn't completely healed, he was strong enough, skilled enough, to survive on the trail. Men like him who served with the Rangers were tougher than most. As Jamie had said himself, he wouldn't be easy to kill.

But as she looked away from his face to his well-worn hunting shirt, her gaze stopped at the small mended patch in the left shoulder, below the fringed cape. She'd been able to scrub the bloodstains from the cream-colored linen, but the small bullet hole in the front, matched by a larger, more ragged one in the back, would always be there beneath the darker patches she'd whipstitched into place.

A little scrap of fabric, a blotch of bloodied, trampled snow. Both of them were grim reminders of how harsh and unpredictable life—and death—could be in this place.

She swallowed again. "You will stay until I've made you breakfast. And I shall pack your haversack so full you'll scarce be able to lift it."

He smiled, the warmth of it lingering in the gray morning. "Thank you, Rachel Lindsey," he said softly. "You are a rare woman."

She had no heart to smile in return. Instead she sighed, quick and troubled.

"What I said to you before, about being foolish—I didn't mean it the way you must think," she began. "I meant instead that you, or anyone, would be foolish to begin a journey in a snowstorm. I can't explain how I know the storm is coming, but I've lived here long enough that I can almost feel it. That's why I went to do the milking so early, and why I was rigging the lifeline. I swear that's all I meant, and not that you're a great fool, because you're not. You're just . . . oh, you're just not."

As if on command the first fat flakes of snow had begun to drift through the air, swirling around her to land like tiny white diamonds scattered over her dark hair and cloak. To Jamie she seemed not only impossibly beautiful but heartbreakingly vulnerable as well, the musket clutched in her hand an empty, brave symbol of exactly how far the odds were stacked against her survival.

This morning he had been here to save her from the wolf, but what would it be tomorrow? The wolves again, a mountain cat? Or would she be trapped in her lonely cabin by more frightening enemies, her own brother-in-law, or Senecas or Mahicans with a grudge against all English, or another desperate deserter from the war like himself? Or what if that same war spread this far, and she and the boy woke one morning to the same kind of terror that he'd helped bring to the settlers in Cherry Valley, the fire and the slaughter and—

No. By sheer will he fought back the nightmare of the past and focused instead on how tightly Rachel's fingers clasped the gun, her knuckles red and chapped from work and cold. He wanted to keep her safe. That was why he'd intended to leave, to spare her the retribution that would come from harboring him.

But maybe that wasn't the answer.

He'd long ago abandoned the formal faith that belonged in the square meeting house, far away in the Pennsylvania of his childhood, but he hadn't quite stopped believing in fate. Fate could have sent him to Rachel Lindsey for a purpose. With all his being he had longed for a way to make right what he'd done. Nothing he could do would bring back the dead, but to guard this woman and her son could be the second chance his miserable soul didn't deserve.

She stood before him now, the wind swirling her skirts as she waited for him to answer her. She would never ask him for help. Instead he'd have to gamble that she'd put aside her pride and let him stay.

"With the storm and all," he said, "perhaps it's better I stay a bit."

And Rachel nodded, her unexpected smile radiant through the snowflakes. "I'll make johnny-cakes with butter and molasses," she promised as the secret, guilty joy swelled in her breast, "and you, Jamie Ryder, shall eat as many as you please."

Chapter Five

"Tell me again how Mama killed the wolf!" Excitedly Billy rocked back and forth in his tall chair, leaning toward Jamie on the other side of the table. "Please!"

"I should make you tell it instead, lad," said Jamie as he pulled one last dark cherry from the crock of conserve. Rachel could fuss and moan all she wished about how meager a table she offered, but so far he couldn't find a single fault with her hospitality, and the cherries that she'd put up herself, sweet reminders of last summer, were no exception. "You've heard the tale so many times since breakfast that most likely you can say it yourself by rote."

Billy's eyes brightened at the challenge. "The big ol' wolf was after Juno an' the chickens, but Mama shot him instead! Shot him *dead!*"

"That's quite, quite enough," scolded Rachel as she wiped Billy's sticky face with a damp cloth and glared at Jamie over the boy's head. "You'll be having bad dreams if you think on it any longer."

"No, I won't." Briefly Billy managed to dodge the cloth. "Where do wolfs sleep, Jamie?"

Jamie leaned back in the chair, relishing the almost forgotten pleasure of being warm and well fed while the wind howled around them. "When wolves aren't scratching after a warm new bedstead in your mama's barn, they'll sleep snug in secret wolf places, caves and such. Mind, wolves got along tolerably well for years and years without us Englishmen."

"We're not English, Jamie," declared Billy scornfully. "We're *'Merican.*"

"And now you're bound for bed, Billy." With practiced ease Rachel swept the boy from his chair and tucked him securely against her hip. "Say good-night to Jamie, then it's prayers and sleep, and not a word of naysaying."

With uncharacteristic meekness Billy for once did as he was told, and he was already limp and half-asleep by the time Rachel tucked him into the big bed and pulled the curtains closed. Later, when she was ready for sleep herself, she would shift him to his own trundle, but for now the thick curtains of the tall bed acted as a small, cozy bedchamber for the boy.

"He's a good lad, Rachel," said Jamie as she cleared away the last of the supper dishes. How easy it had been to stop using her last name with her first! "You've done well with him."

Rachel flashed him a quick smile of thanks. "I'm sorry he said what he did about being American. He didn't mean it the way it sounded."

"Not another meaning that differs from what was said," he said dryly, his face carefully expressionless.

"You Lindseys have a regular problem with that, don't you?"

"Oh, hush!" Though smiling still, Rachel snapped her dishcloth against his arm. "We don't have any such problems whatsoever. I wished to spare your feelings, that is all, though clearly you don't have any to spare."

"Not a one, Rachel, not a one," he said cheerfully as she flounced away from him, clattering the pewter plates together with a great racket.

But as Jamie watched her bending over the tub, her pale arms bare to the elbows as they dipped in and out of the water, the teasing light faded from his eyes. There was an unexpected intimacy about such a simple act that unsettled him. One day shut inside this house together, and already he and Rachel were acting differently with each other. Again he reminded himself that he was staying on to be her protector, not to replace her husband, yet that was exactly how he felt as he sat in the big armchair at the head of the table.

Unaware of his thoughts, Rachel slipped the last pan into the water to soak. "Whatever else you claim, you'd no right to fill his head with that nonsense about me killing the wolf. No, it was worse than nonsense, it was an out-and-out lie, yet because he's heard it from you now it shall carry the weight of the Gospel itself."

"Ah, well, there's no real harm to it," said Jamie, running his thumb along the edge of the table to avoid looking at her any longer. "You would have killed the beast if your gun had fired clean. Besides, it will make a grand story for him to tell to his pa when he comes home."

"Whenever that shall be, God willing." With a disconsolate sigh, Rachel tossed her apron over the back of Billy's empty chair and dropped heavily into her own. "For all I know William could come through that door tomorrow, whistling 'Lady Smollet's Reel' off-key as if he'd never been away."

With a flash of such pure selfishness that it shamed him, Jamie hoped that William would do no such thing. "When is his time done?"

"His time? You mean how long was his enlistment?" Her mouth twisted with a wry bitterness. "If you knew William, you wouldn't need to ask such a thing. Oh, he was eager enough for the glory of soldiering, as long as it didn't interfere with his other pleasures. He signed on with Captain Walker down at the tavern with all the others, claiming with them, too, that he had to be back by harvest to bring in his crops."

She remembered so well the morning William had left.

She'd found him at dawn drunk and snoring in the yard where he'd slid from his horse, and when she'd tried to sober him enough so he could shave and wash before he was due back with Captain Walker, he'd turned amorous instead, forcing her back on the bed, where he'd taken her one last time while the baby had wailed in his tall chair. For the last time, too, he had cursed her as cold and unfeeling, and with his knife had slashed her mother's bargello cushion, searching for the gold he swore she was keeping from him. He never believed that the gold was gone, and most of her affection besides. She was his wife, and all that was hers— everything—belonged by rights to him.

Later she stood in the tall yellow grass on Wappinger's Hill with the other women of the county, the July sun hot on her shoulders as the baby grew heavy in her arms. The small column of new volunteers rode or marched raggedly behind Captain Walker, and the air was filled with the shrill sound of Paul Jonson's fife and the weeping of the wives and mothers, sweethearts and sisters who were being left behind.

When William passed, Rachel silently held Billy up for him to see. William looked not at the baby but at her, his blue eyes bloodshot and his handsome face slicked with sweat from last night's whiskey. He touched his fingers to his lips in wordless farewell, and with something that might have been regret. But he did not smile and neither did she, nor did she weep a single tear from fearing that he would not return.

They had been married three days shy of eleven weeks.

"A summertime lark," she murmured, her eyes unfocused as she drifted through the memory. "That was what the war was to be for William."

Jamie listened, at once both understanding and appalled. A lark—Lord, what an innocent the poor bastard must have been! "He would not have thought that for long."

"No," said Rachel sadly, "I don't expect he did. Captain Walker and our little company joined with General Nicholas Herkimer's troops on their way to relieve the seige at Fort Stanwix. But they were ambushed at Oriskany by Joseph Brant. Only a dozen of our men returned at the harvest, and their tales were sorrowful indeed."

"Your husband could still return," insisted Jamie, wanting only to ease the burden of her sadness. "If he was wounded, he might only now be able to travel. Two months' delay is nothing in such cases."

Bleakly she smiled again, her head tipped to one side so the firelight turned her cheek to rosy gold and her green eyes gleamed like gems. "Two months I would understand, Jamie. But Oriskany was in July of '77, and here it is nearly the end of 1778. That's seventeen months, and in all that time I've yet to have any word or message from William."

"I'm sorry, Rachel," said Jamie softly, and without thinking he laid his hand over hers on the table.

She stared down at how his hand, so much larger, now covered hers, yet she did not pull away. "If you offer that in sympathy for my loneliness, then I accept it with gratitude," she said with stiff formality. "But if your kindness is given by way of condolence—no, I shall not hear it, for I can't yet believe that William is dead."

"Yet seventeen months is—"

"No!" Now she jerked her hand free, shaking her head furiously, and swept to her feet to clutch the spindle back of the chair. "No. Where I come from, wives will wait years and *years* for their men to return home from the sea. Because they do. I've seen it myself, a husband or son appear on his doorstep at last as if from the dead. Seventeen months is as nothing, a handful of days. I cannot let myself grow faithless over seventeen months. I cannot!"

Swiftly Rachel turned away back toward the hearth before he could see the shame in her eyes. She could not

bear to believe that any ill had befallen William, for it
would be all her fault. She had driven him away.
Though she had tried her hardest those first months,
she hadn't been able to be the wife he needed any more
than he had been able to be the husband she thought
she'd married.

Before a church full of witnesses, before her own
parents, she had sworn to honor William, to cherish and
obey him. Instead she had watched him leave for war
with her heart as hard as stone and as empty of love,
and that night when he'd left she had wished on the first
star that he would never come back.

But she didn't want it to end like this. Lord, not like
this, and not her fault.

Still struggling to control her emotions, she wrapped
a cloth around the handle of the iron kettle, filled a
bowl with hot water and set it on the table beside Jamie, carefully keeping her eyes downcast. She'd been
wrong to confess as much as she had about William.
What did Jamie care of her troubles?

"Let me see to your shoulder, if you please," she said
with what she hoped was brisk efficiency. "Though the
way you've been hopping about today, I doubt you'll
need much more help from me."

He looked at her closely, waiting to see if she'd say
more of her husband. She didn't, and as he pulled off
his sash and drew his checked shirt over his head, he
thoughtfully considered all this new silence of hers
might mean. She was trying her best to be brave—trying too hard, by his lights. Her protests on her husband's behalf had an odd ring to them. That she missed
the man, and wished for his safe return, Jamie didn't

doubt. But not once in all the times she had mentioned him had she spoken of love, and for a woman as young and vibrant as Rachel, Jamie found that strange indeed.

"Turn now," she ordered, "toward the firelight."

This time he managed not to wince or grimace as she unbound the bandage and gently touched her fingers to the nearly healed wound. He'd been lucky, something he appreciated perhaps better than she could. He'd seen too many men die from gunshots for him to believe otherwise.

Though the skin was still bruised and swollen from the ball's savage impact, there was no longer any sign of infection or fever. Although he'd bear an ugly scar for the rest of his life, the ball had neither shattered bone nor pierced his lung, and on its way through his body it had obligingly carried away any bits of torn fabric and gunpowder with it. He'd been lucky, no doubt about it, and the luckiest part had been having her as his surgeon.

"That's very pretty," she said, obviously proud of her own handiwork as she studied his back. "Very, very pretty. You've healed fine as a Turk."

He craned his neck to look at her over his shoulder. "I didn't realize that Turks were particularly known for their healing powers."

"Oh, bother, you know what I mean." She scowled impatiently and shoved a loose strand of hair back from her forehead. "I've never had the honor of meeting a Turk to be able to inquire after his health, but then, I'd wager ten guineas that you haven't, either."

She prodded lightly, and involuntarily he sucked in his breath.

"That pains you?" she asked with concern.

Manfully Jamie shook his head. "Not to speak of, nay," he said, unwilling to admit it to her. "You took me by surprise, that was all."

"Well, then," she said with a renewed cheerfulness that worried him. "I believe you've done well enough that I can relieve you of these stitches."

"*Stitches?*"

"Yes, stitches." Bemused, she rested her hands on her waist above her apron. "You might believe you have a genteel little pinprick in the front of you, Jamie Ryder, but by the time that ball had done its work it left a powerfully big hole on the other side. Of course I had to stitch it closed, or you would surely have bled to death. Didn't you feel the thread pull as it healed before this?"

Before this he hadn't, not under the tightly wrapped bandages, but now that she'd told him he could feel nothing else. Without thinking he reached backward and groped blindly until he felt the frizzled ends of clipped threads coming from his flesh. In immediate response his stomach lurched ominously.

He'd always considered himself stoic enough, able to face down an armed enemy without fearing overly for his own hide, but for some reason the image of her mending him like an old sock turned him squeamish where a knife or pistol wouldn't. Why the devil hadn't she simply cauterized the wound with a hot poker or knife blade and been done with it while he'd been unconscious?

"I'll leave this cloth here to soften the thread while I fetch my scissors," she said, leaving a warm, damp cloth over his shoulder.

The warmth was pleasant. The sickening anticipation of her scissors wasn't.

"Would you like something to drink? I've rum and whiskey both, if either will help."

"Thank you, no." He smiled weakly. Was it really going to be *that* bad? "I've never had the taste for spirits."

"I do believe you're the first man I've ever known who didn't. Mind you hold still now," she said, again with that infernal cheerfulness as she perched on the edge of a three-legged stool behind him. "'Twill be the work of a moment, that's all."

He nodded tersely, even as he felt the beads of moisture gathering on his upper lip. He swallowed as he felt the first tug of her scissors, and tried to concentrate instead on the polished brasses on the mahogany chest of drawers before him. How had they managed to haul such a massive piece of furniture across the trails to—

Damnation, the blasted brasses weren't going to be distraction enough.

"How the devil did you meet your husband, anyway?" he blurted out.

Rachel paused only a moment. Growing up in a family of sailors, she almost expected men to swear in times of stress, and William had done nothing to change her opinion. But the question Jamie was asking along with the oath did surprise her, and not happily, either.

Yet he deserved an answer. Not only would it take his mind off the discomfort of removing the stitches, but after she'd raged on like a madwoman about William earlier, Jamie would most likely welcome hearing something more sensible now that he'd decided to wait out the snowstorm here in her house.

"I met William at an assembly in Providence," she began, unaware of the wistfulness in her voice. "I was very young then, and quite mad for dancing. And oh, William danced so beautifully, I believe I fell in love with him before that first quadrille was done."

That was better, thought Jamie, closing his eyes. He could imagine her dancing, her petticoats twirling gracefully around her ankles. "What color was your— *damn!*—gown?"

"Pale yellow silk sateen," she said slowly, "figured with coral and evergreen carnations. The sash was green as well, and so were the ribbons in my hair and the clocks on my stockings. Those stockings were vastly dear, having been smuggled in from London right there in the middle of the war. Far too dear for Father's pockets just then. But my brother Nickerson—he's a privateer now—was visiting, and he bought them specially for me, most likely because I wept so bitterly from wanting them."

Curtly Jamie nodded, picturing her well-turned legs in those green-clocked stockings and wondering if she tied her garters above the knee or below. Probably above; women with legs as long as hers usually did.

"Was it summer," he said through clenched teeth, "or winter?"

"Spring, because the snowdrops had just begun to bloom outside the kitchen door, and I pinned some into my hair amongst the ribbons. Lord knows how I can remember such foolish things, considering all that's happened since.'' She sighed, bending close to clip and tug the last knot free. "I'm nearly·done, and you've hardly bled at all. Just this last bit, if you can bear it.''

"Of course I can,'' he growled. He took a deep breath, thinking of her in pale yellow silk, the neckline cut beguilingly low over her breasts. "I'll warrant Lindsey was—*damnation!*—mightily taken with you, as well.''

"William?'' she said absently, sitting back on the stool now that she was finished. "Yes, I suppose he was.''

She might remember the snowdrops and the stockings smuggled from London, but with the reality of Jamie Ryder before her she was finding it increasingly difficult to recall William at all. The flickering firelight delineated every muscle in his shoulders and back, lean and strong from hard work and harder living, clear to his narrow waist and hips in close-fitting leggings.

Before the raw new scar below his shoulder there had been other wounds, as well: another puckered scar from a bullet on his upper right arm, the jagged seam of an arrowhead or a knife across his left side. Any of them might have been enough to kill him, yet still he'd lived.

Lived to cross his life with hers....

"You've asked so many questions of me about William that I must have bored you to distraction with·my prattle by now,'' she said, her rueful laugh hollow. "Yet I know so little of you. Have you a wife or sweetheart yourself, praying for your safe return?''

"Nay, not I,'' he scoffed, turning in his chair to face her with his shirt bunched in his hand. "You've seen the sum of my worldly goods, and I can't even claim my pittance from rangering for King George any longer."

"A fortune isn't everything."

"Oh, aye, and the sun sets at dawn and rises at the end of the day," he said dryly. Before the war he'd been in line to inherit as fine a fortune as any young man in Chester County, acres and acres of the rich farmland that had been in his family for over a century, and an elegant stone house with it. Only three years ago, and already it seemed more than a lifetime. "No woman in her right senses would willingly shackle herself to a pauper. What would I have to offer a wife, anyway?"

"Don't belittle yourself, Jamie Ryder," said Rachel staunchly. "From what I've seen, you're a good, kind, honest man, and that would be more than enough for most women."

He narrowed his eyes skeptically as he leaned a little closer, his dark chestnut hair falling over his shoulder. "Oh, aye, enough and more. Since when does honesty pay for yellow silk gowns and smuggled stockings?"

She flushed, as much from the nearness of his shirtless chest as from his question. She wished he'd put his shirt back on; it wasn't easy to keep her gaze on his face, where it belonged, but to ask him to do so would prove to him how much his nakedness unsettled her, and she'd no wish to do that, either.

"I told you before, I was very young when I met William. I—I'm not the same as I was then."

"You'd be content without fancy stockings?"

Her flush deepened as she nodded. Now she wore thick wool stockings that she knit herself, and instead of pink slippers with silver buckles she wore William's old shoes with fleece stuffed in the toes. She was a struggling settler's wife, and she looked it. Jamie might only be teasing, but she still wished he could have seen her as she'd been then, in Newport and Providence, fashionable and beautiful enough to turn every gentleman's head as she'd entered that assembly room.

"No more fancy stockings, I swear," she said. "Besides, they wouldn't be nearly warm enough in the snow."

He laughed, a deep, rich sound that she wanted to hear again. "So now you're willing to trade honesty and kindness for smuggled fripperies?"

She smiled wistfully. "That hardly seems an even trade to me. Since when are honesty and kindness worth no more than ribbons and stockings?"

"I didn't ask their worth. I asked whether you'd be willing to settle for such merits alone."

That stung too close to the truth for her to keep her smile. "I've already learned to settle for a great deal in my life, Jamie," she said sorrowfully. "Perhaps too much."

At once his laughter faded, but the warmth remained in his eyes. "Aye, perhaps that's the trouble with us both," he said softly. "Though I'd say we've settled not for too much, but too little, eh?"

He reached out to brush her cheek with the back of his knuckles, his eyes so close to hers that she felt herself tumbling deeper and deeper into their blue depths. At the last minute he twisted his hand, just enough to graze her lips with his thumb, and inadvertently she trembled, the glancing touch enough to remind her of the kiss they'd shared earlier, and how dangerously close she was to letting him kiss her again.

But when she'd fallen into his arms this morning she'd been frightened and confused. Now she had no such excuse, nothing beyond the sheer desire to taste his lips again on hers, to feel the sweet, heady fire he'd brought to her blood, to be touched and cherished and to forget for a moment, just a moment, the aching, empty loneliness of her life.

And that wasn't excuse enough. Lord help her, it couldn't be.

"Sweet Rachel," he murmured as he cradled her face gently in his fingers, his lips now so close to hers that she could feel the heat of his breath on her skin. "You deserve so much more."

"I can't do this, Jamie," she whispered in misery. "Not to William, not until I know for certain."

"William." He drew back slowly, his hands dropping from her face as the warmth drained from his eyes. "William. Of course. Forgive me."

She nodded, turned mute by her wretchedness, and watched as he stood, moving farther, farther away from her. He pulled the shirt over his head, only a little awkward as he forced the wounded arm into its sleeve, then gathered his belongings from the floor at the foot of her bed.

"High time for me to shift to your loft to sleep," he said with a gruff heartiness that she didn't believe for a minute. "If I'm as hale as that old Turk of yours, then my blanket's plenty of comfort for me. Not that I scorn your feather bed, mind, but I think this is best."

"Yes," she echoed, the word emptying in the hollow place inside her. "It will be for the best."

So why, then, did it feel so wrong?

Alec Lindsey thumped his empty tankard down hard on the tavern's battered table. "And I say the bitch is keeping a man there in my brother's place!"

"Mistress Rachel?" Wiping his hands on his apron, John Volk sucked on his pipe as he shook his head. "Your brother's wife?"

"Why else would she keep me standing in the snow," demanded Alec, "denying me all comforts and courtesies as she ordered me on my way?"

"Mebbe she jes' don't like you, Lindsey," called Nate Wye through the hazy tobacco smoke from the far end of the table. "She wouldn't be the first."

Angrily Alec jumped to his feet, reaching for the pistol at his waist, but the tavern keeper was instantly at his side, resting his hand on Alec's.

"We'll have none of that in here, gentlemen," he warned, looking also at Nate, who was grinning and unperturbed, "else I'll stay your credit, the both of you."

Before he continued, Volk waited until Alec slowly sat once again and his hands were both safely around his tankard. "But I say you're wrong about Mistress Rachel Lindsey. She's never been nothing but a lady, not that I've seen. Even poor William boasted about that. I can't see her up and taking some rascal to her bed. No, no. She's too fine by half for that kind of mischief."

"There's no lady alive who's so fine that she doesn't crave what a man can give her," answered Alec sourly. "I know. I've bedded my share of so-called ladies, and they're no different from any other strumpets, once you toss them on their silk-covered backsides."

"Mebbe that's why there be no sweet ladies like Mistress Rachel waitin' on you, Lindsey," called Nate. "You be so busy with your tossin' and tumblin' that you never took the time to learn the little darlings' names."

The other men within hearing roared their amusement, pounding their tankards or their palms on the table while Alec flushed to the top of his neck cloth, only Volk's threat keeping him in his seat. What did this lot of backwoods farmers know of ladies, anyway? He and William were the only real gentlemen in this whole damned county, gentlemen who'd dined and drunk at far better establishments than John Volk's one-room tavern with whiskey, rum and home-brewed beer the only offerings. He'd never even deign to enter the foul place if there was any other within a day's ride, or another in which he could overhear things that could bring him money. Volk himself wouldn't know a claret if he fell into the cask headfirst.

Alec emptied his tankard and then glared furiously around the table. Damn their eyes for laughing, for laughing at *him!* It was beyond bearing, one more sign of how far below their station he and William had fallen. Before the war, when they'd both been students at King's College in the city, the whole world—or at least the rollicking part of it that included New York City—had been theirs for the taking. They'd drunk and gambled and whored with the best young gentlemen in the colony, and life had been very fine indeed.

But then their father had died, damn the wicked old spendthrift to an endless hell, and life as they liked it was over. Instead of the fortune they'd expected, all they'd inherited were the old man's debts on top of their own, and these two forsaken scraps of wilderness.

It had been Alec's idea that they wed heiresses. The New York gentry was out of the question. Their earlier boon companions knew too much of the Lindseys' circumstances to welcome them as suitors to sisters, and there was also that unfortunate business with William's first wife.

Phillipa had been from an old Dutch family, a sweet-faced girl whom William had married in lovesick haste, only to leave her to languish alone in his remote cabin on the farm, where she had finally died in childbirth. Not that William could be blamed for her being peevish and sickly, but the parents of the potential next brides hadn't seemed inclined to agree.

With their creditors at their heels and their genteel manners as their sole introductions, the brothers had headed north to Connecticut. They'd found scant welcome among the dour first families of New Haven, and less in New London, but once they'd crossed the border to Rhode Island, their luck had turned wildly in their favor.

Within a fortnight William had wooed and won the last daughter of Captain Gabriel Sparhawk, reputed to be one of New England's wealthiest men. If the settlement the old captain offered was less than Alec had hoped, there was the promise of far more in the future.

Besides, William was so besotted with the girl that Alec hadn't had the heart to deny him.

But as soon as they'd used her money to pay off what they could and retreated back here, the old problems had started again. Without the diverting pleasures of a city, William had soon grown restless in his new marriage, just as he had in the old one. What gentleman wouldn't? But unlike Phillipa Vanderslyke, Rachel Sparhawk hadn't wept and cowered. She'd fought back.

And she was fighting still, even after she'd driven poor William away with her petulance and shrewish tongue. As far as Alec was concerned, cuckolding his brother was exactly the sort of thing Rachel would do from sheer spite. Not that she would win, in this or anything else. William might have been weak and lovesick, but Alec had no such scruples. He'd already found ways to punish Rachel for what she'd done, and he wouldn't stop until he'd broken her spirit for good.

And he'd do it. He'd show these barnyard wits exactly how common their sainted Mistress Rachel could be, and then, *then* he'd be the one who laughed last, and best.

Chapter Six

Once the snow stopped, it took Rachel and Jamie two days to shovel out the house and barnyard, as well as the path that ran between them. Though the shoveling made Jamie's shoulder ache and made him realize, too, how weak he still was, he welcomed the heavy work that took his mind from the woman who was tantalizingly beside him, yet destined always to be out of his reach.

By the end of the first day he was so exhausted that he fell asleep between bites at supper, his head slipping back openmouthed against his chair, yet he'd welcomed that, too. At least then he hadn't been faced with another awful, awkward good-night to Rachel.

He still groaned inwardly when he remembered that the only way she'd had to stop him had been to say her husband's name. Her *husband,* for God's sake! It didn't matter that the man was most likely dead; precious few Americans had made it out of Oriskany alive. Rachel believed he wasn't, and no matter how troubled their marriage had been, she had a right to honor her husband however she saw fit. If Jamie had any decency left in his body at all, he'd either have to respect that or leave. His choice was as simple, and as painful, as that.

He dropped another shovelful of snow and straightened, breathing hard as he leaned heavily on the shovel's long handle. All around him Rachel's little flock of black-speckled chickens clucked and scurried excitedly as they pecked at whatever dried bits of last year's grass poked through the frozen ground, their crimson wattles and combs bright against the white snow.

Smiling at their jerky little motions, Jamie lifted his hat to wipe his sleeve across the sweat on his forehead. The sky overhead was a brilliant enameled blue, the new snow sparkling in a sun warm enough to drip long, glistening icicles from the eaves.

"Jamie! Jamie, look!"

He turned and squinted to where Billy was standing proudly behind a long, lumpy wall of snow, complete with a small arsenal of snowballs beside it for defense. Why was it, wondered Jamie, that regardless of whether the country was at peace or at war, all little boys—even Quaker boys—built fortresses from snow? The attraction was a powerful one for big boys, too, and with a grin Jamie thrust the shovel into a snowbank, grabbed his rifle and bounded across the snow to join Billy in his fort.

The boy beamed shyly, scooting to one side as Jamie tried to lower his large frame behind the icy wall with him. Mama had warned him not to bother the tall man, but here he was without him having said a single word.

"Who's your enemy today, lad?" he asked as he laid his rifle down and crouched as best he could behind the icy wall next to the boy.

"Don't know," admitted Billy, perplexed. "Can't be 'Mericans, 'cause Mama an' me an' Papa an' everyone else are 'Mericans. But can't be Britishers, neither, 'cause Mama says you're one of them, even though you don't wear a red coat."

"Well, now, that is a problem." Jamie frowned, packing the top of the wall a little more tightly. "They could be Frenchmen—Frenchmen are most always enemies—or maybe Abenakis. They're plenty mean enough to merit a snowball or two."

Billy nodded seriously, though it was clear enough to Jamie that he'd heard of neither Frenchmen nor Abenakis. Good for Rachel, thought Jamie with pleased surprise. Though there was no way to keep the boy entirely innocent of the war around him, there was also no reason to teach him to hate all who were different.

"Maybe we should just use that old rooster of your Mama's as our target," he suggested. "The one who's always so high-and-mighty with the rest of the flock. Look at him there now! I've barely scraped that patch of ground clear, and he's prancing and pecking at those poor hens like he owns the whole farm!"

Scooping up one of Billy's snowballs, Jamie winked at the boy, took careful aim and lobbed the snowball down toward the rooster. Close, but not a hit, as the rooster danced to one side.

"He's a bad one, that ol' rooster," said Billy, leaning forward with excitement. "But you can get him."

"I'll do my best, lad." Narrowing his eyes with concentration, Jamie tried again, and this time he struck the rooster squarely on its speckled back.

"You did it, Jamie!" whooped Billy. "You did it!"

The bird squawked indignantly, wings flapping and feathers flying, and then raced after one of his hens to take out his mortification on her.

"Aye," agreed Jamie, his face stern, "but I think he could be brought down another rung or two, don't you?"

"Yes, please, Jamie, oh, yes!" Without waiting for an answer, Billy scrambled back to where the snow was still untrampled, and returned with a clump of snow so big he needed both mittened hands to hold it to his chest.

"That should teach him, eh, lad?" Trying hard not to laugh, Jamie carefully took the huge snowball and launched it at the rooster. Though most of the loosely packed lump disintegrated in midair, enough remained to drop onto the rooster's black tail feathers with a satisfying dusting of white powder. Once again the beleaguered bird squawked with outrage, while Billy shrieked with delight.

"You taught him, Jamie!" he cried. "You said you would, and you did!"

Jamie laughed, too, amazed by how much he was enjoying himself. How long had it been since he'd laughed out loud with a child over something as foolish as a wet, angry chicken? "I suppose we did teach him, lad," he said, "though exactly what he learned, I'll be damned—I mean daft if I could say."

But as swiftly as Billy's infectious giggling had begun, it now had stopped. He sniffed loudly, rubbing his nose with his mitten while his mouth twisted anxiously.

"What is it, Billy?" asked Jamie uneasily. "Is it, ah, a trip to the privy?"

Fiercely the little boy shook his head. "Don't go, Jamie."

Jamie smiled with relief. "I'm not about to go anywhere, not until we're finished with that rooster and his lessons."

"No, Jamie." Impulsively he reached out to tug the fringe on Jamie's shirt. "Don't go from *here*. Don't leave me and Mama."

"Well, now." Jamie cleared his throat uncomfortably, remembering with painful clarity how Rachel had warned him not to hurt her son, and here he was, doing exactly that. "I'd say that's more up to your mother than to me."

"Mama said you had to leave," said Billy anxiously. "She said you had to, as soon as you felt better."

Lord, he hadn't expected this. "Was that when she told you how I'd been fighting with the British," he asked carefully, "and that I was your enemy?"

The boy shook his head forlornly and sat back in the snow with his hands clasped tightly around his knees. "Mama jus' said you couldn't stay. But she's wrong, Jamie. You make her an' me an' Blackie happy. You make Mama smile. Why would you hafta go?"

Jamie looked down into the unhappy little face, his own emotions twisting in much the same way as the boy's. He'd thought that Rachel was pleased to have him stay. At least, that was how it had seemed to him, and apparently to Billy, too. But though he could make excuses for staying from now to Judgment Day, even Billy recognized him as a Britisher, one of the enemy, and Rachel didn't need any more reason than that to wish him gone.

"Your mama said I could stay until this storm was cleared away and traveling would be easier," he began, "and I've stayed on a bit to help her out with the snow and all, but then she'll—"

"You'll go." Billy's voice was flat, but the tears of disappointment in his eyes were all too clear. "You'll go, jus' like Papa. Only Uncle Alec stays, an' I hate him."

"Billy, it's not that—"

"Bil-ly!" called Rachel as she came around the corner of the house, her hands cupped around her mouth. She spotted them in the fort and waved, her blue mittens bright as flags in the brilliant sunshine. "Billy, it's time!"

Instantly Billy was on his feet, more than ready to run away from Jamie and to his mother. But in the same moment Rachel suddenly toppled flat into the snow, still, horribly still, on her back with her arms thrown out to either side.

"No," whispered Jamie. "God, no, not her!"

He hadn't heard a shot, but that meant nothing to his war-tuned instincts. Sweeping his gaze along the hillside and the trees beyond for any sign of the attacker, he grabbed Billy and yanked him down behind his pretend fort.

"You *stay*," he ordered hoarsely, seizing his rifle. "You stay here with your head down until I say otherwise."

Without pausing, he ran toward Rachel, zigzagging across the open yard as he continued to search the hills, the barn, the roof of the house for whoever must be hiding. His heart was pounding, sick with dread.

She can't be dead, not like this, not so fast, not when he'd sworn to keep her safe. She can't be....

He dropped to his knees in the snow beside her. Her eyes were closed, her body lifeless. "Rachel, lass," he murmured urgently, afraid to touch her until he knew where she'd been hurt. "Can you hear me, Rachel?"

Her eyes flew open, green and startled. "Of course I can, Jamie," she said. "Why couldn't I?"

Too stunned to be relieved, Jamie could only shake his head in disbelief. "What in God's name are you doing? What's the matter with you?"

"Nothing whatsoever, which is more than can be said of you." She pushed herself up on her elbows, bits of snow clinging to her white cap and black hair. "I told you you've been trying to do too much too soon. Why don't you go inside and lie down, and I'll wake you for supper."

"Damnation, Rachel, don't coddle me!" He was shouting, and he couldn't help it. "I thought you'd been shot, I thought you were lying dead, here in the snow!"

"Don't be ridiculous," she said sharply, her own voice rising to match his as she sat upright and shoved back the hood of her cloak. "How could I be dead here in the middle of the afternoon, practically on my own doorstep?"

"Snow angels, Mama!" Breathless from running across the yard, Billy flopped down in the snow beside her. Giggling with delight, he began pumping his arms up and down to make the imprint of the angel's wings in the snow, and swinging his legs back and forth for the robe. "My turn, like you said!"

Immediately Jamie wheeled around to face him. "What the devil are you doing here, Billy?" he demanded, unable to stop himself. "I told you to stay where you'd be safe, and I damned well meant it!"

Billy shrank back, his eyes huge in his face and his mouth pinched, and at once Rachel was on her feet.

"Don't you dare speak to him like that!" she said furiously. She seized Jamie's sleeve, dragging him out of Billy's hearing. "You have absolutely no right to do so, none at all! I won't have you swearing before my child, and I won't have you telling him he's in some sort of danger, because he's *not!*"

Jamie stared at her, overwhelmed, as anger and fear and shame and black memory all churned together within him and her face blurred before him.

"This is our home, Mr. Ryder," she said fiercely. "Can't you understand that? This is our *home*, and I never want Billy to feel afraid while he's here!"

"Damnation, Rachel, words alone won't make it so!"

"I never said they would. I'm not a fool. Merciful heavens, why else do I sleep with a loaded musket beside my bed?"

"Rachel—"

"No, you listen to me!" Rachel gulped a deep breath, struggling to keep her voice from shaking from both anger and emotion. Jamie might have been raised a Friend, but at heart he was now a soldier. The way he'd come racing across the yard to her, the deadly assurance with which he handled his rifle were more than proof. How could a man like that, accustomed to killing and destruction, ever understand how much she had at stake in this farm?

"I know that wishing and words alone can't keep me safe. But words—*your* words, Mr. Ryder—can undermine all I've done to make this a haven for Billy and for me, too, and I won't have it. I can't, not unless I want to spend the rest of my days huddled in fear behind shutters and locks. *I can't.*"

He shook his head again, and caught sight of Billy, huddled forlornly in the angel print in the snow behind his mother.

That other mother had thought she'd been safe, too, she and her children together, and then she'd been struck down in her apron among her breakfast dishes, corn-bread crumbs and smeared butter and blood, Lord, so much blood on her apron and in the sweet rushes she'd strewn on her floor, and—

No, he would not think of it again! That woman had died, but Rachel lived. Rachel lived and Billy with her, and that was what must matter now.

"You're wrong, Rachel," he said, desperate for a way to convince her that she'd accept. "There's so damned much that could happen to you here alone. Didn't you learn anything from the wolf?"

She raised her chin defensively. "There's never been a wolf before, and there won't be again."

"Then next time it will be something else!" He grabbed her by the shoulders, determined to make her understand. "For God's sake, Rachel, why are you being so stubborn about this?"

"Why?" Her eyes went instantly cold, her black lashes narrowing them. She'd had enough of taking orders from William. "You're not my husband, and you're not my father. The way I see it, I don't have to do one blessed thing you tell me to. Now let me go."

His fingers flew from her shoulders as if they'd been burned. What she said was true: he'd no right to expect her obedience, let alone to touch her. Deep inside he knew the only way he could convince her was to tell her what he knew, what he'd seen, what he'd done. But to his shame, he couldn't do it. Words alone weren't enough, at least not the words he knew.

His mouth was set and grim. "You'll insist on remaining here, even if it means putting your own life and Billy's at risk?"

"Yes." She crossed her arms and tucked her hands beneath them to hide her trembling. He was asking her questions, hard questions, that no one else had ever bothered to ask, and though she answered without hesitation, the answers she gave frightened her. "From everything I hear of this wretched war, Billy and I are safer here than we'd be most places."

"But Rachel—"

"We all make choices," she said, steadfastly meeting his gaze. His eyes seemed strangely empty, the warmth she'd come to expect gone. "This one is mine. I don't ask why you decided to do what you did, and I'll thank you not to question mine."

"Mama, look!" called Billy, standing in the middle of his snow angel to point down the hillside. "Look who's coming!"

Though she half expected Billy's visitor to be no more than a squirrel, Rachel turned, glad for the excuse to break away from Jamie. She shaded her eyes with her hand to look at the three horses slowly making their way up the hill. Horses—dear Lord, let it not be Alec again, not today with Jamie so hot and ready to pick a fight.

But then a figure swung down from the first horse to walk it up the hill, lifting her flat-brimmed hat to wave so that Rachel could see the sun glint off the woman's silver-gray hair.

With relief Rachel waved in return, smiling though the woman was still too far away to see her face. "There you are, Jamie," she said without turning, "the proof of exactly how *un*alone I am. That's Mary and Ethan Bowman, my nearest neighbors from down near the river, come to call on me as civilly as if we were in town."

But when he didn't answer, she turned to find he'd vanished. She began to call his name, then stopped. If he wished to sulk and hide, then fine, and if he chose this moment to disappear into the woods as suddenly as he'd come, then that was fine, too. She'd let him. She wasn't going to search for him and she wasn't going to beg, and she certainly wasn't going to let him spoil a visit from the Bowmans.

But she hadn't counted on Billy.

"Where's Jamie?" he asked anxiously as soon as she'd lifted him onto her back and started down the hillside to meet their guests. "Did he go?"

"I don't know where he went," said Rachel more crossly than she intended. "He didn't bother to tell me."

"You made Jamie mad, an' he left," said Billy unhappily. "You said he had to go, Mama, an' he did."

"Oh, Billy, I'm sure he just went into the house or he's in the barn with Juno. Where else could he be?"

Yet still her conscience pricked her. Furious though she'd been with Jamie, she'd have to admit now that he'd spoken from concern for her. No wonder he'd been so angry with her in return. But then she'd made William angry enough to leave, too, and uneasily she wondered if Billy, young though he'd been, could remember the hateful, shouting quarrels they'd had that last week before William had enlisted.

She felt Billy's little sigh against her back, and she knew from his too-long silence that her assurance hadn't been enough.

"Is Jamie a secret from Mr. an' Mrs. Bowman, too?" he asked finally. "Like Uncle Alec?"

Now Rachel sighed. "Yes, I suppose he is," she said reluctantly. It was one thing to lie to Alec, but quite another to do so to friends like Mary and Ethan. "Unless Jamie decides to come out from wherever he's hiding and be sociable, we shouldn't tell the Bowmans he's been here."

"I wish Jamie wasn't a Britisher, Mama," said Billy plaintively, "and I wish he didn't hafta go."

"And I wish for a great many things, too, Billy," said Rachel as she shifted him from her shoulders down to the snow beside her. "Now come, let's put on a cheerful face for Mrs. Bowman."

That, at least, was an easy enough task. It was virtually impossible for Rachel to see Mary's round, weathered face and not to smile. Though she had met the Bowmans when she'd first come west with William, they had not become her friends until the end of last winter, when her life had been at its lowest, most desperate ebb and she'd feared she'd perish from loneliness and shame of what she'd done for Alec.

Shaking from fatigue after walking on the snow-covered trail to their store with Billy in her arms, Rachel had finally broken down and wept over a length of pink ribbon that reminded her of all she'd left behind in Rhode Island. Mary had responded by taking Rachel in her arms until the tears at last were finished, and had kept her firmly under her wing ever since. In many ways the older woman had taken the place of Rachel's own faraway mother, freely offering advice on everything from teaching Billy to drink from a cup to making a poultice of herbs to relieve mosquito bites.

But unlike Rachel's small, round, elegant mother, Mary was a lean and rangy woman who had seen neither a city nor an ocean. As a child she had been captured by Mohawks and had lived with them until she was a young woman. Her clothing had remained unlike any that Rachel had seen in Rhode Island: an English linen apron over a squaw's deerskin leggings, carefully starched white ruffles attached to the sleeves of a man's dark red hunting shirt, a sober pewter cross on a cord tangling with the strings of purple and white wampum beads around her neck, and polished buckles that were purely decorative stitched to the front of her moccasins. She wore her hair in two long plaits, and her laugh was deep and throaty from smoking the white clay pipe that was habitually clenched in her teeth.

Ethan Bowman was more typical of the other settlers Rachel had met. He had come upriver as a trapper and stayed on as the owner of a trading post and shop, and though he'd long ago left the East he'd come from, he still dressed like any other stout English shopkeeper in smallclothes and a waistcoat, albeit a shopkeeper with a long knife sheathed beneath the skirts of his coat and a musket across his saddle. Together he and Mary had raised seven sons and daughters, and they never seemed to be able to agree on exactly how many grandchildren and great-grandchildren they'd acquired as well over the years.

"Good day to you, Rachel!" called Mary as she tugged her horse the last few paces. "And you, Master Billy! I vow you've grown at least a foot since we saw you last."

Rachel leaned forward to kiss the other woman's cheek, deftly dodging her pipe. "Good day to you, too, and welcome! I never dreamed you'd come clear over here so soon after the snow!"

"It's because of that storm that we have come, Rachel," said Ethan as he reached around to take the reins of Mary's horse along with his own. "We wanted to see how you were faring."

"Oh, well enough," said Rachel quickly. "One storm's much the same as another, isn't it?"

"Ha, lass, that's not what you said last winter!" Ethan's grizzled brows rose with surprise beneath the rolled brim of his cocked hat. "Here I'd thought you'd be needing another hand or two to help with the clearing, and faith, you have it all but done on your own!" He ruffled Billy's hair. "You must be helping your mother, eh?"

"I did *that*, Mr. Bowman, sir," said Billy proudly as he pointed to the fort. "Ja—I mean Mama did the rest."

Ethan looked at Billy closely but let it pass. "Did she, now? Your mother's a remarkable woman, lad, and don't you forget it."

"Yes, sir." He tipped his head backward to look quickly at Rachel. "My mama killed the wolf."

Rachel gulped. "Oh, Billy, I don't think the Bowmans wish to hear that tale."

"We most certainly do," declared Mary. "Leastways, I do. A *real* wolf, Billy?"

"Yes, Mrs. Bowman." Billy's eyes were bright as he realized he'd won the attention of all three adults. "She shot that ol' wolf dead 'cause he wanted to eat Juno. I seen the blood all over the snow."

"'Saw,' Billy," said Rachel, vainly hoping to pass over the story. "You saw it, not seen. Now, I'm sure Mr. and Mrs. Bowman would rather come into the house by the fire."

But Mary wasn't so easily put off. "So you killed yourself a wolf, m'dear," she said, beaming as she patted Rachel's arm, "and I say congratulations to you! Time was, not a night would go by when you couldn't hear the creatures howling all mournful in the woods, but now, praise the Lord, they keep to themselves."

"Not this ol' wolf," began Billy again with obvious relish. "He jus'—"

"No more, Billy," said Rachel, her tone warning enough as she swept her mittened hand in the direction of the house with all the graciousness that had been bred into her. "I've cider and spruce beer, or I can make a pot of chocolate in no time."

"Stay a moment, Rachel, and see the other reason for our call." Ethan handed their horses' reins to Mary and walked back to the third horse, a sturdy chestnut gelding with a white blaze along his nose and two sacks of grain tied to his back. "You remember I promised to keep my eye out for a horse for you after I sold Juno's twins for you, and I'd say Proudfoot here is just what you ordered."

Rachel gasped. "You mean he's mine, Ethan? All mine?"

"If you want him, he is." He tugged the horse's bridle, lifting his head for Rachel to see. "But he'll be a good choice for you, lass, and you won't find better for the price."

"Oh, he's beautiful, Ethan," said Rachel as she stroked the horse's velvety nose, "and I don't know how to thank you for finding him."

Mary clucked her tongue. "There you are again, husband, putting a fine gloss on a sorry truth." She shook her head, her long silver braids swinging gently, and turned to Rachel. "The *truth* of the matter, m'dear, is that Mr. Bowman took the nag in trade for an overdue debt from a certain captain given to gaming who should have known better. We don't trade in cattle as a rule and never have, but Mr. Bowman didn't fancy you living out here alone without a horse, so here we are."

Rachel smiled. "You're very kind, Ethan, whatever the reason." Yet even as she spoke, she wondered why she welcomed such concern from the Bowmans while at the same time she resented it so much from Jamie, then thrust aside the question as ludicrous. It made perfect sense: the Bowmans were friends she could trust, while Jamie was a man she scarcely knew. "I'll take him back to the barn and settle him in Thunder's old stall."

"Nay, Billy and I will see to that," said Ethan heartily. "Won't we, Billy?"

Billy wasn't so sure. Wide-eyed, he leaned back against Rachel's skirts as he warily studied this horse that was so much bigger than Blackie.

Rachel patted his shoulders to reassure him as she pushed him gently toward the barn. "I'll come with you and Ethan, lamb. We have to make Proudfoot welcome."

But Mary hooked her arm through Rachel's, drawing her back. "Stay, m'dear, and let them go," she said softly enough for Billy not to hear. "There's things I must tell you that are better for your ears alone."

Half an hour later, as Mary balanced one of Rachel's little French porcelain chocolate cups incongruously in her work-scarred fingers, the older woman told the real reason for her visit.

"We're in trouble, Rachel, every last one of us in this valley and beyond," she said, her face drawn tight with concern. "This lovely war of king and Congress has come 'round to our own doorsteps."

For Rachel it already had, though not that she'd confess it to Mary. She sipped the steaming chocolate, considering how much she could admit without mentioning Jamie. "When last Alec was here," she began tentatively, "he told me there'd been some sort of battle not far from here."

"Alec Lindsey?" Mary snorted with disgust. "I know Alec's your kin, Rachel, but the man wouldn't know a battle from a biscuit, 'less he found them both inside Volk's tavern."

"Then Alec's wrong?" With her little finger Rachel poked at the tiny iridescent bubbles floating on top of the chocolate, taking care not to let her eyes betray to Mary the wild hope she felt swelling within her. If Alec had been wrong about a battle, then maybe he'd been wrong about Jamie, too. "There hasn't been a battle?"

"Nay, m'dear, no battle," said Mary grimly. "Nothing nearly so glorious. Three weeks ago Joseph Brant's Mohawks and a pack of Tory Rangers under that devil's son Walter Butler attacked the settlements at Cherry Valley. Not just the men in the fort, mind. They roamed from house to house in the settlements outside, slaughtering every last living creature they could and setting fire to what they couldn't."

Rachel listened, mute with horror. How could she have harbored and nursed a man who had done such things? Why hadn't Alec told her this? Why hadn't he told her before she'd smiled at and laughed with and *kissed* Jamie Ryder?

"Children, Rachel," continued Mary relentlessly, her words painting a doubly terrifying picture for Rachel, "little innocents like Billy, torn from their dying mothers' skirts and scalped! *Scalped!* All in King George's name, they say, that evil, murderous tyrant! Forty-eight Americans dead when the godless wickedness was done, may all their souls be resting sweet in Heaven now!"

"Amen," whispered Rachel, unable to say more. She thought of how Jamie had never denied being one of Walter Butler's men. The deadly efficiency with which he handled his rifle, the way his face could grow so hard and empty: were those the marks of a man who could ruthlessly murder children for the sake of a king across the ocean? Dear Lord forgive her, the wound she'd so carefully tended could have been caused by a bullet from the musket of a desperate farmer defending his home and family.

Forty-eight dead, and Walter Butler proud enough of the bloodletting to boast of it. But what hideous act could Jamie have done to shock such a man into offering twenty dollars for his capture? Mary might doubt Alec's word, but Rachel didn't, not where money was concerned. She could imagine nothing worse than killing children, and yet Jamie must have gone beyond even that to be so singled out.

Oh, Jamie, how could you have done such things?

She bowed her head beneath the weight of her sorrow and confusion, and her gaze fell upon Blackie, lying forgotten on the floor where Billy had dropped him. With trembling fingers she plucked the toy horse from the floor and cradled him in her lap for comfort. She thought of Jamie's wry smile, the kindness that lit his blue eyes as he played with Billy, the soft-spoken way he teased and made her laugh and how he'd saved her life from the wolf. She'd known next to nothing about him, yet somehow she'd felt she could trust him.

And how horribly, appallingly wrong she'd been.

Oh, Jamie, how could you...

Mary's hand grasped her shoulder. "Steady, Rachel, I did not mean to shock you so. I vow you're white as the snow outside."

"I'll be fine," murmured Rachel as the room seemed to shift and wheel around her, and she squeezed her eyes shut, struggling to make it stop. "Simply... fine."

"Here now, lamb, drink this," ordered Mary as she held the dipper full of water to Rachel's lips. "I know you're city bred and not accustomed to such things, but for Billy's sake you must be brave."

"I will," she whispered hoarsely. "I must."

She would say nothing more. For all she knew, Jamie had left for good when she'd refused his assistance—*assistance,* dear Lord, when he'd brought so much harm to so many others!—for when she'd come into the cabin with Mary she'd seen that the few belongings he'd left in the kitchen were gone.

But he might just as easily be in the loft above, listening to every word and waiting for her to betray him to Mary. She didn't know what he'd do in return, and she refused to risk Mary's life to find out.

"Ethan wants to take you and Billy back home with us," Mary was saying. "That's part of Ethan's reckoning behind Proudfoot, of course. You know the store's more stockade than house from the old wars, and we'll all be safe enough there if the Tories come this far west."

For a long moment Rachel didn't answer. Mary's offer was a tempting one. The Bowmans would let her stay as long as was necessary, until the threat from the British was past. In the meantime she could help Ethan with the store and Mary with the house, and Billy would have the rare company of other children.

But the same reasons she'd given Jamie for staying still held. She'd worked too hard to abandon the house and farm now. It was her home, and here she would—she *would*—be safe.

"I can't, Mary," she said at last, her voice calm though her hands held tight to the little cloth horse in her apron beneath the table. "This is where I belong, and I'm not going to leave."

"That's what I told Ethan." Mary grunted as she fingered the purple and white beads around her neck. "'She won't run like a rabbit,' I says. 'That little Rachel will stay where she is.' But it's not making me happy, not at all."

Rachel shook her head. If Jamie was hiding overhead, she hoped he was listening. "I'm sorry, Mary," she said. "You're most kind and generous and I've no wish to make you unhappy, but I cannot go."

Carefully Mary set down the little chocolate cup. "There's nothing I can say to change your mind, is there?"

"No," said Rachel. "I'll stay."

And merciful Heaven, she prayed silently, let my decision be the right one!

Chapter Seven

Rachel sat up late, unable to sleep, long after she'd tucked Billy into bed and washed the supper dishes and put away the chocolate pot and cups. She'd pulled her chair close to the hearth and laid one last stick on the fire so she'd have enough light for her sewing. She'd also compulsively cleaned and reloaded both her musket, then unloaded and done it again to be sure.

But when the knock came on her door, she still gasped and jumped from her chair, her heart racing as she dropped her mending and grabbed a musket.

"Who is it?" she called through the barred oak, though she could guess perfectly well. Neither Joseph Brant nor Walter Butler would be half so polite as to knock before they set fire to her house.

"It's Jamie Ryder, Rachel." He paused a moment, either waiting for her to open the door or deciding what to say next. "You don't have to let me in, lass, but I'd be much obliged if I could see you one last time."

She knew she shouldn't do it. She tried to think of everything that Mary had told her. He was dangerous to her and to Billy. He was the enemy.

He said he wished to see her one last time.

One last time, and she wished to see him, too.

She lifted the bar from the door and swung it open just enough for him to slip inside with a little gust of icy night air. She fussed with barring the door again, postponing the moment when she'd have to meet his eye, and she kept the musket in her arms.

"You're learning, Rachel," he said softly. "Don't trust anyone."

Troubled, she looked at him at last, and his eyes were heavy lidded, watching her. In his arms he cradled his own rifle, loosely, against his chest the way she held Billy, the firelight winking off the beautifully engraved brass. How ludicrous they must look, she thought, standing here, each of them armed with guns whose barrels measured longer than the distance between them!

"You came back," she said.

"I never left." He shrugged his haversack from his shoulder to the floor with a thump, wincing slightly at the motion. "I heard what your friends said."

"All of it?" Her mouth was dry, her heart beating so fast it almost hurt.

"Enough. They passed near me, and they didn't bother to lower their voices."

"That's because Ethan's hard of hearing in his left ear." Her heartbeat slowed a fraction. He'd been outside, then, hiding in the woods and not in the loft overhead. He wouldn't have heard what Mary had told her.

Or would he? And would it matter if he had?

He reached out his hand to brush back a lock of her hair that had slipped free from her cap, daring to cross the invisible line that the guns had drawn between them.

"Those people care for you, Rachel," he said softly. "They do well to worry over you. Why didn't you go with them as they asked?"

"For the same reason I've given you. This is my home, and I've no wish to leave it."

She lifted her chin, not only from pride but to ease her cheek away from his touch. It only had been a handful of hours since they'd parted, yet already she'd forgotten the perilous currents that seemed to dance and eddy around him, currents that tempted her to plunge into their depths and drown.

The hint of a smile twitched one corner of his mouth. "You're a stubborn woman, Rachel Lindsey."

"My friends told me that, too." She had to end this now, before she became too willing to forget all that Mary had told her, and remembered only the rare sweet warmth that his smile brought to her chilly loneliness.

"Stubbornness can have its merits," he said wryly, keeping his voice low so as not to wake the boy curled up in the bed. He had come here to apologize, and he'd meant it when he'd said it was for the last time. Meant it, that is, until he'd seen her again. "Like the way it turns your eyes so green I can't forget them, even after you've as much as called me a fool for caring about what becomes of you and Billy."

"Oh, dear Lord, help me," she whispered wretchedly. "You must not say such things to me, Jamie. You *can't.*"

"Why not? Do your friends tell you that, as well?"

"Not in those words, no, they don't." She looked down again, horribly aware that it was the only way she could say what she must. "But they did tell me that forty-eight men, women and children were massacred and their homes burned last month at Cherry Valley."

He reeled back, sucking in his breath with a strangled oath. Forty-eight dead. He hadn't known the number would be so high. All he knew was what he'd seen, and that had been enough for any man.

Forty-eight dead. Did Rachel know how many of them had been children? Unable to stop himself, Jamie looked at Billy, his fine, pale hair spread over the coverlet as he slept. When he had heard that the general at Fort Niagara would give six dollars for every American child's scalp, he had scoffed it off as hearsay. He'd fought with the British for two years before that, honorably and without fear, and he knew their ways. Their officers wouldn't sink to murdering children.

But after Cherry Valley, he'd never doubt again.

"You were there, weren't you?" Rachel was asking, her voice taut. "Three weeks ago the Tories came with the Indians, said Mary, and three weeks ago I found you in the barn. Your gun, and your wound, and—and I— I need to know, Jamie. Did you—were you there with Walter Butler?"

And all he could do was stare at her, at the horror and dread that marked her lovely face. Did she realize how she'd shifted closer to the bed, shielding her sleeping son from the enemy with her skirts and the musket in her hands? She was so much like the others who'd been ready to give their lives without a thought in order to protect their children. He thought of how the Senecas marked the scalps of the mothers they'd killed: white paint, daubed with red tears.

And blood, so much innocent blood.

"I need to know, Jamie," said Rachel again, pleading. "Even if you go, I need to know if you did—if you were with the others at Cherry Valley?"

"Aye," he said hoarsely. "I was."

He saw how her face crumpled, and he couldn't bear to stay for more. He threw open the door and stumbled outside, slamming it shut behind him as he gulped at the cold, sharp night air.

He'd been a coward once before, and he was a coward again. He steadied himself against the rough walls of the house, breathing hard. So much for sweet farewells, for smiles and teasing compliments. He should consider himself fortunate if she didn't turn him in for Butler's bounty. That was what he deserved, the fine reward of cowardice.

Bleakly he looked up at the moon, thinking of the woman and child on the other side of the door. That door was most likely barred to him now, and he couldn't blame Rachel. He'd warned her often enough not to trust him. Now she knew the reason. Rachel could talk all she wanted about her home being her sanctuary; that was exactly what it had become to him. He no more wanted to leave here, to leave her and Billy, than she would want him to stay.

It was the horse's neigh that he heard first, more shrill than it should have been, and he shivered in spite of the heavy coat.

The Senecas had laughed like devils as they'd torched the settlers' barns, trapping the animals inside. As the flames grew higher, they had danced in the firelight, adding their own war cries to the screams of the dying animals. No one could stop them and, what was worse, no one tried.

There was the horse again, louder, and Jamie's hands balled into tight fists as he struggled to deny the sound. Lord help him, why must his memory torture him like this? He shook his head, fighting with himself, and from the corner of his eye saw the too-bright square of the barn's doorway, lit from the flames within.

Rachel's barn. It was Rachel's barn that was on fire. He shook his head, forcing himself to trust what he saw. But what he saw now was the barn and the man running from it, his figure black against the moonlit snow as he plunged clumsily through the deeper drifts and away from the fire.

"Halt, there!" shouted Jamie, already lifting his rifle to his shoulder as he ran himself. "You, halt!"

The man looked over his shoulder at Jamie, nearly stumbling in the snow. But he didn't stop, and as he ran forward Jamie saw him shove back his coat with one hand. Instinctively Jamie knew what would come next, and before the man had stopped to aim the pistol, Jamie fired. The man jerked once as if pulled by a string, then pitched forward into the snow, his running over for good.

"Jamie, what in dear heaven are you—"

"The barn's on fire," he said curtly as he swung his rifle over his shoulder. "We have to save the animals. Damnation, Rachel, hurry!"

He didn't wait, trusting her to follow. He could smell the smoke now, and hear the little pops and cracks of the fire along with the sounds of the terrified animals trapped inside. The rooster and some of the hens had already fluttered through the smoke and out the open door.

That open door was Jamie's best hope. He guessed that he'd surprised the man who'd set the fire into fleeing before he could close the door after him, and before, prayed Jamie, the fire had had a chance to take hold. He ripped the powder horn from around his neck and dropped it along with his rifle to the ground, not wishing to blow himself and the barn skyward. Then swiftly he pressed his kerchief in the snow to wet it before he tied it over his mouth and nose, and headed into the barn.

The smoke was thick and acrid from the damp wood, stinging his eyes. Flames jumped from the hoppers where winter feed was stored and licked, crackling, at the beams. But so far that was all, and if he worked fast he might be able to save the barn as well as the animals.

Disoriented by the smoke, he felt his way as swiftly as he could toward the gelding trapped in the corner stall. He tripped over something soft that squawked and skittered away—another hen?—and heard Rachel mutter crossly behind him when the chicken collided with her, as well. He hadn't expected her to follow him into the burning barn, and he whipped around to send her back. To his surprise she had tied a scarf over her face as well, and had wrapped a wool scarf over her cap and hair against the drifting sparks. For a split second he wondered how and where a sea captain's daughter like her had learned such sensible precautions, until she suddenly vanished into the smoke.

"Rachel? Rachel!" His voice was muffled by the handkerchief and the dull roar of the fire, and there was no response from her in turn. *"Rachel!"*

"Stop bellowing, Jamie," she called back hoarsely, popping up once more before him, her face smudged with soot. She grimaced and tugged at the rope that was twisted around both hands. "It's only this contrary animal that's—"

She slipped down again, pulled off her feet before she could finish. Jamie glimpsed the cow's white-rimmed eyes and her long horns with their brass tips as she swung her head and tried to break free. He seized the rope around the animal's neck to find Rachel. Grabbing her arm, he dragged her, coughing and sputtering, back to her feet.

"Are you all right?" he demanded.

"Of course I am," she rasped indignantly.

"Then hang on." He jerked Juno's head in the direction of the open door, and with the flat of his hand smacked the cow's bony flank as hard as he could. With a final frightened lowing, Juno bolted forward with Rachel close at her side, into the smoke and through the door to safety.

He hoped the gelding would be as easily persuaded. The horse was thrashing his hooves wildly against the sides of the stall, frantically seeking a way to escape.

"Easy now, lad, easy," crooned Jamie as he pulled off his coat to cover the terrified animal's eyes. He wished he was able to move more slowly to reassure the animal, but there simply wasn't time. "No one's going to hurt you."

He reached up to tie the coat over the horse's forehead. The gelding began to rear back, but Jamie moved swiftly, hiding the fire from the horse's rolling eyes with the cloth.

"I told you everything will be fine, didn't I?" said Jamie as he quickly slipped beside the horse to lead it from the barn. He patted the gelding's shoulder to reassure it, the animal's coat glazed with foam despite the winter night. "Lively now, lad, so we don't worry Rachel."

Trembling, the horse reluctantly followed Jamie from the stall and toward the door. Jamie's eyes stung from the smoke, and as they passed near the flame, his throat burned despite the handkerchief. He coughed, a rough, ragged gasp for air, and felt the horse quiver in anxious response and begin to pull away. Fiercely he tightened his grip on the bundled coat that was his makeshift harness, forcing himself and the horse step by step toward the door. He was almost there: he could feel the chill of the night begin to pierce the heat of the fire.

Another step, another step, another prayer that the horse wouldn't bolt and his lungs wouldn't burst.

"Jamie!" Rachel was there, a bucket of water swinging heavily from each hand. "Oh, Jamie, look at you!"

"I'm fine," he croaked, breathing deeply of the cold, sharp air to clear his head. "The horse—"

"I'll take him back to the lean-to with Juno," she said quickly, setting the buckets down to take the horse from Jamie. "Come with me, brave boy. Handsomely, now, handsomely! Such a grand, fine horse!"

She looked over her shoulder at Jamie, her face taut with concern despite the caressing tone she kept for the horse. "I'll be back in a moment, and I'll bring more water from the well."

"Nay, there's no time." They'd already given the fire more time than they should have while they'd saved the animals. The well was beside the house, and with only the two of them to ferry the heavy buckets back and forth, the barn would be ashes before they'd be able to bring enough water to douse the flames.

But there was another way, and Jamie forced his aching body to run across the yard to where he'd left his shovel, still thrust in the snow after he'd gone to join Billy at his fort—could it really have been only this morning? He grabbed the shovel, and dug deeply into the bank beside the door.

The snow was heavy and wet as he carried it into the barn, and when he tossed it into the fire it landed with a hiss of steam, blanketing the flame with the sheer weight of the frozen water. Swiftly he returned with another shovelful of snow, and another, each one smothering another corner of the fire. He was only half aware that Rachel had joined him, matching his efforts with her own shovel. He didn't even realize that the fire was finally out until the barn seemed strangely dark around him, the bright flames replaced by moonlight on the drifting bits of smoke and steam.

"We did it," said Rachel hoarsely. "*You* did it."

She snuffled loudly as she dropped her shovel and rubbed her palms across her cheeks. Her face was streaked with soot and her eyes were red from smoke, and with her spark-pocked skirts hanging damply around her she looked every bit as bedraggled as the hens now pecking forlornly at her feet.

Close to exhaustion, Jamie slowly shook his head. "Nay, lass, you were on the mark the first time. I couldn't have done it alone any more than could you."

"But I was the one who let it happen." Her shoulders sagged as she looked at the damage around them. "I can't imagine how I was so careless. I must have left the lantern too near the forage when I was milking."

"It wasn't your fault, Rachel, and it wasn't an accident."

"But how else could it have happened," she said, waving her arm at the charred wood, "from the inside like this?"

"Someone set it, that's how."

She stared at him, fear mixed with disbelief. Now that the immediate danger of the fire was gone, she felt weak-kneed and shaky. She could have lost so much, and she shuddered to think of how Juno and Proudfoot would have suffered. She was tired and frightened, and all she wanted now was for Jamie to take her into his arms again and hold her, just hold her, the way he had before, and not scare her more with threats she was now too weak to deny.

"That's ridiculous," she said hoarsely. "Who would do such a thing?"

"You tell me." He was watching her closely, his eyes in the moonlight an unearthly blue in his soot-blackened face.

She swallowed convulsively. "Mary said the Indians and the Tories set fire to farms."

"Tories like me?" His laugh was harsh. "Nay, Rachel, this one you can't blame on me, nor on Brant and his men, either. Our orders are to fire the buildings only after the enemy—meaning you and Billy, sweetheart—has been subdued or captured."

"But who else?" Even in the middle of the fire she hadn't felt as helpless as she did now. "Who else could it have been?"

"You tell me," he said again. "You know. I won't."

And at last he took her arm, not for comforting but to lead her from the barn. She didn't want to go, not like this.

"I have to go to Billy," she cried as she tried to pull free. "He'll be frightened if I'm not there."

"You haven't been there the last hour," he said, his grip on her arm as relentless as the expression that hardened his face. "You've said yourself the boy can sleep through most anything."

"I have to go back to the house, Jamie, I have to go now!"

"You can go to Billy soon enough, Rachel," he said as he swept up his rifle and powder horn from the snow. "This will take but a moment."

"No, Jamie, please, no!" she wailed as he dragged her stumbling through the snow. With sickening certainty she knew he was going to show her something she didn't want to see. Now she remembered the single shot that had made her race to open the door, the shot fired from Jamie's rifle. She didn't want to know where that ball had gone, any more than she wanted to know the meaning of that long, still, black lump lying in the snow before them. "Oh, please, Jamie, don't make me do this!"

"I have to, Rachel." He held her steady, forcing her gently to look at the body in the snow. "Who is it, sweetheart? Did you know him?"

The man was of middling size, of middling age, unshaven and unwashed. His hat had been tossed to one side, his thinning sandy hair dusted with snow, and his staring, clouding eyes were brown and bulged slightly outward, like a frog's. The battered pistol was still clutched in his frozen fingers, and the front of his gray coat was soaked dark with blood. All that blood from one little hole, a single shot that must have pierced his heart as neatly as shooting seeds from an apple.

"You knew this man, didn't you, Rachel?" asked Jamie. "What was his name?"

"Fredrich Gelrichs," said Rachel, her voice hollow. "He works—*worked*—on Alec's farm."

She didn't doubt for a moment that Alec had sent him here to set fire to her barn. Gelrichs had been a shiftless rascal whose single merit was the ability to outdrink Alec and still be able to fetch him home from Volk's tavern; he would have had neither reason nor incentive to attack her on his own. He had no home, no family, and no one in the county would mourn his death, if anyone even bothered to notice he was missing.

"I'm sorry, Rachel," said Jamie softly. "But it was better for you to know for certain."

She looked up at him then, his face as surely marked with sadness as it was with soot while he waited for her to decide what would come next between them. If Gelrichs had been one reminder of the uncertainty of her life, then Jamie Ryder had been another, bringing with him all the pain and horror of the war she'd wanted so desperately to escape.

It was better for you to know for certain. Surely he'd meant Gelrichs and Alec, but he could have included his own past, as well. She knew now that he was her enemy, that he could kill another man ruthlessly and without remorse, that he'd been a part of the massacre at Cherry Valley.

She knew all these things. But she also knew that again and again he'd risked his own life for hers when another man would have walked away, that he'd been unerringly kind to Billy and honest and fair to her. When he had kissed her, he had made what should have been sinfully wrong seem impossibly, inevitably right.

He wasn't perfect, but neither was she. She was still William's wife until she knew for certain she was his widow. But if Jamie left now, he'd take with him not only her spirit but her heart, as well.

Uncertainly she reached out to rest her hand on his arm. "Will you go now?"

"Nay," he said slowly. "I don't believe I will."

And finally he drew her into his arms and held her, just held her.

Chapter Eight

Rachel waited three days, telling herself she must hold off until they'd finished cleaning and repairing the barn after the fire, and then she waited again until Billy had gone to sleep. She almost waited too long, for Jamie had already begun to climb the ladder to the loft to sleep before she finally blurted it out.

"I'm going to speak with Alec in the morning about the fire."

Jamie stopped, his hand on the rung. "You most certainly are not," he said. "Have you lost your wits?"

"I've made up my mind, Jamie," she said. Busily she reached into the workbasket beside her chair for some hand sewing, pretending there was nothing unusual about her plans. "I don't have to go clear to his house, only to Volk's. Alec practically lives there, anyway. I should go now, before another storm closes the trails again. I'll take Proudfoot and be home in plenty of time to fetch supper."

"Fetching supper has nothing whatsoever to do with it." He came back to stand before her, trying not to notice the elegant, vulnerable curve of the nape of her neck in the firelight. Each day he purposefully had worked himself to the edge of exhaustion to keep himself from thinking of her like this, and each day he'd failed miserably.

"Rachel, we've been over this same ground before. If you go anywhere, it should be to the magistrate. I don't care if Alec is your husband's brother. He wishes you ill enough to send some rogue with a flint to burn your barn. For all you know, he might have set fire to your house as well if I hadn't surprised him."

She looked up sharply. "Alec wouldn't have hurt me or Billy. That's not what he wants."

"I can't damned well think of another explanation for what he did."

But Rachel could, and she swiftly lowered her face back to her sewing. Jamie still had his secrets, and this shameful one was hers. She'd already said too much.

"Alec is a proud man," she began, choosing her words now with greater care. "I should not have kept him from the house when last he came. To be turned away by a woman with a musket must have been very hard for him to bear."

"Rachel, I saw what happened," said Jamie impatiently. "Lindsey threatened you, you and Billy both. You had every right to order him off your land. If he hadn't left you alone when he had, he would have had me to answer to, instead."

"And would you have shot him, too, as you did Fredrich Gelrichs?" Her green eyes blazed furiously. "There are other ways to solve problems than shooting at them."

"Not in wartime there aren't," he said, his own anger flashing in an instant to match hers. Long ago his father had told him much the same thing, and Jamie had only to remember what had become of his parents to see how wrong the old man had been. "I say you stay here, where I know you'll be safe."

"And I say I won't be made a prisoner in my own home!"

"Damnation, Rachel, I'm only trying—"

"Hush!" She sliced her hand through the air to silence him, her own voice lowered once again to a fierce whisper. "Don't you dare wake Billy with your ravings!"

With a great effort he bit back his temper. "All I'm saying is that these are dangerous times, and Lindsey has proven himself to be a dangerous man."

She saw how much that stifled temper cost him, and it touched her more than all the anger in the world.

"Jamie, all I mean to do is speak to Alec, nothing more," she pleaded. "I want this—this misunderstanding between him and me to end here, and not to worsen. He's William's brother, and I am William's wife. I can't forget that, at least for Billy's sake. I'll apologize if that's what Alec wants, and play the meek little lady if that's enough to salve his pride."

Grimly she knew it wouldn't be as simple as that, not by half, but she'd no intention of telling Jamie the real cost of keeping peace with Alec. "I'll meet him at the tavern, I'll speak to him and then I'll come home. That's all there is, Jamie. Truly."

"Then I'll come with you." He crouched before her chair, impulsively seizing her hands in his so that her sewing fell forgotten to her lap. "You're a lady, Rachel, and you don't belong in some rough tavern by yourself any more than you belong on that trail alone."

His large hands were warm and strong around hers, swallowing up her slender fingers. How much she longed to put her life and troubles into those gentle, capable hands forever!

"I'd never ask that of you, Jamie," she said softly. "You forget that Alec knows who you are, even if he doesn't know exactly where to find you. It wouldn't matter that we're in American territory. With all the men in the tavern to help him, he would have you in chains and back to your Colonel Butler before you could blink. He won't forget that reward, and he won't forget your name or description, either."

Jamie groaned with frustration. "What good am I to you like this?"

"More than you know, Jamie Ryder." She smiled wistfully, gently rubbing her thumb across the red-gold hairs on the back of his hand. In a moment she'd pull her fingers free of his.

In just one more long, infinitely sweet moment.

"Billy and I will leave after breakfast," she said softly, "and I promise we'll be back again before you've had the chance to miss us."

His brows rose with surprise. "You'll take Billy? Why not leave the lad here with me? You know he'd prefer it to being jostled all morning on the saddle before you."

"Oh, no," said Rachel, smiling with bemusement at his suggestion. "Of course he'll come with me. I'd never leave him behind with you."

"Of course you wouldn't." Abruptly he pulled his hands away from hers. "Too much of a risk."

Swiftly Rachel shook her head. "I didn't mean it like that, Jamie, I swear it! I've never trusted myself to leave Billy with anyone."

"You don't have to explain, Rachel," he said curtly, all the warmth gone from his eyes as he rose to his feet. "I've told you often enough not to trust me, and it seems at last you're listening."

Miserably Rachel gathered up the sewing she'd let fall. She couldn't begin to explain to him how precious Billy was to her, any more than she could make him understand that her concern for the boy had nothing to do with him.

"What the devil is that trumpery you've been fussing with, anyway?"

Reluctantly she held up her work for him to see, the stuffed head and body of a little white horse with scraps of red wool for the mane. "It's for Billy, a mare to keep company with Blackie. 'Tis nearly Christmas, you know."

"Christmas." He loaded the word with scorn. "What a foolish, papist waste of an honest day that is."

"Not in this house, it isn't," she said defensively, "and certainly not with Billy. Don't turn pious with me, Jamie Ryder. Any Friend who swears as much as you do and who's fought in an army has lost all right to turn his nose up at celebrating Christmas."

He sighed and ran his fingers wearily through his hair. "I'm too tired to quarrel with you any longer, Rachel, and I don't want to do it."

"Then don't." She wrapped the unfinished toy in a scrap of fabric to keep it hidden from Billy and tucked it back into her workbasket. "I'll leave as soon as it's light. But pray, don't trouble yourself to rise on my account. I'll manage perfectly well by myself."

And as Jamie slowly climbed the ladder to the loft, with despair he didn't doubt that she could.

"Are we there yet, Mama?" whined Billy, wriggling impatiently on the saddle before her. "We've been riding *forever.*"

"Hush, Billy," said Rachel crossly. "It only seems like forever because you keep demanding every step of the way how far we've come and how far we've still to go. If you could just sit quietly and see how pretty the trees look with the snow on them, why, the time would pass much more quickly for us both."

"Don't wanna look at trees," said Billy rebelliously. "I hate trees, an' I hate snow."

"What you're going to hate even more," warned Rachel, "is the switching I'll give you if you don't start behaving yourself directly."

At the end of her patience, she struggled to balance Billy with one arm while she held the reins with the other, and tried as well to keep him from swinging his feet into the musket she had tied to the saddle. If Billy had begun to count every step that poor Proudfoot made on the snowy trail from the time they'd lost sight of their chimney, then she'd been little better. The only difference was that she didn't have to count out loud.

By her reckoning they were nearly there. If she remembered the way correctly, over the next hillside she'd be able to see the smoke from the fire of the smith who kept a small shop beside the stream, and just beyond that would be Mr. Volk's tavern.

Except for Billy's impatience, their trip had been uneventful. When she'd started out, with the warnings from both Mary and Jamie fresh in her ears, she'd scanned every tree and rock with edgy thoroughness for stray Tory soldiers or Indians. But with the land around them reduced to stark bare trees against white snow, she had soon decided that no one could hide and track them without her seeing them immediately, and so she'd been able to relax her guard and concentrate on Billy instead.

"What's Jamie doin' now, Mama?" he asked, his second-favorite question and one that was perhaps even more annoying to Rachel.

"I don't know, Billy," she said with an irritable sigh. She didn't want to think about Jamie this morning, let alone talk about him. They'd scarcely exchanged five words over breakfast, and when he'd waved goodbye she'd sensed it was more for Billy than herself. So why, then, could she only think of the way her hands had fit into his, and the warmth in his blue eyes as he'd knelt before her?

She sighed again, more softly this time. "Maybe Jamie's still working on building the new bins for the barn or maybe he's gone on to splitting wood. All of the usual things that he does. Why does it matter?"

"Wish I'd stayed home, too," said Billy glumly. "You said it'd be fun t'ride on Proudfoot, an' it's not."

"Then it's a good thing we're almost at the tavern so you can get down." She pointed ahead, as relieved as

Billy to be at the end of the journey. "There, that little building is Mr. Volk's tavern."

"That's not little," said Billy, impressed, as he straightened to see better. "That's big."

To eyes as untraveled as Billy's, Rachel supposed the square log building did seem big, bigger than their own house, nearly as big as their barn. But to Rachel, who remembered the handsome clapboard taverns and coffeehouses at Newport with their gold-trimmed signboards, assembly rooms for hosting grand dances and beds enough to sleep a score of guests in comfort, Volk's tavern seemed small and mean indeed.

She had been here only once before, with William when he'd come to seek out Alec on some errand or another. Like the Bowmans' store, the tavern was more of a fortified stockade than a welcoming place for refreshment. Though a rough covered porch had been added on the front, there was still only one small window beside the stout, cross-barred door, and no tavern sign or marking. But the unconscious man sprawled across one of the outside benches spelled it out clearly enough, as did the well-trampled path to the door and the shards of broken bottles and crockery mugs that littered it.

"Is that man sleeping?" asked Billy with loud interest. "Why's he outside? Isn't he cold?"

"He's had too much to drink, and that made him fall asleep." All too well Rachel recalled finding Billy's father often in much the same situation, but at least the boy didn't seem to remember it as well. "He's outside because that's where he fell asleep, or perhaps that's where Mr. Volk put him last night when he wished to close the tavern. And, no, I don't think he's feeling cold at all.''

Billy nodded, considering. ''He should wake up now. It's morning.''

Rachel sighed. ''Well, yes, I suppose he should, but fortunately it's not our task to wake him.''

As object lessons went, she told herself it could have been worse. There were a great many other tavern scenes that would have been harder to explain, and she was grateful, too, that the snoring man on the bench wasn't Alec.

Stiffly she climbed down from the horse to lead him around the tavern to the lean-to that served as a stable. She hadn't ridden in months, and every muscle in her legs and back ached in protest. At last a red-haired boy with a game leg limped forward to first take her shilling for Proudfoot's oats and water and then the reins from her hand.

She slung her musket over her shoulder before she reached up to help Billy, barely stopping him from gleefully sliding down the polished leather saddle and tumbling straight to the ground. She clasped his mittened hand firmly in hers, but saved the scolding for later.

''Can you tell me if Mr. Alec Lindsey is within?'' she asked the ostler's boy.

''Mr. Lindsey?'' he repeated laconically. ''Oh, aye, Mr. Lindsey be here. Don't think he never left last night on account o' the gaming. That be his bay, there at the end.''

''Thank you.'' With her back as straight as she could make it, Rachel marched across the yard to the tavern door with Billy skipping alongside to keep up. Though she was relieved that Alec was in fact here, the news that he'd been here all night was hardly welcome, and she prayed he wasn't so drunk that he wouldn't be able to hear and understand all she meant to say.

"Can I play th' games, too, Mama?" asked Billy excitedly. "I like games, even if I hafta play with Uncle Alec."

"Uncle Alec doesn't play games for children, Billy," she said absently, inwardly marshaling her arguments for Alec. "All fours or whist, games like that with cards, or maybe tossing dice."

"Oh." The single disappointed syllable was dragged from deep within him.

Belatedly Rachel saw how Billy's little face had fallen, and she bent long enough to give him a swift hug. She wasn't the only one who'd been lonely in their isolated house. Billy wasn't a baby any longer, and he was reaching the age when he needed other children to play with. If William had stayed, Billy would likely have had a new brother or sister, but now that seemed a possibility as distant as finding another house with children.

"Tonight after supper we'll play any game you wish," she promised. "Hide-and-seek with Blackie, or hussel-cap?"

His expression brightened. "Can Jamie play, too?"

"You may ask him," she said, hedging. After Jamie's sour response to Christmas, she didn't want to guess what he'd say to something as frivolous as a game of hussel-cap. "But come, let's find Uncle Alec."

The heavy door groaned in protest as she swung it open, and she paused in the narrow hall to let her eyes grow accustomed to the gloom after the bright sun on the snow. Her nose needed time, too, to accept the appalling stench that assailed her: stale tobacco, spilled beer, overcooked onions and the lingering ripe aroma of men who bathed only when they fell into a river. However could Alec, who fancied himself such a gentleman, bear to frequent such a place?

"Mistress Lindsey, good day to you," said the tavern keep as he hurried to greet them, hastily pulling a red knitted cap down over his bald head. Volk's face was round and white, as if he seldom moved beyond his own tavern, and his eyes and brows were ink black, brows that were now drawn together in obvious unhappiness.

"Mistress Lindsey," he began again. "Ma'am. It's a pleasure to see you, a very great pleasure indeed."

"And good day to you, too, Mr. Volk." Rachel smiled, ignoring his discomfiture though her heart was racing. She didn't want to be here, and she didn't want to have what was bound to be an unpleasant conversation with Alec. But she'd learned long ago from her mother's example how best to deal with Newport's recalcitrant tradesmen, and Mr. Volk would be little challenge compared to them.

"'Tis a pleasure, ma'am, but still 'tis wrong," he said, wiping his fingers anxiously on his green apron. He glanced pointedly at her musket. "To put it blunt, ma'am, you're a lady, and your boy here's a child, and them gentlemen what makes up my custom don't want to be troubled by neither ladies nor children when they come through my door."

Rachel's pleasant smile remained firmly in place. "The only gentleman I wish to trouble is my husband's brother, Mr. Alec Lindsey."

"I can't allow it, ma'am, indeed—"

His words were drowned out by a great roar of shouts and applause and thumped glasses from the room to the left. Eagerly Billy crept forward to peek inside, and Rachel yanked him back with her hands firmly on his shoulders.

"I've traveled a considerable distance, Mr. Volk," she said with the merest hint of insistence, "and my business is most urgent. If you cannot bring yourself to trouble Mr. Lindsey, why, then, I shall do so myself."

"Nay, ma'am, I can't—"

"My dearest Rachel, what a charming surprise," said Alec as he suddenly filled the room's doorway. "I vowed I'd heard your sweet voice."

He leaned against the doorframe with a practiced insouciance, sipping from the pewter pot in his hand. He had shed his coat and loosened his neck cloth in the heat of his game, but beyond a fresh day's growth of beard on his jaw and eyes red-rimmed from lack of sleep, he looked none the worse.

And he *was* sober, noted Rachel as she mentally raised her guard. Or what passed for sober in Alec.

The smile she'd given to Volk vanished abruptly. "I've come to speak to you, Alec. In private."

"Have you indeed, sister," he mused, his eyes narrowing over the rim of the pot. "Then why bring my brother's boy to this place with you? You recall William, Volk. Mark the likeness, eh? No matter how hard

Mistress Rachel tries to make the child over in her own image, he's still William's spawn to the core.''

Billy shrank back against Rachel's skirts, and now her hands on his shoulders were there to reassure him.

"Of course I've brought Billy with me," she said defensively. "You know perfectly well I could not leave him alone in the house with no one to care for him."

"No one?" asked Alec with mocking surprise. "And here I'd heard otherwise."

To her shame, Rachel flushed. "In private, Alec. I won't speak before an audience."

Alec sighed dramatically as he shoved himself away from the doorway. "Forgive us, old Volk, but she means you. I'll take her into the other room, and I give you my word I'll keep her from tippling your stock behind the grate. Take the boy back to your wife in the kitchen, will you? She can give him biscuits or whatever it is boys eat these days."

"That's not necessary, Alec," said Rachel quickly. "Billy can stay with me."

Alec cocked one brow. "What are you afraid of, Rachel? That I'll spirit him away through the back door?"

That was exactly what she feared. But if Alec could jest about it here before the tavern keeper, then surely he'd no intention of stealing Billy from her today.

"Don't wanna leave you, Mama," began Billy anxiously, grabbing a fistful of her skirt.

"Just for a few minutes, lamb, I promise." She bent to give him a quick kiss and smooth his hair, and tried to ignore the frightened reproach on his face as Volk led him toward the kitchen.

She suspected her own expression probably wasn't much different as she joined Alec in the empty common room. Three tables, two benches and a half-dozen rickety chairs were the only furnishings, and Rachel chose to stand, her gloved hands clasped tightly together.

She waited only until Alec had shut the door. "Why did you wish to destroy my barn and my livestock, Alec?"

His face went blandly quizzical. "Sister, you make no sense."

"Then I'll make it as clear as I can," she snapped. "Why did you send Fredrich Gelrichs to set fire to my barn four nights ago?"

Alec emptied the tankard and set it on the mantelpiece. The grate was empty, the air in the room chilly enough for their breath to show as if they were still outside. "So Gelrichs told you, did he? He must not have been successful, either, since I saw you arrive on horseback. No wonder the worthless bastard's run away."

Rachel didn't bother to correct him. Jamie had made Gelrichs's body disappear, and she hadn't wanted to know where. "Listen to me, Alec. I want this to end here, now. We're even. I don't need any more of your 'help,' as you call it, and I don't want it."

"Ah, but Rachel," he said softly, "what if I still want yours?"

"I'm not going to do it again, Alec!" she cried. "Last year I trusted you because Billy and I were hungry and needed food, and you were William's brother. But now that I know the truth, I won't do it again. Never, Alec. *Never!*"

He smiled at her. "Brave words, dear sister. But I feel sure you can still be persuaded."

"Then you're wrong." Her voice shook with fury as she lifted her chin in defiance. "Those 'errands' you made me do were treason, Alec. It doesn't matter that I'm a woman. If I'd been caught crossing the lines with your little messages, the army would have tried and hung me for a spy, the same as they would a man."

"Everything in life is a risk, Rachel."

"Not for you, it wasn't!"

"Rachel, be reasonable." Impatiently he tapped one finger against the mantel. "I've offered to share the profits of these little adventures with you, haven't I? I've seen how this miserable rebellion is collapsing beneath its own weight. When the crown finally wins, as it inevitably must, then I, for one, mean to be in the best position to benefit. Poor men like me can't afford the luxury of high-flown sentiments."

In his silk-embroidered waistcoat and Holland linen shirt, Alec looked far from the pauper he claimed to be. Rachel thought of how dearly it had cost her father to scrape together the gold for her dowry, gold that had gone to pay not for her new life but for the London clothes and Thoroughbred horses that William and Alec refused to do without.

"You may be able to think only of yourself, Alec, but I cannot," she said bitterly. "In the name of your greed, you made me shamefully betray the same cause that my father and my brothers are risking their lives to defend."

"Oh, shame, shame," he scoffed. "Do you think I really care about you and your tedious family?"

"Then what of your own?" She hadn't meant to argue with him, sensing the danger of it, but once she'd begun she found it impossible to stop. "What about William? He believes enough in the war to fight for it. Doesn't that mean anything to you, Alec?"

If she hadn't been blinded by her own anger, she would have seen the hatred that glittered in his half-closed eyes.

"And how have you served my brother, Rachel?" he said. "It wasn't enough that you drove him to the army with your shrewishness. Now you've decorated him with full patriotic honors, a splendid rack of cuckold's horns."

She gasped with shock. "How dare you accuse me of such a thing! How *dare* you!"

"Don't deny it, Rachel, I'm not a fool," he said with disgust. "So who is this man you're so jealously guarding in my poor brother's bed? Some former sweetheart come to visit? Or perhaps it's that deserter from Butler's men. According to William, your carnal excesses are more suited to some low backwoods scoundrel than to a gentleman who expected a lady-wife."

"How hateful you are, Alec, vile and spiteful and hateful!" Her cheeks flushed with shame, not only for what William had told his brother of their lovemaking, but also for the mean unfairness of his accusations about her and Jamie. "I don't have to stay here and listen to your—your *ravings!*"

But as she turned on her heel to leave, Alec grabbed her arm and jerked her back. "Do you really think I'd let you walk away that easily, Rachel?"

She tried to pull free, but he held her fast. "I don't need you any longer, Alec," she said, practically spitting the words into his face. "I don't need you, and you can't make me do your bidding any longer."

"True enough," he said at last. "But I do have Billy."

With a frightened cry she struggled to break away, desperate to get to Billy, twisting and lashing out at Alec until he shoved her back against the door, pinning her there beneath the weight of his body with her hands clasped roughly at her waist.

"You can't take him from me," she said wildly. "Not even you would take a child from his mother!"

"Then what a pity, Rachel," said Alec, his smile thin and humorless, "that little Billy's not your son."

"Billy *is* mine!" she cried as her eyes filled with hot tears of anguish. "I'm the only mother he's ever known! From the first time I held him in my arms, I have loved Billy as my own son!"

"But he isn't your son, my dear, no matter what you choose to believe. He was born to William and Phillipa, not to you."

Alec pressed closer, clearly enjoying the advantage he had over her. "If I were to swear in court that you were an improper mother, then as the boy's only blood kin I would become his guardian until William returns. He would come live with me, and if you tried to come near him, I could have you arrested."

At last he released her, and with a broken sob Rachel twisted away from him. She stumbled across the room until she reached the window, then sank to her knees with her cheek against the sill.

He could accuse her of being sordidly unfaithful to William, and she would hold her head high and ignore it. He could destroy her barn and her livestock, and she would fight back to protect the home that was hers. But if he stole Billy from her, he would take away the center of her existence, the little person whose unquestioning love had given her life both the joy and meaning that her empty marriage had failed so miserably to do.

Without Billy she would have nothing.

Nothing.

"If you but glance out that window, Rachel," said Alec evenly, as if he hadn't just threatened to rip her life to bits, "you'll see two of my newest, ah, business associates. More reliable, I believe, than Gelrichs proved to be, and the taller one has a sister who's a regular houri. And if you or that man of yours would be so foolish as to try to abscond with the boy, my dear, you can be sure those two savages would welcome the chance to fetch you back."

Slowly she raised her gaze to the window, and through the haze of her tears she saw the two Indians sitting cross-legged on a bench outside the lean-to stable and smoking long-stemmed pipes in silence, their greased, bristling hair the mark of Senecas. Over their hunting shirts and leggings they wore mantles of raccoon pelts, and in addition to the rifles resting beside them—long-barreled rifles strikingly similar to Jamie's—they wore tomahawks tied to their waists.

With a shudder she remembered what Mary had told her, and what Senecas like these had done with their tomahawks to the women and children of Cherry Valley. Alec was right: such men wouldn't run away like Fredrich Gelrichs, and Rachel's despair plunged even deeper.

Behind her she heard the latch click as Alec opened the door. "How glad I am that you came to me today, Rachel," he said. "You can expect me to repay the courtesy as soon as I have another of my little errands for you. At New Year's, shall we say? Ah, Billy, here you are!"

Swiftly Rachel wiped away her tears on her sleeve and turned in time to find Billy hurtling through the doorway and into her open arms. His hands and face were sticky with cider and the sugar icing from gingerbread that Mrs. Volk had given him, but Rachel didn't care. She hugged him as tightly as she could, rocking back and forth as she fought the fresh tears that burned behind her eyes.

It didn't matter that she hadn't birthed him. He was her Billy, her baby, her son, and she would do anything not to lose him.

Anything.

She was hugging him still as they rode from the tavern yard, hugging him close as they began the long trip back home.

"Mrs. Volk's cat has kittens, Mama," chattered Billy happily. "Three black an' one white an' one yellow. The yellow one liked me best, Mama. I made him eat milk, Mama, an' he said meow, meow, meow!"

She hugged him close and listened to him, trying not to imagine the heartbreaking silence if Alec did as he threatened.

"Meow, meow, meow, Mama, an' I said— Oh, look, Mama, it's Jamie!" Billy wriggled with delight. "Where'd *you* come from, Jamie?"

"I've been with you all along," said Jamie, grinning as he came to walk beside them, his rifle cradled in his arms. He wore the heavy white coat trimmed in blue, and before this Rachel hadn't noticed how exactly the bright indigo stripes matched the color of his eyes. "You just weren't looking in the right places."

"That's not possible," said Rachel, her unhappiness making her speak more sharply than she realized. "I would have seen you."

"Only if I'd wanted you to." He pulled off his black hat with the turkey feather and reached up to plunk it onto Billy's head, and the boy laughed. "And I didn't."

"Jamie, I told you not to come with us," she said, remembering all too clearly the two Senecas outside the tavern, their tomahawks and their rifles and their frighteningly blank faces. "I—I don't want anything to happen to you."

He searched her face, his smile fading as he heard the little catch in her voice. "I didn't come *with* you, Rachel. I was watching *over* you. I don't fancy any harm coming your way, either."

Billy clutched the brim of the hat with both hands to tip it back from his face so he could see. "Jamie, Mrs. Volk's cat had kittens, an' the yellow one liked me, an' he said meow, meow, *meow!*"

"Cats will do that, won't they, lad?" he replied, but his gaze remained on Rachel's face. "Did you see Lindsey, Rachel?"

"Yes." She looked away, over Jamie's head, and her arms tightened once again around the child in her lap. "Yes, I did."

And though her heart ached to tell him everything, she didn't.

Chapter Nine

"Mama said I could ask you," said Billy as he stood before Jamie with a little red cloth bag in his hands. "Can you play hussel-cap with me an' Mama?"

"Say please, Billy," said Rachel over her shoulder as she dried the last of the supper dishes. "No one will ever wish to play with you if you're ill-mannered. Say 'Would you please play hussel-cap with Mama and me, Jamie?'"

Billy nodded solemnly, swinging the bag in his hands so the coins inside jingled together. "Would you please play hussel-cap with Mama an' me, Jamie, 'cause I know how to win over her an' you?"

"Billy!" said Rachel with dismay, but Jamie only laughed.

"Most likely you will, Billy," he said, "since I've never played, and you sound like a great gamester."

"Never?" Billy looked at him doubtfully. "Everyone plays hussel-cap."

"Not if everyone's father disapproves of games of chance with wagering," said Jamie mildly. "I'm the greenest of greenhorns when it comes to gaming, lad."

"We're hardly sitting down to the tables at White's, Jamie," said Rachel as she joined them. She took the bag of coins from Billy and shook it hard, keeping the open end closed with her fingers. "Say cross or pile."

Jamie tipped his head to one side to look at her suspiciously. "Do I have to say it or be judged too ill-mannered to play?"

"No, you ninny, that's how you play," said Rachel, smacking his arm with the bag to make her point. "You must choose either cross—that's for heads—or pile—for tails—while I'm shaking the coins."

"That's the husseling," said Billy with satisfaction. "I like that best."

Rachel tapped him with the bag, too, for good measure and to make him giggle. "Choose, Jamie, or I must keep doing this all night."

"All right, then, I'll choose cross."

He was glad to see Rachel smile again as she teased Billy. Whatever her conversation had been with her brother-in-law, he'd guessed that it hadn't gone well. She'd been sad and withdrawn ever since she and Billy had returned, so obviously distraught that Jamie almost wished he'd shot the man when he'd had the chance.

"Then cross it is, gentlemen." With a flourish of her wrist she dumped the coins out onto the table. "Stay back until they've settled, Billy!"

But Billy was already scouring the motley assortment of a dozen coins—English, French and Spanish, pennies, francs and a single battered pistole with shaved edges—busily separating the crosses from the piles.

"You got seven, Jamie," he said with a certain grudging admiration. "Now me."

Rachel scooped the coins back into the bag, this time letting Billy do the shaking and tossing after he'd called pile. But to Billy's severe disappointment, and not without a few covertly prodded coins, he only earned a five.

"You an' I could still win, Jamie," he said philosophically as he husseled the coins for Rachel, "if Mama does worse."

"How wondrously kind of you, Master Billy," protested Rachel, but when her coins were counted she'd finished with a sorry score of three.

"You lost *bad*," announced Billy with more relish than tact. "Now you hafta pay Jamie a forfeit."

Rachel's cheeks grew pink. "Not tonight, lamb," she said, flustered. "Since this is the first time Jamie's played, we'll skip the forfeits."

"Nay, Rachel, don't do it on my account," protested Jamie soundly. Though he hadn't a clue as to what these forfeits might be, Rachel's blush was enough to intrigue him.

She shook her head, that blush rising from her cheeks clear to her forehead. "It's the purest silliness, Jamie, of no account. If we played the game properly, you'd get to keep the seven coins plus the three you won from me. But since these are all the coins we have, Billy and I invented our own foolish system of stakes, or forfeits. I told you, it's of no account, and we won't do it tonight."

"Yes, we will, Mama," insisted Billy. "Jamie said so. He won an' you lost, an' now you hafta *kiss* him."

"Is that a fact." Jamie leaned his arms on the table, bringing himself near enough to Rachel that he could count every one of her black, silky lashes. "Your mama must kiss me?"

From the corner of his eye Jamie saw Billy nodding vigorously. He was too occupied with Rachel to notice anything more.

That charming little blush had blossomed and turned Rachel's whole face so bright that he wondered if she'd any blood left in the rest of her body. She sat there straight as a ramrod and wide-eyed as a hare before a hunter, her palms flat on the table as she waited for him to claim his dreadful forfeit. He watched her anxiety grow as he let the anticipation stretch longer and longer between them, and by the time she nervously flicked her tongue around her lips and swallowed he almost groaned himself.

But somehow he managed to wait until she'd finally begun to inch forward over the table before he sat back in his own chair with a sigh.

"I'm sorry, Billy, but I fear I must agree with your mama on this," he said, making a great, stern show of shaking his head. "'Tis one thing to play for the sport alone, but turning it into a kissing game with these so-called forfeits—nay, I cannot be party to that."

It took what little remained of Jamie's self-possession not to laugh out loud at the strangled look on Rachel's face: acute relief warring with equally acute disappointment. He'd told the truth when he'd said he'd never been much for gaming, but after seeing that particular expression and realizing she'd wanted to kiss him as much as he did her—well, he might be willing to reconsider.

At Rachel's hurried suggestion, they switched to keeping track of the games with marks on a slate instead of forfeits. Yet even that was not enough to calm the pace of the game, not with Billy growing wilder and wilder as he husseled the coins, spilling more on the floor than on the table. After Alec's threat that morning, Rachel was willing to indulge Billy more than usual. But when the pistole flew so far afield that Jamie had to retrieve it from the coals in the hearth, with a long-handled meat fork, she finally scooped up Billy instead of the coins and began to ready him for bed.

It was one of Jamie's favorite times of the day, and as he did every night he retreated to the chimney corner with his back against the warm bricks and a crockery mug of steamed chocolate in his hand. He found a deep satisfaction in watching Rachel's small rituals with her son, every night the same pattern of face washing and hair combing and prayers beside the bed. Then after she'd pulled the covers up snug over the little boy and his stuffed horse, she'd sit beside the bed with his hand in hers and sing to him until, at last, his eyes would drowsily slip shut.

Though there'd been no music in Jamie's own house as a child—music, like games, having been regarded as an idle, worldly pastime—he knew that what Rachel sang to Billy were no ordinary lullabies. The songs were dark and moody, filled with storms and passion, grieving lovers and unkind fates, songs that clearly spoke more to her own longings than those of a child. Yet as Jamie watched Rachel's head bowed over the low bed, her profile caressed by the firelight as she softly crooned the last song of the night, he knew no child could ever feel more safe or better loved than Billy Lindsey did as he drifted off to sleep.

Rachel bent to kiss the child's forehead, then rose wearily to her feet, rubbing the back of her neck. It had been a long, exhausting day, and she intended to go to bed herself as soon as she banked the fire for the night. Humming to herself the song she'd just sung to Billy, she began to sweep the hussel coins from the table into her palm.

"Leave them," said Jamie softly. "Fetch your cloak and come outside with me."

Startled at first, she relaxed and smiled sheepishly. "Lord, I am tired. I clear forgot you were sitting there."

"How you flatter me, Rachel." He stood and set his empty mug on the table. "And here I thought I was the lord king of hussel-cap himself."

"You are. You won, and handsomely, too." She laughed quietly, not wishing to wake Billy. "Isn't that enough, my Lord Hussel-Cap?"

He bowed with a rough elegance, and again she laughed into her hand. He had thrown himself wholeheartedly into the high silliness of their game, shouting over good throws and moaning over poor ones with an enthusiasm that had delighted Billy. She was grateful for that; it was good for Billy to see men who weren't too proud to laugh or tease. Strange how she'd stopped worrying that Jamie would leave them. He had fit so easily into their tiny household that it seemed in a way he'd always been there, and always would be.

"Lords expect to be obeyed," he said imperiously, though the way his tousled hair fell rakishly across his forehead was hardly fit for court. "Come, Lady Rachel. Your tidying can wait."

Still she hesitated, torn between longing to share his company and fearing the consequences if she did. Alec's awful accusation still rang in her ears. She'd never considered herself immoral or low, and he'd shocked her by saying she'd cuckolded William. A shocking word for a shocking deed.

And yet, and yet...

To be with Jamie seemed right, not wrong. She'd told herself how good it was for Billy to be with so kind a man. Couldn't the same be said for herself, as well? She'd felt the same way earlier, when she'd believed she must kiss Jamie for losing. Had he guessed how shamelessly she'd wanted to feel his lips against hers again, even before Billy?

"Don't keep me waiting, Lady Rachel," he warned. He held up a pair of fingers. "I've two reasons of my own for demanding your obedience. Now fetch that cloak."

"Aye, aye, your lordship," she said with a curtsy that would have done her mother's training proud. No harm could come of this, she told herself as she took her cloak from the peg. If he hadn't kissed her during the game when he'd been handed a reason, then he wasn't going to do it now. Besides, it was likely so cold that it would be impossible to linger outdoors for any real mischief.

And the seventeen months since William's departure was a long, long time.

The night was cold as she expected, with that peculiar stillness that came only when there was snow on the ground to muffle all sound. Yet no more snow would fall tonight, with the sky as clear as the air was still.

"Have you ever seen so many stars?" she asked as Jamie gently shut the door behind them, leaving it unlatched so they'd be able to hear Billy if he cried out. She turned in a slow circle, her face upturned. "Like diamonds spilled on midnight velvet."

"I'd have to say it was the other way around," he said. "If I were ever to see these blessed diamonds on velvet, I'd say they looked like a winter sky with a crescent moon."

"Be careful, Jamie," she teased as she stepped farther away from the house. "You're sounding perilously close to poetical."

He wanted to say that she made him feel that way, that all the diamonds beneath all the stars would never have the brilliance of her smile. He wanted to, but didn't, afraid she'd flee and break the spell of that new crescent moon.

"Where are you going?" he asked instead.

"Only to search for the North Star," she said, "and there—*there*—it is."

She freed her hand from her cloak just long enough to point to the brightest star overhead. "When I was little, my father would take me into the garden every night on his shoulders and make me find it in the sky. It's like a signpost to a sailor, you see, the one sure way he has to find his way back home."

"It's the same for landsmen in the forest," said Jamie. She had tipped her head back so far that, unbeknownst to her, her little white cap had fallen off. Her hair seemed black as the sky above, her pale skin gleaming with all the magic of moonlight.

No stars would help him now, he thought with a bittersweet longing, neither at land nor at sea. He was hopelessly lost, and Rachel was the reason.

"Make a wish," he said, so softly that she turned to look at him, questioning. "Go on. That's the first of my two commands. Make a wish."

She smiled at him uncertainly, the yearning in his voice taking her by surprise. She never knew what to expect from Jamie, and it was one of the things she liked best about him. He could not step two paces from the door without bringing his rifle, the barrel gleaming dully across his back in the moonlight, yet still he wanted to wish on stars.

He smiled in return, lazy and seductive in ways that made her heart flutter within her breast. "You found your star, didn't you? Now wish upon it."

"Very well." She found the North Star again, took a deep breath and shut her eyes. After Alec's threat, she was sure there could be only one wish, and effortlessly she remembered the star-wishing rhyme from childhood.

Lord of stars, lord on high,
Grant this, my wish, before I die:
Watch over my Billy,
Keep him safe and with me!

Yet even as she whispered the magic words to herself, she knew that wasn't all. The tall man with the burnished hair who stood waiting before her had earned a special place in that wish as well, and quickly she amended it.

Watch over Billy and Jamie,
Keep them both safe and with me!

"What did you wish for, lass?" he asked, his voice low. He'd silently stepped closer, and his words were as soft as that velvety sky. "Was it for William's safe return?"

Instantly her eyes flew open, her cheeks warm with guilty shame. She'd forgotten William entirely. She hadn't even considered him in her wish, not for a moment.

"I—I cannot tell you," she stammered miserably. "If I do, the wish can't come true. You know that."

Mentally he swore long and hard, furious with himself for asking such a thoughtless question.

"I thought maybe Alec had given you fresh news of William," he said, struggling to explain without wounding her further. "You seemed so unhappy when you returned that I thought—"

"Don't ask me, Jamie, because I can't tell you." She drew her cloak more closely about her shoulders, as much vainly striving to keep herself free of sorrow as from the chill. "It's time we went back into the house, anyway. I'm cold.".

"Then I'll warm you." Gently he took her hands and pulled her toward him. When he'd come outside he hadn't bothered to close his heavy woolen coat, and now he drew her arms inside, around his waist, as he wrapped the coat around them both like a blanket.

"Jamie, no," she protested weakly. His body next to hers was warm and strong, the intimate tent of his coat wrapping her in his scent. "This isn't right."

"You're not warmer?"

"Yes, but—"

"Then it's right enough by me." He hadn't meant to hold her this way, but then he hadn't wanted to lose her just yet, either. "And it should be by you, as well."

And to the traitorous part of her that had no conscience, it was more than right enough. Seemingly on their own her hands curled more tightly around his waist, pulling them closer together as she stared down at the triangle of curling hair at the low, open neck of his shirt. Above it she could see his pulse beating in the shallow hollow at the base of his throat, and foolishly she longed to press her lips to the spot, to taste his skin and feel if his heart could race as fast as her own.

"Do you recall, Rachel, that I'd two reasons for asking you here?"

"Two reasons," she repeated, strangely breathless as she turned her face up toward his. She didn't know when she'd lost her cap, and without its restraint the unpinned coil of her hair had fallen free, tumbling wantonly over her shoulders and down her back.

"The first was so I could see the stars in your eyes," he said, his hands slipping beneath her cloak and around her waist to draw her closer. "Can you guess the second reason, lass?"

She shook her head, her unbound hair swaying against her cheeks. Her breasts felt heavy against the warm, hard pressure of his chest, and instinctively she arched her body into his.

"You could guess if you tried, Rachel. Most likely Billy could. 'Twas his idea, after all."

"The forfeit," she breathed. "You want to claim your forfeit now."

"Clever lass," he murmured indulgently, tracing the bow of her lips with his thumb. "Clever, clever lass."

She shivered beneath his touch, weak-kneed with anticipation. "I thought you said you'd be no party to kissing games. I thought you said they were foolish."

"They are." His voice was low and dark, his mouth already lowering to seek her sweetness. "Because when I kiss you, we won't be playing games."

The next moment Rachel felt the gentle force of his lips as they brushed across hers, coaxing them to part for him. Willingly she obeyed, and her breath caught in her throat with a husky whimper as she relished the texture of his tongue against hers, the soft warmth framed by the roughness of his beard.

Jamie tasted warm and potent and undeniably male, and she knew she'd never weary of it. With hungry need she opened and took him in deeper, threading her fingers into the coppery silkiness of his hair.

She wasn't an untried girl. She thought she'd known what to expect from men and their passions, their desires. But nothing in her past had prepared her for this, the moment she learned how much more there could be.

"Rachel, lass, you are so sweet, so warm," he murmured. "How can you burn like this in the snow?"

He brushed his lips lightly across hers, the heat of her breath stealing the chill from his skin. It beckoned him deeper, this warmth of hers when all else was wrapped in ice and snow, her mouth and body a welcoming sanctuary. Her fire could make him whole again, if he could only lose himself in it.

In *her*.

"Do you know what you do to me, Rachel?" he said raggedly as he sought the secret, sensitive place beneath her ear. "Do you know the power of your sorcery?"

"It's you, Jamie, not me." She shivered as his lips nipped at her throat. "It was never like this for me before."

"Kiss me," he ordered roughly, "and I promise you 'twill happen again."

She did, and he kissed her harder, deeper, branding her as much as he could with his mouth alone. She moaned, and he took her pleasure into his mouth, her body twisting sinuously against his inside the warm cocoon of his coat.

It wasn't enough. With her it never would be, and with a low, impatient growl he lifted her back against the house to sit on the wide sill of the window. She gasped softly with surprise, her hands fluttering as she tried to balance herself and not topple off into the snow.

"You think I'd let you slip away from me, Rachel?" he asked as he steadied her. "If I could, I'd never let you go."

"Then don't, Jamie Ryder," she whispered, her green eyes dark with passion. "Don't ever let me go."

Her hands came to rest on his shoulders and slid around the back of his neck as she drew him back, their faces and their mouths now on a level. She gasped again as he slid his hands along the curve of her waist, molding the full, round swell of the flesh below. He pulled her closer, her legs falling open on either side of his hips, then closer still, so she could feel his own heat, hard and ready, pressed low against her belly. She felt his large hands on her thighs, easing them apart as he moved against her. With a shudder she moaned and arched against him, her hair tangling over her face, heedless of everything but the raw, aching need that he'd brought to her blood.

All she heard was the sound of her own heart beating the rhythm of desire, matched by Jamie's harsh breathing in the tangle of her hair. She didn't hear the uncertain little thumps behind the door, or the squeaking protest of the iron hinges as it opened.

But she heard the one word that would rouse her from anything.

"Mama?" asked Billy, his cheeks flushed with sleep as he stared, uncomprehending, at her and Jamie. "Mama?"

"*Billy!*" All too easily she could imagine herself as Billy must be seeing her: moaning and panting like an animal in the moonlight, her cap gone and her hair loose, her skirts tossed up like the disgraceful slattern she was, and her legs wrapped around a man's waist, a man who wasn't his father.

A man who wasn't William.

And oh, dear, dear Lord, what Alec would make of this if he could but know!

"Mama," said Billy again, scowling as he rubbed at his eyes with his hand. "Can't find Blackie."

"He can't have gotten far, lad," said Jamie as he eased himself free of her, as if being caught like this before her son was the most normal thing in the world. "Most likely he's just wandered from his pasture a bit, that's all. We'll find him soon enough, once we—"

"No." Swiftly Rachel pushed herself away from Jamie, refusing to look at him in her shame. Billy was her son, not his, and it must be for her to comfort him. She bent to gather the child into her arms and carry him back to his own bed.

"Come along, lamb," she murmured as Billy burrowed against her shoulder with a trust that tore at her heart. "Let's find that old Blackie."

Helplessly Jamie watched her go, her cheek nestled next to her child's and her back squarely turned to him as she pushed the door shut between them. He couldn't begrudge her that stiff, straight back any more than he could the closed door, not after the way he'd treated her.

But his body still throbbed with need, every nerve raging like a bull in rut, and as soon as she was safely inside he slammed his fist as hard as he could into the windowsill where she'd just sat. The shattering pain made him swear, but that at least was something real, something tangible. Nothing like the raw, aching emptiness she'd left in his soul.

He hadn't meant it to be this way when he'd brought her out here. All he'd intended was to kiss her lightly, quickly, a fitting conclusion to the teasing way he'd denied her forfeit earlier before the boy. He'd wanted to cheer her after whatever had happened with her brother-in-law, and to take the sadness that had marked her face. He'd promised himself he'd keep it safely meaningless, a moment of stolen, passing pleasure.

That was what he'd meant to do. But the instant his lips touched hers he'd realized exactly how hopelessly impossible those intentions had been. So much fire in her, so much passion, enough to melt all the snow on this hillside, and he nearly struck the sill again in despair. Why the devil hadn't he been able to stop at that one kiss?

Miserably he groaned, and swore again. He should go to the barn to sleep tonight; that was where he belonged, with the other beasts.

Yet still he stood there. He could just make out her voice, the same sad, wild lament he'd heard her sing earlier. Gently he touched the door. She'd closed it, true, but she hadn't barred it against him. As quietly as he could he pushed it open and slipped inside, coming to stand behind her.

She sat crouched beside the low bed, her face hidden by the dark curtain of her unbound hair. With infinite tenderness she stroked Billy's cheek, her song scarce more than crooning. He was once again asleep, curled up on his side around the stuffed horse, yet still she crooned softly to him until the song was finished and the peaceful silence settled over him like another coverlet.

At last Rachel sighed and sat back, her gaze still bound to the sleeping child. "I cannot lose him, Jamie," she said forlornly. "I can't risk Alec taking him away."

"Why would he take Billy? You're his mother."

"But I'm not." She twisted around to face him, and he saw the tears that marked her cheeks. "I'm William's second wife. His first was Billy's true mother. She died giving birth to him. I'm—I'm nothing."

"Oh, Rachel, don't ever say that." He sat beside her, gently taking her hand in his. He was surprised, but not shocked, the way she seemed to expect him to be. By marrying again, William Lindsey had merely done what most widowed men did when left with a young child. "You're Billy's mother. No one seeing you two together would ever believe otherwise."

She laced her fingers into his, staring down at their joined hands. "That is the finest thing anyone has ever said to me."

"It's true," he said firmly. "Certainly to Billy you are. William would be proud."

She shook her head sadly, the firelight glinting off the little gold hoops in her ears. "William didn't want him. After Phillipa died—that was her name—he and Alec left the baby and three bottles of whiskey with an old Indian woman. When he married me, he never even mentioned he'd a child, he was that certain the baby would be dead by the time he returned."

"Then why would Alec want to take Billy now?" demanded Jamie angrily. "Clearly he cares nothing for him."

"Because he blames me for William enlisting," she said haltingly. "Because he thinks I drove him away. If I don't—don't remain faithful to William while he is gone, the way Alec believes I should, then he'll swear to the magistrate that I'm not fit to be Billy's mother, and they will take him away."

She stopped there, not daring to tell Jamie the rest. But what she'd said was more than enough.

"He can't do that," said Jamie angrily. "No other woman could ever love this child more than you do. And you've done nothing—*nothing*—wrong."

She pulled her fingers free of his to clasp her hands together in her lap, shaking her head unhappily. "But he's right, Jamie. Look at me. Haven't I been unfaithful to William this very night? I'm weak and wanton, else I never would have kissed you the way I did."

"You are none of those things, Rachel! If William still lived, then Alec might have a right to meddle in your life, but—"

"But I don't know that he's dead, Jamie!" she cried softly, the words wrenched from her. "I don't know if I'm a widow or a wife, I don't know if I'm Billy's mother, I don't even know when or how or why I've come to care so much for you!"

Jamie went very still, his heart reeling crazily at what she'd said. He had so little to offer her, nothing beyond himself, and she had so much to give.

"You care for me?" he asked carefully, wanting to be sure he hadn't imagined it. "You are not sure how or why, but still you care for me?"

She nodded reluctantly, afraid to look at his face. "I think I've—I've cared for you from the first, when I found you in the barn." Her hands twisted in her apron. "Oh, Jamie, forgive me, I know it's wrong and I never should have spoken."

"Nay, lass, it's right," he said as he eased one of her clasped hands free and slowly raised it to his lips. "It's very, very right, for I've come to...care for you, too, Rachel Lindsey. Rachel *Sparhawk* Lindsey."

At last she dared to raise her eyes to his. Her face was wet with tears, her tangled hair clinging to her damp cheeks, and she trembled as his lips pressed against the pale veins in the crook of her wrist.

"Oh, Jamie," she said, her heart close to breaking from despair. There was so much he didn't know about her, so much that could destroy any hope for happiness. "I don't want to lose you, too."

"You won't." He slipped his arm around her shoulders and pulled her close, and she went to lie against his chest with a broken little sigh. "If you need time to find your peace with William, then you shall have it. For I never want to lose you, either."

Chapter Ten

"Well, now, Billy, look at that," marveled Jamie as he set the boy, blissfully covered with snow that was already beginning to melt and drip, on the floor before the hearth for Rachel to undress. "I'd say your mama's gone to a great deal of trouble and toil, but I'll be a double-blasted goose if I can say exactly what it is."

He shrugged the heavy coat from his shoulders, the damp wool steaming in the warmth of the fire, and stared with something close to amazement at the elaborate display that Rachel had made while he and Billy had been tending both to the stock and a new snow fort.

Cropped branches of evergreen had been bent and tied together into a hoop with scraps of colored yarn and hung over the hearth. More boughs were tucked along the chimneypiece, and around the bases of a pair of gleaming silver candlesticks. The candles themselves weren't the usual tallow, but a muted green, scented with bayberry, and from the way the candles were no longer quite straight Jamie guessed Rachel had kept them carefully stored away since she'd come from Rhode Island as a bride. Festooned from one side of the chimneypiece, across the wreath and down the other side was a delicate cutwork chain of white paper that must have taken Rachel hours to cut and paste together.

"It's Christmas, Jamie," said Rachel warmly, at once defensive and wounded by his response to her handiwork. "Christmas Eve, to be exact, and I wanted to surprise you with something pretty and special. I told you before that you don't have to celebrate with Billy and me if you don't want to, but I would appreciate it if you'd keep to yourself your comments about idleness and popery and goodness knows what else!"

Her cheeks were pink and she was practically quivering with outrage, kneeling on the flagstones with Billy's wet socks clutched in her hand. Belatedly Jamie realized how seriously he'd blundered.

"Hold a moment, Rachel," he said carefully. "Was I saying anything of that sort now?"

She lifted her chin. "You were going to. You'd begun to wear your prim and righteous look."

"Then I'll take it right off." He slid his palm over his face and smiled, duly transformed.

Billy giggled. Rachel didn't.

And Jamie sighed. "It's a beautiful, ah, display, Rachel," he said. "I doubt there's another one like it anywhere in this county. It took me by surprise, that was all, on account of being so unexpected. The chain looks particularly fine."

"Thank you," she said stiffly, mollified for now. "I had the devil's own time with that chain. Nothing I tried for glue would stick, and the ends of the links kept popping apart until I very nearly tossed the whole wretched mess into the fire.''

She tied the waistband on Billy's dry breeches, patted him fondly on the bottom and rose, her hands on her hips as she studied the decorations.

''I wish I had ribbons instead of the yarn,'' she said critically. ''Ribbons make a better showing. Mama always used ribbons when she dressed the house at Crescent Hill for Christmas, yards and yards of ribbon, enough that Father groused that he'd personally made the fortune of every milliner in Newport.''

''I doubt it looked one whit better than this,'' declared Jamie staunchly, though he thought privately how appalled his own mother would have been by the excessiveness of all those yards and yards of Newport ribbon.

''Truly?'' She glanced at him sideways.

''Truly.''

''Good. And you weren't really being that hateful, at least not yet.'' She smiled at last, almost mischievously, and slipped her hand into his. ''I'll wager last summer you never dreamed you'd ever celebrate Christmas, did you?''

''Nay, lass,'' he answered truthfully, ''that I didn't.''

But then, celebrating Christmas was the least of the changes in his life. Last summer he'd been eating peaches filched from the orchard at Fort Niagara, wenching and brawling to stave off the boredom while he and the rest of the Rangers in his company waited for the officers to decide where they'd strike next. Last summer all he'd wanted was another chance to lash out at his enemy, the same enemy who'd destroyed his dreams and his family with the empty, false promise of liberty for all men.

Last summer he'd never heard of a place called Cherry Valley....

But last summer, too, he hadn't known the woman who now stood beside him. It was almost unimaginable now, that life before Rachel and Billy, a dream— and a nightmare—that each day seemed to grow fainter and fainter. What would his old companions think to see him here, splitting firewood and mending harnesses and squandering his rare gift for marksmanship on hunting rabbits for the suppertime ragout? And how they'd laugh, Lord, they'd roar out loud to learn that he'd lived almost two months beneath a beautiful young widow's roof without bedding her.

He didn't quite believe it himself.

He had never desired a woman more than he did Rachel. The memory of how passionately she'd returned his kiss, the sinuous, seductive way she'd wrapped her limbs around him beneath the warm shelter of his coat, the taste of her mouth and the scent of her flesh, all of it haunted him, day and night. Her constant nearness both tempted and tortured him, and he never knew when some innocent motion or gesture would nearly reduce him to a stammering, overwrought idiot.

He had promised he would grant her time to find peace with herself, and he had. He *was*. Though he was convinced she was a widow, she needed to accept her husband's death for herself. Jamie loved her enough to understand that. Grief took time to heal. When at last she came to him, he wanted to be the only man in her heart.

But surely he couldn't be faulted for praying it would be sooner, not later.

"I thought we'd have our pudding tonight," she was saying. "Tomorrow, if it's not too cold, I hoped we'd be able to go to visit Mary and Ethan."

Jamie frowned. "All that way? Just you and Billy?"

She looked at him hopefully. "I'd rather thought you'd come, too."

But the look he gave her reminded her exactly why not.

"Twenty dollars for my neck, and happy Christmas to you, too," he said dryly. "I'd like to be excused, if you don't mind."

Quickly Rachel glanced to Billy, praying that he hadn't understood. "You're right, of course. Mary was counting on a whole crowd of guests to come to read the Christmas scripture and drink a cup of punch. Without a proper meeting house or minister, I'm afraid that's the best we can do in the valley for now."

"Scriptures and rum punch," murmured Jamie, unable to resist though he did know better. "Nothing heathen about that."

Rachel shot him a single murderous glance.

"What about th' presents?" asked Billy hopefully. He held up Blackie, waggling the front leg to make the little horse wave. "Blackie likes Christmas presents."

Rachel laughed. "Oh, pooh, Billy, last year Blackie was your Christmas present! But seeing as tomorrow we'll be gone from the house, I thought perhaps tonight you'd have your present. If, that is, you and Blackie can manage to be very, very good."

"I promise," said Billy solemnly. "I'll be very, very, *very* good."

And he was, better than Rachel had ever dreamed he could be, scarcely fidgeting at all through supper while Jamie had extra servings of the turkey he'd shot and she'd roasted. But by the time she brought the pudding to the table—a pudding of which she was inordinately proud, having taken her last hoarded stock of raisins, a pound each of suet and flour, the eight eggs the hens had obligingly laid and a pint of heavy cream from Juno, all boiled to perfection for exactly five hours— Billy was beside himself with expectation, his legs flailing against his chair and Blackie neighing constantly.

With a sigh Rachel set down her spoon and pushed back her chair. Her glorious pudding could wait a bit longer. From the highest drawer of the mahogany chest she pulled out three packages, wrapped in scraps of muslin and tied with yarn, and brought them to the table.

The littlest one went first to Billy, a striped blanket for Blackie. Too excited to linger over that, he immediately tore open the second, larger package, and gasped with wonder. The little white horse was a perfect match for Blackie, and without a word Billy took them together into his arms in a fierce, ecstatic hug. For once, Rachel didn't insist on his saying thank-you; the look on his face was thanks enough.

She looked down at the third, last present, plucking at the yarn. To ignore Jamie on Christmas would have been inconceivable to her, yet with all his fussing about heathen rituals, she wasn't sure how he was going to respond. Before her second thoughts overwhelmed her, she walked around the table and shyly placed the package on the table before him.

"For me?" he asked, knowing full well it was but not sure what else to say.

"For you." She bent swiftly, her lips closing sweetly over his. She meant it only as a quick salute, a greeting of the season between friends.

But though she was swift, he was swifter. In the same instant she'd meant to pull away he reached up to cradle her head and hold the kiss another dizzying, delicious beat longer than she'd intended. When at last he released her, she could do no more than grin foolishly until the room stopped spinning around her.

"Happy Christmas, sweetheart," he said for her ears alone as his fingers brushed across her lips, still tingling where he'd kissed her.

"Oh—*oh*, that is, a happy Christmas to you, too, Jamie," she stammered breathlessly, her voice rich and low with the longing he'd stirred in her blood.

Then she retreated, before she said or did more. Wrong though it might be, she had missed kissing him, and from the way he was watching her now, his blue eyes narrowed and openly predatory and that teasing, inviting smile on his lips, she knew he'd missed it, too. When she'd hung the pine boughs over the chimneypiece, she'd fretted that she hadn't a sprig of mistletoe to hang from a beam overhead. Now she was glad there wasn't one, not with the heat flaring up between them like sparks to dry powder.

"Aren't you going to open it?" she asked, wishing her voice didn't sound so odd and thick. "The present, I mean."

He raked his fingers back through his hair and grinned at her, stopping just short of winking but looking wicked enough to make her blush anyway. He was, she thought indignantly, a fine one to talk about rum punch and scriptures when he was looking at her like *that* over their Christmas pudding.

Unaware that anything had changed, Billy slid off his chair with the two horses and his spoon and crowded himself next to Jamie. He coughed, and then belatedly covered his mouth, looking quickly to Rachel to see if he'd been caught.

Jamie picked up the package and shook it. "What do you think it is, lad?" he asked. "A new pair of moccasins? Stockings? A white horse for me, too, to keep Proudfoot company?"

Billy shook his head and tapped his sticky spoon on the table with a hearty snuffle. "It's a scarf."

"Billy!" cried Rachel with dismay, but Jamie was already unfolding the muslin and drawing out the scarf she'd knitted, white with indigo stripes to match his coat and extra long to wrap twice around his throat. He stared down at it, saying nothing, and her second thoughts leapfrogged to thirds and fourths.

"I thought you needed a scarf," she said with a nervous little laugh. "The winters here are so very cold, and you've never had a scarf that I've seen."

"Do you know how long it's been, Rachel, since anyone made something for me?" he asked quietly, and when he looked at her now what she saw in his eyes wasn't teasing and it wasn't wicked, only bold and simple and so direct that it stole her breath clear away.

"Mama made it," said Billy cheerfully. "Do you like it?"

"Aye, lad, that I do," he said, wrapping it around his neck. "It could well be the best, most perfect scarf in the entire state of New York. It's so perfect, in fact, that I'm going to have to put it to the test right now."

Speechless, Rachel watched as Jamie jumped up from the table and bolted out the door. She didn't care if it was the most perfect scarf in the state. He'd no right to go racing away from her table and off into the night like a madman. Even worse was neglecting her precious pudding, the raisins already beginning to sink forlornly deeper into the glistening mass as it cooled on their plates.

Muttering one of her father's choicer oaths, she began to clear the plates from the table. At least Jamie wouldn't be gone long. All he had for warmth against the cold was that wretched scarf, his coat hanging forgotten on the peg by the door, but, more important, he'd left without his rifle, something he almost never did.

Pointedly she left the serving of untouched pudding at his place. Rude, ill-mannered oaf, she grumbled crossly, leering at her as if she were some common serving wench, then racing off without so much as a by-your-leave when—

Suddenly the door opened again with a rush of cold air, and Jamie reappeared, the new scarf fluttering from around his neck.

"Didn't want to be outdone," he said, grinning and unabashed. With a flourish he drew a new wooden sled from beneath his arm. "Here you go, Billy, and a happy Christmas and all such things."

Too stunned to answer, Billy raced forward. He was practically dancing with excitement as Jamie set the sled on the floor for him to sit upon, and his eyes were shining with unbridled joy.

"We'll have to wait until tomorrow to try it out proper," promised Jamie as Billy perched the two little horses on the front of the sled, "but I'll warrant she'll be fast as blazes on that hill near the barn."

Billy nodded, bending low over the sled as he imagined himself already flying down the slope, and Jamie next turned to Rachel.

"Thank you, Jamie," she said softly, all her earlier displeasure forgotten and forgiven at the sight of Billy with the sled. "However did you do it?"

"'Twasn't easy, I'll grant you that, not with the sorry sort of tools left in your barn," he said, "and not with you and Billy in and out often enough to make keeping secrets nigh on impossible."

She smiled at him fondly. "Not that, you great clodpate. I already suspect you could rebuild this entire house from the stones upward if you'd a mind to. I meant how could you bring yourself to celebrate our foolish, idle holiday like this?"

His smile faded. "If you don't know that by now, Rachel," he said with a frankness that took her by surprise, "then there's little hope for either of us. But here, I haven't neglected you, either."

He took her hand and turned it across his, then dropped a small bundle of cloth into her open palm.

"Well, sweetheart," he said dryly as she hesitated. "As a wise woman once said, 'Aren't you going to open it?' "

She ducked her head with embarrassment, pulled open the little knot of cloth and gasped. In her palm lay an exquisitely carved heart, creamy white and polished like old ivory, engraved with a filigree of flowers and vines.

He cleared his throat self-consciously. "I know a scrap of old bone isn't as fine as you're accustomed to," he said, his own insecurity now mirroring hers, "but I thought if you hung it from a ribbon or somesuch, it would look comely enough."

"It's beautiful, Jamie," she breathed. "*Beyond* beautiful, and I won't hear you say otherwise."

She hurried to rummage through one of the drawers until she found a length of narrow blue silk that she threaded through the little hole bored into the top of the heart. She handed it back to him again and spun around, poised for him to tie it around her neck.

Carefully he took the ends of the ribbon from her. Presented to him like this, the nape of her neck was smooth and pale and achingly vulnerable, begging him to press his lips against the warm, flawless skin. She trusted him so much it frightened him. Now these same fingers of his that had so deftly carved the filigree heart fumbled clumsily as they tied a bow in the ribbon, done in by the trust and the pale skin and the tiny, wispy curls that escaped from beneath her cap.

She twisted around to face him, her fingers touching the heart that now nestled in the hollow of her throat.

"You've made this day so special, Jamie," she said softly as she glanced at Billy, busily dragging his new sled with the two equine passengers across the floorboards. "You can't know the difference you've made. But when I think of all you've done for us these last weeks—oh, my, I can't begin to thank you."

"Of course you could, Rachel," he said softly, seductively. "You know how."

She looked at him, really looked at him, at his summer blue eyes with the little rays worn from the sun and weather, at the smile with the single dimple that could be sweet enough to make the angels sigh or so sinfully wicked that the devils must claim him for their own. Vainly she searched for a hold to save herself from the currents of emotion she felt swirling and roiling around them once again. Around them, and over her, pulling her down. What had he done to make her feel this way all over again?

William, think of William and your vows and Alec and the consequences if you don't!

"I don't know what you're talking about, Jamie," she said, though she did. Why else would her heart be hammering even though his hands were safely at his sides?

"Oh, aye, you do," he said, his words laced with a soft-spoken but unquestionable assurance. "If you care for me as much as you claim, then you know. And so, sweetheart, do I."

He reached out to trace the outline of the pendant on her skin, his touch so light on her skin yet more than enough to make her shiver.

"And Rachel?"

She nodded, unwilling to answer and risk breaking the spell he had cast so effortlessly around her.

Jamie leaned forward, and this time all he kissed was her cheek. "Happy Christmas, Rachel. Happy, happy Christmas."

Jamie had come back to this place in his dreams before, and he recognized it.

He had been among the last to leave the woods, his job to keep clear the path of retreat in case relief troops came from the fort. But Butler's surprise had been complete, and the two settlers who had tried to run for help had not even reached the clearing.

He had run fast and low through the smoke of the burning houses and outbuildings. He had hardened himself to the screams of the dying and the wails of those that still lived. It was Butler's way to strike the lone settlements, to destroy the ring of support for the Continental armies and push back their lines. The orders were always the same: kill those men who resisted and make prisoners of all others, burn the crops and the standing structures to the ground.

But this time something had gone wrong. The mutilated bodies that lay before the burning houses or tumbled in the kitchen gardens wore petticoats or leading strings: women and children, babies and white-haired elders, mangled and slaughtered together where they'd fallen. He saw two of the Senecas who were the Rangers' allies chase a woman across an empty field until she stumbled and they struck her down, their war cries frenzied as they claimed her scalp.

Where was Brant? Why hadn't he done as he'd promised, and kept his warriors from wanton killing?

Still Jamie ran, through the smoke and the screams and the horror that pushed against him like another enemy.

"Ryder!" bawled Sergeant Herrick, waving furiously for Jamie to follow. "Here!"

He ran to the house, following the sergeant through the shattered door, following orders. In the hallway he passed a tall mahogany chest of drawers, the polished front crudely hacked by a tomahawk, and on the floor beside it, dropped by a child, lay a little black stuffed horse.

Not here, he thought wildly, *not here....*

He kicked the kitchen door open, his rifle raised.

"Jamie!" screamed Billy, his little arms raised desperately toward Jamie as the tall Seneca with the feathered scalp lock raised his tomahawk and swung it down and—

"Jamie, wake up!" said Rachel as she struggled to calm him. "Jamie, love, please, it's only a dream!"

His eyes flew open, wild with horror and fear as instinctively he rolled to one side to reach for his knife.

"Jamie, love, you're safe!" she said urgently. "You're here with me, Rachel, and I won't let anyone hurt you!"

His chest heaving, he stopped fighting and stared at her, his face slick with sweat.

"Rachel," he said thickly. "Praise God they didn't catch you."

"Of course they didn't," said Rachel. "Why would they even try, anyway?"

"It was the Senecas again." Slowly he was breaking free of the nightmare's grip. He was in Rachel's loft, beneath the bundles of dried herbs and braided onions that hung from the rafters in her house. This was his blanket, and his rifle and his knife within reach beside him.

Down the ladder the tall mahogany chest would be where it belonged, its polished front smooth and unscathed. Blackie and his new mate would be tucked safely into the trundle bed beside Billy, who would be curled up on his side with his face flushed with sleep.

And Rachel was here, too, sitting on the floor beside him, her green eyes huge by the wavering light of the lantern at her feet. Bare feet, bare toes, and he realized she'd come to him from her own bed, for she wore only her night rail, a shawl clutched loosely over her shoulders. Beneath the linen he could see the full, round shape of her breasts, and he thought how much he'd give to press his face there, now, to lose himself in the peace that only she could give him.

"Are you all right now?" she asked gently. "I came when I heard you cry out."

He sighed, ashamed to let her see him like this. "It was a dream, that was all. I'm sorry to have wakened you at all."

"I was awake already." She tried to smile, her mouth wobbling and finally crumpling so miserably that she pressed her hand over her lips to hide it. Now he noticed how her face was tight with concern, her eyes shadowed with weariness.

"Oh, Jamie, it's Billy," she said. "He's sick. Very, very sick."

Chapter Eleven

Billy had been sick before, the usual childhood sniffles and stomachaches, but Rachel had never seen anything make him this ill this fast. He had crawled up into her bed, whining that his throat hurt. She had taken him under the covers with her, and realized at once how dry and hot his skin was with fever. She had tried to give him warm sweetened milk to sip and he had fought her, coughing it back up and crying. His eyes grew dull and his breathing more labored, and his skin burned hotter. By the time Jamie came down to be with her, the child was whimpering from the pain of the dry, wheezing coughs that racked his little body.

With Jamie's help she was able to see how red and swollen Billy's throat had become, and her heart twisted when she saw the thick white streaks that marked true quinsy. Quinsy was always dangerous; in a child as young as Billy, it could be fatal. While Jamie held Billy still, she swabbed the child's throat with a mixture of beaten yolk, sage and alum, trying not to weep herself at the fear and pain in Billy's tearful eyes.

For the rest of the night and most of the following day she walked him back and forth across the cabin, cradling him in her arms as she had when he'd been a baby and singing softly to try to make him sleep. But by late afternoon he was worse, not better, each breath a ragged fight for air as the pus threatened to choke him.

"Let me take him for a while, Rachel," said Jamie gently. "You won't help him at all if you're so worn out you fall ill yourself."

In anguished silence she shook her head, pulling the coverlet higher around the child's shoulders as she swayed back and forth in the rhythm that had always soothed Billy before.

Jamie touched the back of his hand lightly to Billy's brow. "I don't believe he's any warmer. We can thank God for that."

"It's not the fever that worries me," said Rachel unhappily. "It's how putrid his throat is. There was a family in Newport who lost four children to quinsy, all daughters, in the span of a single morning."

"Billy's a strong lad, Rachel," said Jamie, as much to convince himself as her. He wasn't of the temperament to put much stock in dreams, but again and again he kept remembering how in his nightmare Billy had held his arms up to him to be saved. "If any child can fight this, 'tis Billy."

"If only I could do more for him," she said, her voice brittle from fear and exhaustion. "When he was a babe, that physick with the egg and alum cured him of thrush like a marvel, and Mary said I was to remember it for quinsy, too. But I don't think it's done him any good at all this time."

"Then take him to Mary now, if you think she could help you again."

She sighed, plagued with uncertainty. "I wouldn't want to risk carrying him so far in the cold, not with the fever."

"Then I'll go for you," said Jamie firmly, relieved at last to be doing something to help. He was accustomed to solving problems with action; waiting seemed to him as good as nothing.

"You can't, Jamie! You said so yourself!" She gasped, recognizing the sacrifice he was willing to make for Billy's sake. "The Bowmans' house will be filled with people, and someone's bound to realize who you are!"

He reached for his coat, his mouth firm. "And what if they do, Rachel? Do you truly believe that matters to me more than Billy's life? Nay, I'll fetch Mary back here to you, along with whatever herbs and such she needs."

"No, Jamie, don't!" she cried. "I doubt there's anything that Mary could do that we haven't tried ourselves, and I—and I—oh, Jamie, I don't want to be left here alone, not now!"

With an anguished sob she sank onto the edge of the bed, bent over the sick child in her lap. She hadn't taken the time to dress, and she'd barely paused to eat or drink. She still wore her night rail with the shawl tied over it, her plait half unraveled and her hair tousled around her face. She looked beaten and exhausted, and very, very frightened.

She didn't have to say more. Jamie understood. The next few hours were likely to be the most critical for the little boy's survival. If Jamie left now, he could well be between here and the Bowmans' house when the crisis came. He couldn't blame Rachel for not wishing to weather that moment alone, any more than he wanted to abandon her when she might need him the most.

Slowly he hung his coat back on the peg and came to sit beside her on the bed. Billy was drowsing now, curled into the crook of Rachel's arm, his tortured, rattling breathing the only sound in the cabin.

With great gentleness Jamie smoothed the child's silky, pale hair back from his forehead. He'd become too sick even to wish for Blackie, forgotten along with the new white horse on the pillow of the trundle, and Jamie's own throat tightened when he remembered the plans that he and the little boy had made for testing the Christmas sled today.

"How could I have thought that giving Billy up to Alec would be the worst that could befall us?" said Rachel in a hoarse whisper of despair. She took one of Billy's little hands in her own, stroking the limp, chubby fingers that were so dear to her. "To lose him forever like this on Christmas Day—"

"Nay, Rachel, stop," said Jamie harshly. "You haven't lost him. Don't give up hope, mind? Don't give up!"

Her eyes were swimming with tears as Billy stirred restlessly against her. "I don't want to, Jamie," she whispered. "Merciful heaven, he's my baby!"

"Then think of something else, Rachel!" ordered Jamie. "Think of—damnation, I don't know, another time when you were happy! Think of one of those Christmases when your mother was wrapping every blessed thing in your house with white ribbons!"

Rachel sniffed with a shudder. "She didn't wrap everything with ribbon," she said. "Only the sprigs of mistletoe that she hung in the doorways. But isn't it time we swabbed Billy's throat again and—

"You just did it, sweetheart, not an hour past," said Jamie. He rested his hand over hers and Billy's, easily covering them both. "Now tell me instead about your mother and the mistletoe."

"But Jamie—"

"Tell me about the mistletoe."

She sighed, looking down at Billy in her lap. "It wasn't every Christmas," she began at last. "Mama didn't begin using the ribbons until my sister Bethany was married on Christmas Day. That was ten years ago, when I was only fourteen, but still I got to help Mama pile the oranges in the silver bowls and make the paper chains for the fruit cakes."

"So that was where you learned that pretty trick," he murmured, coaxing her back to a happier past. He couldn't help glancing at the chains she'd made for this year, still hanging over the chimneypiece, and thinking how happy the three of them, too, had been only last night. "A wedding on Christmas Day. No wonder you think of punch in the same breath with it."

"Of course we had punch." She gave a final little hiccuping sob. "Father was famous for his receipt. Sparhawk rum from his own distillery, sherry, brandy, a dozen whipped eggs and cream."

"Doubtless he was also famous for the drunkenness of his guests, serving a brew like that."

"Well, perhaps some of the gentlemen did take too much," she admitted, "but only very late, after I'd gone to bed. I had my first real lady's gown for the grand party on Christmas Eve, and I was allowed to stay for all the dancing. We always had the best music because Father hired the fiddlers from his ships. And there was a puppet show, too—I helped with that. Not a common Punch show, but a play with the most beautiful carved puppets on strings that had come clear from Italy."

Her eyes were shining, lost in the memory. As Jamie had dared to hope, Billy seemed to be less restless in her arms, too, his sleep growing more peaceful as the anxiety left his mother's voice.

"It must have been a very grand occasion," he said, thinking how very different her life had been from his, "even for a place as worldly as Newport."

"Oh, it was! Over fifty guests came for the wedding, and that with snow on the ground, too. And the supper we had! Lord, Mama and the cook outdid themselves!"

"Aye, I've no doubt that they did," he agreed, and asked her next to recall the dishes that had been served, and then the details of the ladies' gowns. By the time she'd recited the names of the dances that the ships' fiddlers had played and the partners she'd had for each one, it was past nightfall.

"It was the last Christmas we were all together," she said wistfully. "Of the six of us children, there's not a one of us left in Newport, nor Mama and Father, either. We began by scattering ourselves, and the war's done the rest. But that Christmas, Jamie, that one was the best."

"For showiness, aye, there's no doubt it was," he said softly, "but for miracles, I'll take this one. Look."

He pressed her hand to Billy's forehead, damp now but mercifully cool. "I'd say the fever's broken, wouldn't you? And mind how easy his breathing's become. He hasn't coughed in a quarter hour."

"Oh, Jamie, you're right!" She was going to cry all over again, but this time the tears were from happy relief, not grief. "He's going to be all right, isn't he? He truly is, isn't he?"

Jamie grinned, and when his lips met hers over Billy's head their kiss was sweet and filled with joy.

"Happy Christmas again, Rachel," he murmured. "It's a foolish holiday, aye, but I think in time I might come to like it."

"Where's your breakfast, Rachel?" asked Jamie, frowning at her over his own plate of eggs and corn bread.

"I ate earlier, while you were in the barn," she said quickly, not wanting him to worry.

His frown deepened with concern. "That's not like you, sweetheart."

"It is this morning," she said. "We were all so late rising that I was too hungry to wait."

She busied herself with crushing Billy's corn bread into a bowl with milk, making a mush that would be gentle to his throat. Though this morning all that seemed to remain of the quinsy was a voice like a baby bullfrog's, Rachel meant to keep him inside and in bed, not wishing to risk a relapse.

Billy, however, had other ideas. "Don't like mush," he croaked, turning away from the first spoonful she offered. "Mush is for babies."

"Mush is for boys who've been very sick," she said, trying to sound stern despite the fire in her own throat. When Jamie went out again, she would dose herself with the same medicine that had worked so well for Billy. She was a grown woman, not a child, and she expected she'd be well enough again by supper. She had to be; Jamie and Billy depended on her too much for her to be sick. If only she wasn't so impossibly tired, she'd be fine.

She held the spoon out to Billy again. "Now come. If you wish to get well enough to ride on that new sled with Jamie, you must eat."

Unconvinced, Billy eyed the mush suspiciously, his mouth firmly shut.

"If I put jam on it?" pleaded Rachel. "A spoonful on top?"

He nodded, and with a weary sigh Rachel rose to get the crock with the blackberry jam. But as she did, her head seemed to turn light as goose down and her legs lost all will to hold her, and she'd barely set the bowl with the mush on the table before her legs gave way completely.

"Rachel!" Jamie caught her as she fell, scooping his arm underneath her knees to carry her to the bed. "You're sick now, too, aren't you?"

Weakly she pushed herself up. "I'm fine, Jamie. I'm tired from tending Billy, that's all."

"I don't believe a word of it." Grimly he rested his hand on her forehead. "You're hot as blazes, and if you open that stubborn little mouth of yours long enough for me to look inside I know I'll see your throat's as bad as Billy's was yesterday."

"You've no right to carry me about as if I were Billy," she protested feebly. "I'm perfectly fine."

But she wasn't fine, and as the day wore on she realized how far from fine she truly was. She burned with fever, and her head ached abominably. Her throat hurt so that she could bear to eat nothing, and could only sip at the weak herb tea that Jamie brought her. She let him swab her throat with the same physick she'd used on Billy, and like Billy she wept from the friction of the cloth-wrapped stick on her raw, infected throat. She drifted in and out of feverish sleep, only vaguely aware that Jamie was always at her side when she woke.

Nothing could have forced Jamie to be anywhere else. He could see that she was weakening, the infection sapping away her strength as she fought against the pain. Her breathing became as ragged and labored as Billy's had been, but unlike Billy she failed to improve, instead sinking deeper and deeper into the quinsy's grip. On the second morning he used the last of the physick she'd made for Billy's throat. He had no idea what had gone into it, or how to make more.

He had never felt more helpless, or more useless, in his entire life.

"Mama's still sick?" asked Billy anxiously as soon as he'd wakened and peered into Rachel's bed. "Still?"

"Aye, lad, I'm afraid she is," he said, lifting the boy up into his arms. Though he'd been fond of Billy before, Rachel's illness had put them constantly in each other's company, and the bond between them had grown and strengthened. "Hush, now, we'd do well to let her sleep while she can."

"Why doesn't Mama get better, Jamie?" Unhappily Billy looked down at his flushed, feverish mother, and hugged Blackie and Whitie. "I got better. Why doesn't she?"

"I don't know," said Jamie, making up his mind even as he spoke. "But I believe it's high time we took her to someone who does. Do you think we can find our way to Ethan and Mary Bowman's house?"

"Mr. an' Mrs. Bowman's house?" Billy twisted his mouth uncertainly. "You an' me? With Mama?"

"Aye. Once she pointed out the smoke from their chimney to me. We'll find it."

But Billy shook his head. "You can't go there, Jamie. Mama said you're s'posed to be a secret."

"Am I, now?" He smiled grimly. "Well, then, for your Mama's sake, I warrant I'm not going to be a secret much longer."

The snow danced around her, every flake an icy, welcome kiss on her hot cheeks.

Rachel wanted to dance, too, to spin around and around the way she had when she was a little girl. She could hear the fiddlers tuning their instruments, the sliding whine that would soon turn into the sweetest tunes imaginable. How she loved to dance! She would wear a white dress and a white sash, and she would twirl through the air just like the snowflakes.

"Hold on, Rachel," Jamie was saying. "Only a little longer."

She didn't want to hold on. Why should she? Didn't he understand that she wanted to be free of the earth and dance on the wind?

"We're almost there, lass," promised Jamie. "Just beyond those trees."

She looked up and saw the white ribbons tied to every branch, and smiled. Mama must have done that for her, just as Mama would have looped back the cherry-colored hangings of her bed to air it out for her homecoming, and put roses from the garden on the bedside table. Mama must have known that she'd be coming back to Crescent Hill tonight, in time for the dancing. She hoped the first dance would be one of the new Scottish reels; those were her favorites above all others. She tried to look past Jamie's arm, eager for the first glimpse of the tall chimneys of the house.

It had been so very long since she'd been home. Now, at last, she was almost there.

The two men came running up to Jamie through the snow flurries even before he'd drawn Proudfoot to a halt. The older one in the black coat he recognized as Ethan Bowman; the other, a leaner, pink-cheeked version with the same face, he guessed must be a Bowman son.

"Holy fire, it's Rachel Lindsey," said Ethan as he reached up with his son to take her carefully from Jamie. She was barely conscious, limp in their arms, her long, black hair trailing from beneath the hood of her cloak. "What's happened, sir?"

"She's ill," said Jamie. "A putrid quinsy she caught from the boy. I hoped your wife might help her."

"Of course she will, sir, don't you doubt it," said Ethan. "Mary! Mary, you're needed!"

But the older woman was already rushing from the house, her silver braids flopping over her shoulders.

"Bring her into the house at once, Abel," she said, shooing her hand at the son who held Rachel in his arms. "Into the front room, where there's a fire. Hurry, hurry, you great lummox, the poor sweet creature must be perishing from the cold!"

From Proudfoot's back Jamie watched the bustle of activity, painfully aware of how much an outsider he was. Rachel wasn't his alone any longer. These people were her friends, and they had far more right to watch over her than he would ever have. He had concentrated so hard on keeping Rachel alive until they reached the Bowmans' that now, safely here, he felt empty and curiously bereft.

He hadn't realized how tensely he'd been holding Rachel until they'd taken her from him. His arms throbbed as he straightened them for the first time in hours, and he braced himself as he slowly climbed down from the horse, taking care not to wake Billy, lashed to his back.

"Bless you, you've brought little Billy, too," said Mary. "Aren't you the very saint!"

Jamie didn't answer, left at a loss by being called a saint. Not that Mary noticed his silence. She was already busily undoing the lashes that held Billy inside the makeshift carrier, fashioned from Jamie's knapsack.

"Come here, sweet baby," she crooned as she took him into her arms. Billy stirred sleepily, his cheek still marked red where he'd slept against his arm, and his knitted cap dusted with snow. "You come with Mary, and I'll see you have cider and honeycakes."

She'd turned away to bear him into the house like another trophy by the time Jamie called out to her.

"You'll be wanting these," he said, stepping forward. He pulled the two stuffed horses from the pocket of his coat and self-consciously held them out to her. "The black one's Blackie and the white one's, well, Whitie. Billy doesn't go far without either one."

Mary's weathered face softened into a surprised, radiant smile, and Jamie realized that when she'd been younger she must have been a beauty.

"You're very right, sir," she said warmly, "and for the child's sake—and our peace—I thank you for remembering. But now I must see to Mrs. Lindsey."

Then she was gone, disappearing into the house with the toy horses as well as Rachel and Billy and, it seemed, Jamie's two main reasons for living.

"We owe you a debt, sir," said Ethan, his hands tucked beneath the skirts of his old-fashioned coat to warm them. "Mary and I fancy Mrs. Lindsey like one of our own brood, and we're obliged to you for rescuing her. Benjamin, boy, come see to this gentleman's horse!"

One more Bowman instantly appeared, most likely a grandson, took Proudfoot's reins from Jamie's hand and led the gelding away to the barn.

Jamie watched the horse go, and then looked up at the rambling house before him. For a man this far west, Bowman had prospered. The left side of the house was clearly the older—low and square like a stockade and built of peeled, chinked logs much like Rachel's cabin.

From the hanging signboard painted with a fanciful E.B. and a trading pelt, Jamie guessed that this first house had now become the Bowmans' shop.

The addition was really an entirely new house, built in the latest fashion, with planed clapboards, twin brick chimneys and double-sashed windows that must have made a long, perilous journey from London. It was, he thought glumly, the kind of worldly house in which Rachel would feel entirely at home, and where he'd always be at odds. He wondered if they had dances with fiddlers here, and if Mary Bowman, as eccentric as she seemed, had tied ribbons around mistletoe for Christmas.

But while Jamie had been studying the Bowmans' house, Ethan had in turn been studying Jamie.

"So, tell me, sir," he said. "Which company do you serve with?"

Though the question was asked politely enough, Jamie immediately went on his guard. He'd been so worried over Rachel that he'd forgotten the risk he was taking by coming here. He'd do better to remember it.

"None," he answered. "None at present."

Ethan cocked his head to one side and scratched behind his ear. "Yet that coat you're wearing, sir. It's most particular, and not of a kind we see often in this county. The indigo stripes, the hood, those little rosettes at the waist in back—it all puts me to mind of the kind of coats King George hands out to keep his most special soldiers warm. Capotes, the Frenchmen call them."

"Perhaps the last man to wear it was one of those soldiers," said Jamie carefully. Though long parted from the meeting house, his conscience still laid perverse traps for him. One of them was a complete inability to lie, though he could contrive these most elaborate ways of expressing the truth that were probably as bad as out-and-out lying. And he wasn't lying now to Ethan Bowman, not really. The coat had always belonged to him and him alone, making him both the first and the last man to wear it. "That would explain it."

"I'll wager a guinea the man was a soldier serving in Canada," declared Ethan. "Most likely a Ranger, at that. No paltry infantryman gets himself a coat that fine."

Jamie's face remained impassive. "It suits me well enough, and it keeps me warm."

"And who, sir, can quarrel with that?" Shrewdly Ethan's glance slipped lower, lingering next on Jamie's rifle with an interest that Jamie didn't miss. If Ethan knew enough to question the overcoat, then there'd be no chance he'd overlook a gun as overtly, elegantly lethal as Jamie's rifle. The curiosity in his gaze already spoke volumes.

But to Jamie's surprise, Ethan said nothing about the gun. Instead he merely patted his amply filled waistcoat, then waved in the direction of the house.

"Forgive me, sir, chattering on about woolen coats like the shopkeeper I am," he said with a rueful chuckle as Jamie followed him inside. "Coat or no, you must be chilled yourself. Pray step inside with me and I'll fetch you a glass of something handsome, sure to take the cold from your bones."

"A dipper full of water will do well enough," said Jamie as he took off his hat at the doorway and shook it free of the snow. "Though if your wife has more of the cider she offered to Billy, I'd welcome it."

Ethan grunted. "Not a drinker, eh?"

"Oh, I drink," said Jamie with a faint smile. "Every man and beast does. It's spirits I keep clear of."

"Holy fire, isn't Mary going to love you," said Ethan, shaking his head as he led Jamie into the kitchen. "First you remember to bring little Billy's toys, and now you choose water over my whiskey."

He smacked a sleeping cat from a Windsor chair and motioned for Jamie to sit while he took two glasses from the cupboard.

But Jamie hesitated, glancing back down the hallway to where he could faintly make out Mary's voice. "I'd like to see how Rachel's faring first," he said. "She was weak enough when we left home."

Home. Lord, he could have ripped out his own tongue for that slip! He saw how Ethan's brow quirked up, but again the other man chose not to comment.

"She's in the best of hands, sir," he said instead. "The boy, too. You did right to bring them here."

Jamie wavered, straining his ears for Rachel's voice. "Still and all, I'd like to see for myself."

"Mary won't let you in even if you try," said Ethan. "You must trust her. My wife knows cures for every ill and ailment the flesh is heir to, better than any town-bred surgeon. It's from her time with the squaws, you know."

He motioned to the chair again, this time more pointedly. "Now sit, sir, so we can talk properly."

Instinctively Jamie tensed. "I'm not a man much given to talking."

"And I'm one who is," said Ethan. "Now you can stay and we can discuss this matter civilly, or you can take your leave. It matters little to me. But I'll tell you this first, sir—you'll see neither Mrs. Lindsey nor the boy again until you hear me out, and not even that wicked-looking rifle of yours is going to change my mind."

To Jamie, the choice couldn't be more simple. He could walk from this house a free man and lose Rachel, or he could put aside his pride to stay and gamble his life against the chance of seeing her.

He stayed, and sat in the Windsor chair while Ethan poured a whiskey. He stayed, but he didn't put aside the gun, and the long knife hidden beneath his coat was a comfort, too. Right now he needed all the comforts he could find.

Ethan dropped heavily into the opposite chair, his glass cupped in his hand. "Why don't we begin with you telling me your name."

Jamie didn't flinch. "I don't see that my name is your affair."

"When you're in my house, it damned well is my affair," said Ethan warmly, "and it's even more my concern because of Rachel Lindsey."

"Who I am has nothing to do with Rachel!"

"The hell it doesn't! How long have you been living under her roof? One month? Two? At least since Mary and I brought her the gelding. Not only was she nervous as a cat, but there was no way she could have done all the work around her place that she claimed."

"And where's the sin in that?" demanded Jamie.

"You tell me where the sin lies, and it best not be in her bed!" Angrily Ethan thumped his glass down on the arm of his chair, hard enough to sprinkle whiskey over the floorboards. "You can't guess how that poor girl in there has suffered, shackled with a useless, whoring drunkard for a husband! The last thing she needs in her life is some footloose Tory deserter with a price on his scalp!"

"Twenty dollars," said Jamie, his eyes like chips of ice. "Do you mean to collect it yourself, Ethan Bowman?"

"Not unless Rachel tells me to!" snapped Ethan. "Do you think I care if you killed some bastard officer, Ryder? That's one less bloody Englishman we'll have to kill ourselves!"

If that were only all of it, thought Jamie grimly. *If that were all to what had happened that day...*

His eyes narrowed, watching Ethan. "Then you know who I am?"

"How the devil could I not?" Ethan shrugged impatiently. "Alec Lindsey's trumpeting your name and description to everyone who'll listen, he's that eager to claim the reward."

"He'll know where to find me now, won't he?"

Ethan shook his head. "He won't hear it from me. Like most sensible people, I believe that the Lindseys have gotten their way far too long as it is."

He looked at Jamie shrewdly. "But you didn't know that when you brought Rachel here, did you? For all you knew, I'd stick a pistol in your ribs and haul you off for the reward."

"That's right," said Jamie wearily. "But Rachel's life seemed worth a good deal more to me than my own."

Ethan nodded, and Jamie sensed the older man's hostility beginning to slip away. Clearly the Bowmans cared as much about Rachel as they said, and Ethan could hardly be faulted for wishing to protect her.

Briefly Jamie considered telling him about the barn fire and how Rachel feared Alec would try to take Billy from her. But then he thought better of it. The Bowmans were Rachel's friends; if she wanted them to know all her troubles with Alec, she'd tell them herself.

"So why hasn't anyone taken the Lindseys down a notch before this?" He asked. "Most bullies benefit from a good thrashing."

"Influence, sir," said Ethan sourly. "Influence. The old man was a judge or some such in Albany, and though the devil's long ago claimed him as his own, his friends still favor the boys. Add the disorder of the war, burdening folks with troubles of their own, and Alec is left to do fair well whatever ill he wishes. 'Tis best to be careful where you tread around that particular rattle-snake. Watch your back, and Rachel's, too. But rest assured that there'd be plenty who'd cheer if you aimed your rifle at the rascal next."

"I very nearly did. You can ask Rachel. She's taken a few shots at him, as well."

Ethan snorted with disgust. "Pity neither of you finished the job. She's Alec's own sister-in-law, yet last winter when William didn't return home, he nearly let her and the boy starve to death."

"But you and Mary didn't let that happen, did you?"

"Of course not, not after we'd discovered the sorry state she was in," admitted Ethan gruffly. "It wasn't easy, arranging matters to save her pride, but we contrived."

Jamie looked down at his gun, running his fingers lightly along the barrel as if smoothing away some infinitesimal smudge was more important than his next question. "Do you believe William is still alive?"

"Ha, so that's the rub, eh?" Ethan swirled the last of the whiskey in his glass. "You've been rangering with the Tories. I don't have to tell you what Brant's savages did to the men they caught at Oriskany. Why take a prisoner when a scalp's so much more convenient?"

Jamie nodded. Oh, he knew about what Brant's men could do. He *knew*. "She still believes William's coming back."

"She'll keep right on believing it until she has a reason to stop," said Ethan with a sigh. "It's been hard on her, the poor, tenderhearted lass. I tell you, we worry over her. She's like one of our own."

And like his own, too, thought Jamie. Blindly he stared into the fire, realizing all over again how much Rachel had come to mean to him. Her merry laugh and how her smile lit her green eyes, the scarf she'd knitted to surprise him and the songs she sang to Billy each night, the way she'd chosen to trust him—*him!*—over all others and the way she kissed with a fire that licked and burned at his soul. His Rachel, he thought with wonder, his generous, impulsive, loyal, stubborn and very beautiful Rachel.

Had it really taken the threat of losing her forever to make him realize how much he wanted to be part of her life?

If she would have him. Dear Lord, if only she would have him!

"Will it be enough, Ethan Bowman, if I tell you I'll never knowingly bring her pain or sorrow?" asked Jamie quietly. "Will you believe me when I say there will never be another woman more dear to me than she?"

"Don't tell me, Ryder," said Ethan. "Tell Rachel."

Chapter Twelve

Rachel crawled to the end of the bed, eagerly craning her neck so she could see more of the Bowmans' yard from the window. One of the Bowman daughters had returned to live with her parents while her husband was away with the army to the east, and she had brought her five children with her. All five of them, plus several more drawn from neighboring houses, were now engaged in a monumental sledding and sliding contest on the hill beside the orchard, while a few of the older, more daring children raced through the orchard itself, dodging the apple trees as they shrieked and screamed their way to the bottom.

In the thick of the activity was Billy, the exceptionally proud and gleeful owner of the best Christmas sled on the slope. The sled's maker was there, too, dragging Billy again and again up the hill to give him—and any other child that wished it—a firm push for a start. Though he towered over them, Jamie was clearly enjoying himself as much as any of the children, roaring and laughing and scrunching himself up to take his turn on Billy's sled, his new striped scarf streaming after him.

Rachel laughed, too, delighted by Billy's obvious happiness. If it had been her decision, she probably wouldn't have let him play outdoors so soon after the quinsy, but to see him sliding and tumbling with the other children made her long to be out there, too.

But her delight also included Jamie. Not so long ago, he wouldn't have been able to relax enough to enjoy such foolishness, and she remembered all too well how he'd berated her over making the snow angels. He'd promised to give her time until she found her peace; was it possible that in the meantime he'd been able to find a little peace with himself, as well?

"And where do you think you're headed, m'dear?" scolded Mary as she shoved open the bedchamber door with her shoulder, a tray with Rachel's dinner in her hands. "Back beneath the covers this instant, before I must come and stuff you under them myself!"

"Oh, but Mary, look outside!" pleaded Rachel, her voice still a dry croak. "And look at Billy! I've never seen him have such a grand time!"

As she spoke Billy was careening down the hill with a little girl on the sled before him, both of them screaming with joy as the unsteered sled—Billy still had much to learn in that department, no matter how many times Jamie had put the ropes into his little mittened hands—ground to a clumsy halt in a snowbank and dumped both giggling children into the drift.

Mary set the tray down on the bed before she went to the window, hands at the waist of her apron. "The reason you've never seen him like this before, missy, is because you've never seen him with young ones his own age."

Rachel sighed, settling back against the pillows and pulling the covers up over her knees. After the first three days, when her fever had finally broken and she was over the worst of the quinsy, she'd felt guilty about having Mary wait on her like this, but after nearly a week of it she'd come to enjoy it, too, for the time it meant that she and Mary would have together to chat.

"I know that, Mary, but I can't pluck playmates for him out of the air, can I?" She sighed again, hugging her knees. "When we go home tomorrow, he's going to be so beside himself with loneliness."

"Then leave him here with us for another week," said Mary cheerfully, pouring herb tea from the pewter pot for both Rachel and herself. "I'd rather keep you, too, snug and safe, but I know better than to ask that again, especially now that I know you've Jamie to look after you. But having Billy stay with us a bit longer would be good for you both. And what's another child with the mob we have under our roof at present?"

Rachel shook her head. "Oh, no, Mary, I couldn't! You're most kind to offer, of course, but I—I've never left him with anyone else."

"Then it's high time you did," said Mary promptly. "You'll have a week to build up your strength without him tugging at your apron, and he'll be happy as a skunk. Ethan and I will bring him home to you in a sennight."

To hear Mary, the plan made perfect sense, but still Rachel hesitated. "He's only just three, Mary. Don't you think he's too young to leave me?"

"No, I do not," declared Mary as she poured her tea from her cup to the dish to cool. "Rachel, you're quite the most devoted mother I know, but you can't be the whole world to Billy. And neither, m'dear, can he be yours."

A particularly loud cheer rose from the children outside, disintegrating into uncontrollable laughter, and Mary leaned toward the window.

"Saints, but you should see what that man of yours did!" she said. "Took the shingles the Wilson boys were using for sliding and tried to scoot down the hill standing upright. Didn't get too far, though. There's nothing children find more comical than to see another fall smack flat on his backside."

Rachel blushed and ducked her chin. "Jamie's not 'my' man, Mary. You shouldn't call him that."

But Mary didn't hear, or pretended not to. "Still, I'm not about to fault a man who favors children. It's a good sign he's generally gentle and tractable in other ways, too. To see him out there now, I'll wager your Jamie's the oldest one in his family, the big brother to a whole nest of little ones."

Rachel's chin sank lower, her hair slipping forward on either side of her face like blinders.

"Well, is he or not?" persisted Mary. "I'm seldom wrong in such matters."

Rebelliously Rachel grumbled low in her throat. "I don't know."

"Then where is his home, pray?" Mary's smile was meant to disarm, but all it did was put Rachel even more on edge. "Surely, m'dear, you know that much."

"Unlike most men, Jamie's not a braggart," said Rachel defensively. "He seldom speaks of himself."

"He certainly speaks enough of you." Mary set her empty dish on the tray and went to light a rush from the fireplace. Taking her pipe from the top buttonhole of her shirt, she touched the rush to the bowl, puffing gently until the weed lit. Inhaling, she smiled to herself and let her eyes flicker briefly shut on the other side of the smoke, all the while keeping Rachel openmouthed with anxious curiosity.

"'How is Rachel this morn? How much is she suffering? What can I do to ease her pain? Has she asked after me?'" Mary tipped her head slyly. "I do believe he asked that one every day."

"Truly?" asked Rachel breathlessly. "He truly wished to know?"

After living with Jamie in the single room of her house for so long, she had seen next to nothing of him here at the Bowmans'. It wasn't only that Mary kept his well-chaperoned visits to her sickroom at a minimum to keep her from tiring, or that he spent hours each day traveling back and forth from her farm to tend to her stock.

It was more—and worse—than that. He had seemed oddly formal in her company, falling back on the unnervingly polite reserve that she'd remembered from the beginning. He had held his black hat in his hands and refused to sit. Instead he had stood beside the fireplace, saying next to nothing, and was seemingly more interested in studying the checkered bed hangings than in speaking with her. It had hurt her, that bewildering distance, and more than once she'd wept into her pillow after he'd left.

But now, to hear Mary's telling, she'd been wrong to weep, and he'd been wonderfully interested in her after all.

"Oh, aye, questions left and right," said Mary carelessly. "But why should any of that matter to you, sitting like a queen and sipping your thistle juice?"

"But it does!" Rachel set her dish down with an anxious clatter. "I want to know! I *need* to know!"

Mary drew deeply on the pipe, ignoring Rachel's outburst. "If Jamie Ryder isn't much given to speaking of himself, Rachel, then maybe it's because you're not much given to asking him to do so. How you ever let yourself fall in love with the man without knowing the first thing about him is beyond all reckoning."

"I do so know about him!" cried Rachel, her froggy voice squeaking with indignation. "I know that he is good and kind and generous, and that he has a smile more beautiful than any other man alive! I know that he treats Billy better than his own father ever did, and I know he isn't afraid of work or wolves or admitting that he's wrong! I know he can shoot the seeds from an apple, and that he likes to let his steamed chocolate settle until there's a skin on the top that he can eat with a spoon!"

She took another deep breath, not finished yet. "I do *so* know about him, Mary, bad things as well as the good! I know that because he's a Tory my father most likely wouldn't let him through the door to our house! I know that he used to be one of Walter Butler's Rangers, and that he was with them at the massacre at Cherry

Valley, and that he's likely—likely done a great many very awful things because of being a Ranger. But I also know he's been hurt, not just his shoulder but deep inside, where the scars don't show except in his eyes. But he's a good man, Mary, a good, honest man, and I won't hear you say I know *nothing* about him!''

"Then at least you admit you're in love with him," said Mary with unconcealed triumph. "Saints, I've never seen a more smitten nor more stubborn pair than the two of you!"

But the joy that had filled Rachel's eyes when she'd spoken of Jamie vanished. "I can't be in love with Jamie, Mary," she said forlornly. "You know that, no matter how much you like making matches. I can't be half of a pair with him for anything."

"Oh, m'dear," said Mary softly. "Whyever not?"

"Because of William," said Rachel, her heart like lead in her breast. "To fall in love with any other man when I do not know if he—"

"Rachel, listen to me." Mary pushed aside the tray and sat beside Rachel, taking both her hands. She looked down, deliberating with herself, as she gently rubbed her thumbs across the younger woman's hands. "Rachel, I haven't told you this before because I hoped I wouldn't have to. But you're not leaving me much choice."

"What is it, Mary?" asked Rachel uneasily, though part of her already knew. Part of her had known for months, over a year.

"When you were so distraught last winter, Ethan made certain inquiries about William's fate after the ambush at Oriskany. Those few pitiful men who'd gone off with Captain Walker and returned were right, Rachel. Brant's men took no prisoners that day, and they killed and scalped all the wounded, including—''

"Please don't say it aloud, Mary," said Rachel hoarsely. "I don't think I could bear it."

The pressure of Mary's hands increased in silent sympathy. "You can bear it, m'dear, because you must. God doesn't give us any sorrows without giving us the strength to bear them, as well."

"But I made him do it!" cried Rachel. "If it hadn't been for me, William would never have gone for a soldier with Captain Walker, and never have been there in Oriskany to be killed! Even Alec says so!"

"Then Alec Lindsey is an even greater ass than I thought before," said Mary grimly. "Now, listen to me, and listen well. William's death is not your fault. Life's a frail, uncertain thing at best, and William could have just as easily broken his neck falling from his horse after a night drinking himself stupid at Volk's. More likely, anyway."

"But Mary—"

"I said you were to listen to me, Rachel! William is dead, and you've been his widow far longer than you were his wife. You can spend the rest of your nights and days mourning him and blaming yourself until you don't have a life left at all, or you can start asking Jamie Ryder exactly how many brothers and sisters he has in his family."

Mary's voice softened, almost pleading. "It's your life, m'dear, and it's your choice. I can't make it for you. But please, Rachel, promise me you'll consider what will make you happy. That's all I ask for my own daughters, and all I want for you. To be happy.''

Rachel stared at the plain pewter cross that hung at Mary's neck. It was swinging now with the force of Mary's words, catching the winter light from the window as it swung back and forth, back and forth.

William was dead, and she wasn't.

And for the first time since her husband had marched unsteadily away from her on that long-gone summer day, Rachel shed tears that were meant for William alone.

It was Rachel who wept again, and not Billy, when she and Jamie left the Bowmans' house on the following morning to return to the farm. She had finally agreed with Mary to leave Billy behind for a short visit, with the stipulation that Ethan would bring him back immediately if he grew homesick or cried at night.

But as Rachel had hugged him close while Jamie waited, Billy had wriggled impatiently and looked past her to his new best friend, Thomas, and the snowman they were making together. With a sigh Rachel had finally let him run off, his short, round figure in the red knitted cap blurring as she watched through her tears.

''He'll be fine,'' said Jamie as she turned to look over her shoulder one final time. Secretly he longed to look back, too. He was going to miss the boy as much as she was. ''Better than fine, with all those other boys to play with.''

''I know,'' said Rachel with a plaintive sniff. ''But I'm his mama and he's my baby, and I've every right to be sad about this if I want, even if I know that he'd much rather stay behind."

Jamie grunted, tugging hard on his horse's reins to bring him back in line. While Rachel rode Proudfoot, Ethan had lent him another horse for the ride home, to be collected when they returned Billy. The gelding didn't like the burden of carrying a man of Jamie's size, and he was showing his unhappiness by shying off the trail whenever he thought Jamie wouldn't notice.

Rachel sighed, knowing he'd have to pay more attention to the horse than to her. She wanted so much for this ride home with Jamie and the week afterward to be special. She realized that Mary, shameless matchmaker that she was trying to be, had given this time without Billy to her as a gift, and she prayed she'd be able to find that rare happiness with Jamie that Mary had promised.

Watching Jamie from the corner of her eye, she wasn't sure it was going to be possible. But she was determined to try her best and, swallowing her own misgivings, she decided to follow the advice that the older woman had given her.

"You seem so at ease with children," she said, wincing inwardly at how unnaturally cheerful her voice sounded. "Do you come from a large family?"

Still wrestling to control his horse, Jamie only half heard her, though what he heard registered as odd. "Nay, not large."

Ask him questions and he'll answer, Mary had promised, and stubbornly Rachel tried again. "Are you the oldest son?"

"Aye."

"How many brothers and sisters do you have?"

"I *had* one brother and one sister, both dead of smallpox, and my mother with them."

"Oh, Jamie," she said softly, touched as much by his bluntness as by what he'd said. No wonder he'd never spoken of his siblings! "I'm so sorry."

At last he swung around to look across the narrow space that divided them, his expression hard and studiously empty. "Why should you be sorry? It wasn't your fault."

In the two years since Sam, Sarajane and his mother had died, Jamie had never once spoken of it to another. Why the devil had he done so now? Surely Rachel didn't want to be burdened with his old grief any more than he wished to share it.

"I know it's not my fault, Jamie, but if there's anything I—"

"Now, does all this querying of yours have some point to it?" he interrupted. "Something to do with leaving Billy behind with the Bowmans?"

She sighed forlornly, recognizing a stone wall when she charged into it. "No. No, I suppose it doesn't."

For a long time they rode in miserable silence, Jamie with his shoulders hunched and his hat pulled low and Rachel with her head bowed within her hood as she tried not to weep.

Jamie swore to himself, his mood blacker and blacker. He hadn't wanted this morning to disintegrate like this; far from it. Not a fortnight past he had carried Rachel in his arms on this same trail, making every promise to heaven that he could think of in exchange for her life, and now he was treating her as if she meant nothing at all to him. It wasn't her fault that she'd asked after his family; for most people such a question would have been innocent enough, even polite. Before this he'd always found her the easiest woman in the world to talk to. Why now, when so much was at stake, could he think of nothing to say?

At last he cleared his throat, and she turned with swift expectation. "You know," he began, trying to remember the speech he'd prepared the night before, "you know, you're the one I expected to stay behind at the Bowmans', not Billy. That house must have put you to mind of all you left behind in Newport."

"In Newport?" repeated Rachel, confused. "Why would staying at the Bowmans' house because I was ill remind me of Newport?"

"I meant the house itself," said Jamie, feeling as clumsy as if he'd been riding the horse while standing on his head. "I meant what a grand, fine place it is, like that house of yours in Newport that you're always talking about."

There, thought Jamie, he'd finally said it, the single biggest doubt that had been eating at him ever since he'd brought her here. Seeing Rachel in the Bowmans' house, looking pale and fragile and impossibly beautiful as she sat in the middle of an enormous curtained bed with a half-dozen bolsters behind her, had made him realize how much more she belonged in a place like that than in the tiny, rough cabin she now was forced to call home, and where she'd saved his worthless life.

The problem was that she hadn't looked anything like *his* Rachel, the one who made her own butter and chopped firewood and swung her musket at a wolf, and the difference had made him withdraw into himself with uncertainty. On New Year's Day the Bowmans had brought their celebration to her bedside, and he had seen how she'd laughed and reveled in the toasts and fiddle music. It wasn't that Jamie disapproved of such worldly celebrations for others; it was that they always made him feel like an outsider, an interloper with no life of his own. As soon as he could, he had slipped away to go outside and stare at the stars, and he was quite sure no one, especially not Rachel, had noticed that he'd left.

"I won't argue that Mary and Ethan's house is quite the finest in the county," said Rachel slowly, reluctant to mention her own family after she'd blundered so badly over his. "It's certainly larger than mine. But my mother would have had your head for comparing it to ours in Newport. One of Mama's greatest joys was sending Father and my brothers off on shopping expeditions in every port they visited, and our house showed exactly how successful they'd been."

At first Jamie didn't answer. So the house in Newport was even richer and grander than the Bowmans'. What of it? Hadn't Rachel told him herself that worldly riches didn't matter to her any longer? Hadn't she said she'd willingly give up silk stockings and silver buckles for an honest man who loved her?

And yet, and yet . . .

"Why didn't you go back there?" he asked, his voice harsher than he realized. "When William left, why didn't you take Billy and return home to Newport?"

"Because there's no home to return to," she said quietly, looking straight ahead. "When the British landed, my parents and I fled to Providence with little more than the clothes we were wearing. Father was most outspoken against the crown—he still is—and the wretched lobsterbacks would have hung him for a traitor if they'd caught us."

Hung for a traitor. The words echoed through Jamie's soul, matching the furious beat of his own heart as he listened. If he had known this was the hideous truth, he would never have asked her. Her innocent question about his brother and sister paled beside it.

Hung for a traitor....

"As it was, they seized our house and everything in it, all of Mama's treasures, as forfeit," she continued, her voice calm and hollow. "They tore up the arbors and cut down the cherry trees in the garden for firewood, and they let their horses eat Mama's roses. I'm sure whatever they haven't destroyed with their boots and sabres they've packed up and shipped back home to England as plunder. All because Father dared to speak what he believes is right, to choose freedom over tyranny, and now—now they've left him and Mama nothing."

"He has his life, his wife and his family," said Jamie hoarsely. "My father thought he was safe in his beliefs, and did not run. And aye, they did hang him for a traitor, and now he has nothing."

Rachel gasped, wheeling Proudfoot around to a halt. "Jamie, look at me. *Look at me!*"

She reached out and seized his reins, clumsily jerking his horse's head around to stop him, too. "Jamie, is this true? The British murdered your father?"

The raw, bitter anguish she found in his eyes shocked her. "Nay, Rachel, the British didn't do it. The *Americans* did."

"But I don't understand how that could be possible! It's the British who are the tyrants, the ones who wish against freedom!"

"It's men who do it, Rachel," he said harshly, "and it damn well doesn't matter which flag they're under. My father was a Friend. He could no more countenance what that so-called Congress was doing in Philadelphia than he could sever his own arm, and he said so, preaching peace and caution in our Meeting and to all others who would listen. And the wrong men did, Rachel. I tried to warn him. I tried, because I'd heard the rumors, but—"

He broke off, overcome, shaking his head as if he still could not believe what had happened next. With a muttered oath he flung his leg over the side of the horse and dropped to the ground, stalking away from her, running from her into the snow.

"Jamie!" she called frantically, sliding from Proudfoot's back so she could follow him on foot. "Jamie, please, don't go!"

He plunged on another few ragged steps before at last he stopped, drawn back by her voice, and swung around to face her as she hurried toward him, her skirts dragging through the snow.

"I quarrelled with him, Rachel," he said raggedly. "He believed that words would be enough to stop the madness. I didn't, and went north, to join with the British and fight for what I believed was right. How could I know what they would do to him, Rachel? How could I know?"

He was breathing hard, almost sobbing, as the past he could not change racked him. "Because Father would not swear to support the American cause, he was accused of sedition and treason, his lands confiscated and his family dispossessed. Just like your father, Rachel. Except they took mine in a cart to the city commons and hung him with as little dignity as they would a horse thief."

He broke off again, gulping for air, and Rachel dared to rest her hand on his arm. For a long moment he stared at her hand, then clumsily covered it with his own, the simple gesture giving him the strength to finish.

"I was stationed at Fort Niagara, and though Mother wrote to me, I never received a single letter, even after she tried to come to me. She had no one left to turn to, and I couldn't help because I didn't know. She and Sara and little Sam had only gone as far as the house of another Friend in Princeton when they all took ill with smallpox."

He shook his head again. "I didn't know, Rachel, else I would have done anything I could to help. You know I would have, don't you?"

"Of course you would have, Jamie," murmured Rachel, her fingers curling around his. She could only imagine what he'd survived, and how he'd blamed himself. "You couldn't have done anything else."

His eyes were bleak. "Oh, aye, and what did I do instead? Put my soul at the service of jackals in gold lace, to fight beside thieves and savages who murder children and women? And even at that I was a failure, one more blasted, blessed *failure.*''

He shook away her hand and swung his arm grandly through the air, his laugh bitter. ''That reward that Butler offered—do you know why he did it? Because in the middle of that hellish morning I tried to stop a Seneca brave from murdering two children. I broke my *orders* and attacked one of my own allies, and when my sergeant saw what I was trying to do, I shot him. I shot him, Rachel, shot him dead where he stood. And eventually I did, I was still too late to save the children.''

''Oh, Jamie,'' she murmured, her heart weeping for him in his sorrow. She thought of how much he cared for Billy, how much he'd enjoyed playing with the children at the Bowmans'. How much those two children lost at Cherry Valley must haunt him!

He laughed again, an aching cry of despair. ''Now you know the worst, Rachel. You know it all. What better proof is there that I'm every bit the wastrel my father always said I was?''

''But that's not true, Jamie, none of it!'' cried Rachel as she seized him by the shoulders to force him to look at her. ''You're not like that, and you never have been, not to me or to Billy! This war has made us all do things we might not have done otherwise. It's not you. It never could have been. You're a good man, Jamie Ryder, and I won't hear you say otherwise of yourself!''

He searched her face, desperately wanting to believe her. He had expected to find revulsion and horror, yet all he saw in her eyes was understanding and sympathy, and something more, something his battered soul craved and dared not ask for.

"I've made mistakes, Rachel," he said haltingly, "mistakes no man should make."

"And I've made more than my share, as well," she said, reaching up to smooth his hair back from his forehead. "But together, Jamie, perhaps we can do some things that are right."

"Together." The word fell leaden from his lips. "Rachel, I have nothing to offer you."

Her mouth tried to twist into a smile, and he realized her eyes were bright with tears. "You have yourself, Jamie, and that's all I want," she said softly. "I love you, and I believe I always will."

Gently he reached for her and kissed her, her lips warm and sweet with the promise of everything she offered.

"I love you, too, Rachel," he said, his voice low and hoarse with the words he'd never spoken to another woman. "I love you."

She smiled up at him through her tears. "Then take me home, Jamie. Now, love. Let's go home together."

Chapter Thirteen

He insisted on carrying her from her horse into the cabin, reminding her sternly of how ill she'd been and how she must not take any further risks.

"You're as bad as Mary!" scolded Rachel, trying to be serious as he unbuckled her shoes for her and slipped them from her feet. Her toes were very ticklish, a fact she hoped he wouldn't discover just yet. "I'm not a bit of fancy porcelain, Jamie. I'll hardly break to bits if you look at me wrong!"

"You're *my* bit of fancy porcelain, and I'll look at you however I please." He drew the coverlet over her and tucked it under the edge of the mattress, leaving her dressed even to her cloak. After standing empty for over a week, the cabin felt even colder than the air outside. "You're going to stay right there until I get a fire going."

From the bed she watched him bending over the fireplace, and the warmth she felt had nothing to do with the coverlet.

"That's my hearth, you know," she said. "You've as

much right to be there as I would to tinker with your rifle.''

"If you want anything to eat or drink that you don't have to chip free of ice, then you won't complain.'' The spark he'd started flamed brighter in the tinder, and with a nod of satisfaction he rose. "And if you wish to learn how to fire my rifle, all you must do is ask. I'd just rather you didn't 'tinker' with it on your own.''

"Oh, pooh,'' she scoffed. "You might recall that I'm not a complete ninny with a musket. How different can a rifle be?''

"Different enough. I'm partial to you as you are without seeing you shoot off a hand or foot.'' He came to sit on the edge of the bed, his face turning serious as he reached out to brush her cheek with the back of his hand.

"Do you know how precious you are to me, Rachel?'' he asked softly. "I could have roamed all over this world and never found another woman like you.''

"I'd rather hoped your roaming days were over,'' said Rachel wistfully, slipping her hand up under his hair to rest on the back of his neck.

"I'll warrant they are, sweetheart,'' he said. "You've given me all the reason I need to stay in one place. But that's not to say that I'd object to a bit of persuasion to make me sure.''

But as he bent to kiss her, she held her fingers up to stop him. "There is one other thing, Jamie,'' she said, choosing her words carefully. "Something Mary told me.''

"What, more grim warnings?'' he teased.

"No, Jamie, this is—this is *serious*." She swallowed, wondering why this should be so hard. "It's about William. Mary said that Ethan had made inquiries clear to Canada about him for me, and that though—though his body wasn't ever found, they are very sure that William died at Oriskany, and I—oh, Jamie, I promised myself I wouldn't cry!"

"Shh, love, it's all right," he said tenderly. "You don't have to say more if you don't wish to."

Bravely she shook her head. "No, I must say this. Truly." She gave a little hiccuping sob, then plunged on. "I now know for certain that William is dead and that I am his—his widow. Part of me gave up hope long ago when he didn't come home with the others, but for William's sake I had to be sure."

She rubbed away her tears with the heel of her hand and tried to smile. "For William, and for you, Jamie," she said shyly, "because now, at last, I'm free to love you. Life's too uncertain and short for me—for *us*—to wait any longer."

He looked at her almost in disbelief, his heart full with love. "Oh, Rachel," he murmured. "What did I do to deserve you?"

He bent to kiss her, and she smiled through what remained of her tears even as his lips found hers. She wasn't going to cry anymore. William was gone and Jamie was here, and now at last she was going to be happy.

With a contented little sigh she pulled Jamie down lower, tangling her fingers in his hair as she stroked the back of his neck. His mouth moved lazily over hers, and she parted her lips to draw him in, longing for more.

Kissing Jamie had always made her feel deliciously wicked, but to kiss him like this, lying down, seemed doubly so.

And he was the one who finally broke away, his breathing already uneven.

"That's enough for now, lass," he said as he tapped an admonitory finger across her lips. "You're making it powerfully difficult for me to remember that you've been ill."

Her lips curved into a smile that was more than half pout. "You said you wished to be convinced to stay," she said. "I wanted to be sure you would."

He chuckled. "You're convincing enough, sweet. *More* than enough."

Her smile warmed as she searched his face, her hand shifting around from his neck to gently stroke his cheek.

"I know this little house can never be the same as what you lost with your family, any more than it's been able to replace Crescent Hill for me," she said softly. "But it's become home to me and Billy, and I pray it can be the same to you, too."

"Ah, Rachel, my love," he murmured. "My home now will always be where I'll find you."

She began to pull him back down again, but instead he reluctantly eased her arms from around his neck to free himself. "No more of your persuading now, sweetheart, I beg you! I meant it about keeping you well. Mary told me you were still perilously fragile, and that I must coddle you to avoid another decline."

Rachel frowned suspiciously. "That doesn't sound like Mary at all. I'll wager she said nothing of the sort to you, for she told *me* I could do whatever I pleased as long as I didn't become overweary.''

''I'd rather be cautious,'' he said as he reached for his hat. ''Besides, I like this notion of coddling you. Now, you stay put while I go tend to the horses, and I'll be back as soon as I can to find us some sort of supper from what Mary sent along.''

Stubbornly she folded her arms over her chest. ''You'll find I can be most demanding where coddling is concerned. *Most* demanding. You may regret this entire arrangement before you're done.''

''Oh, I doubt that.'' He grinned and touched his fingers to his lips as a final salute. ''Though I might need a whit more of that persuading when I return.''

He was grinning as he led the two horses to the barn, and the grin remained firmly in place as he curried and watered and fed them. He was smiling still as he tended to Juno, and he didn't stop as he scattered feed for the poultry.

The truth was that he was happier than he'd been in years, maybe even in his whole life. He couldn't remember feeling this heady mixture of joy and contentment before, or the incredible *rightness* of being with Rachel.

He still couldn't believe all that he had confessed to her this morning, things that he had sworn to himself never to tell. Speaking to her hadn't done away with the pain of his loss or the depth of his shame and sorrow. Nothing would ever completely end that, and he wasn't fool enough to think that even Rachel could do that for him.

But her sympathy and her understanding had some-how begun to put an end to it, a closure, and for the first time since he'd ridden away from his father's house he felt able to look ahead instead of backward. For the first time his life seemed truly to belong to him, and he found the prospect a fine one indeed, especially since Rachel would be there to share it with him.

And then, of course, there was the desire, burning white-hot through his body from nothing more than a single, slanted look from her green eyes. When he kissed her, his whole being ached from wanting her, and when he thought of finally making love to her—and in his mind there was now little doubt that he would—that thought alone was enough to make him groan out loud.

The gist of it was that he loved her and she loved him, and before he realized it he was grinning like a besotted madman all over again. He slung his rifle over his shoulder and pulled the barn door shut. If he'd known how to whistle, he would have done it; instead he be-gan singing, rather tunelessly, one of Rachel's more cheerful bedtime songs for Billy, scattering scolding chickens in his path as he walked through the yard to-ward the house. Another dusting of snow had fallen since he'd come here yesterday, and he knew he should make time after supper to clear it away before it turned to ice. Besides, a bit of snow shoveling might make it easier to keep his promise to Mary Bowman to let Ra-chel rest, and then—

Tracks.

Jamie stopped in an instant, reflexively bringing his rifle around from his back to his shoulder as his gaze swept the hillside. Nothing moved, nothing struck his eye as different, nothing had changed around the cabin with Rachel inside.

Cautiously he knelt, lightly moving his hands over the footprints in the new snow as he studied them. Three men, one with a horse. The one with the horse was an Englishman, or at least wore an Englishman's boots. The other two were Indians, probably Senecas, from the seams along the soles of their moccasins. Whoever they were, they'd made no effort to disguise their prints, that was certain. Had they really been that confident of their welcome, or were they that bold in their surprise?

The more Jamie looked, the more prints he saw, and he cursed himself for being so caught up with Rachel that he'd let himself be this careless. The snow had fallen yesterday morning; from the softness of the prints Jamie guessed the men had come soon afterward, going first to the house, then to the barn and back to the house again before they'd finally left. Unlike the man sent by Alec Lindsey to set fire to the barn, these men had touched nothing that Jamie could see, harmed nothing. They might be no more than travelers or trappers hoping for a warm meal and shelter from the cold for the night.

But Jamie didn't believe it, not for a moment. And if they'd come once, they could well come again, and next time they might not be quite as polite.

His happy grin only a memory now, Jamie returned to the house. He didn't want to worry Rachel, but he wanted her forewarned, and he wanted her to stay in the cabin unless she was with him. He'd come so close to losing her forever to the quinsy; he couldn't bear to risk her life again.

"Rachel!" he called as he pushed open the door. Next time he'd tell her to bar it after him, and take no chances. "Rachel, listen to me, we've—"

His words stopped. There simply weren't any left in his brain to send to his mouth.

"Well, there you are, Jamie," said Rachel cheerfully. "I was beginning to think that you were feeding each one of the hens one millet grain at a time, you've been away so long. It was wondrously flattering to consider that you found them or Juno and Proudfoot more entertaining company than me."

"Rachel," he finally managed to choke out. "What are you doing?"

She smiled, in perfect innocence. "I'm doing exactly what you told me to do. I'm waiting here in bed with the coverlet drawn up, waiting for you to come back."

Maybe she'd been right in the first place, thought Jamie, still struggling to put his words together into sentences. Maybe this coddling business *was* beyond him.

She was waiting in the bed, exactly as he'd told her to be. But clearly she'd spent a good deal of time out of it while he'd been in the barn. She was sitting cross-legged like an Indian, with the coverlet pulled up only over her knees, so he could see exactly what she was—and wasn't—wearing.

Gone were the heavy cloak and thick wool bodice and skirt chosen for warmth alone. Gone, too, were the scarf that Mary had insisted she wrap around and around her throat, and the little white cap that had held the heavy coil of her hair in place beneath her hood.

Now she was wearing a dressing gown of coral-colored silk with a bodice cut so low in front that nearly the entire swell of her breasts was enticingly visible, edged by darker coral lace that emphasized the creaminess of her skin. Narrow black ribbons wove in and out of the lace, little bows that somehow held the bodice together. The snug-fitting sleeves barely hugged the tops of her shoulders, stopping at the elbows, where an exuberant flourish of ruffles framed her graceful arms and hands, one wrist now delicately bent as she sipped chocolate from one of her porcelain cups.

All her hair, more black silk, was piled loosely on top of her head, held in place with a single coral ribbon that begged to be tugged free. Loose tendrils curled around her cheeks in enchanting disarray.

He had never seen her like this before. Damnation, he'd never seen any woman like this before, wrapped up in ribbons and lace like a special present.

She smiled again, her cheeks nearly as pink as the silk.

"Do you like it?" she said, her voice breathy with a hint of uncertainty. "It's from Paris, you know. One of my sisters is married to a Frenchman, and she sent this to me all the way from Martinique as part of my wedding clothes. I wanted to surprise you."

"You've done that, lass, no mistake." His heart was hammering in his chest so hard he was certain she could hear it clear across the room. He'd never had much to do with any Frenchmen, but they certainly seemed to have an excellent sense of how a woman should dress. But for him alone: no other man alive was going to see his Rachel like this.

She let her fingers drift across the line of her collarbone until they stilled on her necklace, the little heart he'd carved for her for Christmas, resting there in the hollow of her throat. She sighed, and he watched her breasts rise and fall above the fragile silk barrier.

"I've surprised you, but you don't approve," she said, twisting her mouth with disappointment. "What is it you say? You can't 'countenance' it. You've got that dreadful stern Quaker face on."

"Nay, Rachel, you're wrong. I approve." He swallowed hard. That stern Quaker face of his was about all he had left of his self-control, and it was barely enough to keep him from leaping onto the bed with her this instant. "I don't believe I could approve much more."

She smiled, her whole face lighting from within. "I wanted to be pretty for you, Jamie," she said wistfully, her eyes a little too bright. "Just once I wanted you to see me without soapsuds on my hands and flour in my hair. I wanted...I wanted... oh, no, what is *wrong* with me?"

She stared down at the cup in her hands, her cheeks bright red as she worked to compose herself. When she lifted her face again, her eyes were clear and her smile even.

"Would you care to join me for a cup of chocolate, Mr. Ryder?" she asked, her air drawing-room polite. She waved her hand at the plate on the chair she'd pulled up beside the bed to serve as a tea table. "I've biscuits and conserve, too. I recall, Mr. Ryder, that the cherry was your favorite."

Jamie hesitated, torn between Rachel and her cherry conserve and the prints of the three men in the snow

outside. He could spend the rest of the afternoon following those tracks, or cleaning her two muskets for her
and testing her shooting skills, maybe even teaching her
to use his rifle, on the chance the men might return today.

Rachel, or the rifle. No sane man would ever want to
face a choice like that.

As he watched and tried to make up his mind, she
stretched her legs out before her, curling them beneath
the coverlet as she bent over to set her cup on the chair.
Unable to look away, he held his breath as her breasts
slipped another fraction farther from the gown's neckline. She took her spoon and dipped it into the conserve, fishing out a single glistening cherry. She tipped
the spoon to her lips, letting the cherry slide inside, and
glanced sideways at Jamie.

"Cherr-wy," she said with a charming little gulp, her
mouth full and the sweet syrup staining her lips. "Your
favorite."

He dropped the latch on the door and swung the bar
over it with a resounding thump.

Her smile widened, and she licked the spoon.

It hadn't been any choice at all.

"You're right, Rachel," he said as he dropped the
rifle and powder horn into the corner by the door and
tore off his coat and then his belt with his knife.
"Cherry is my favorite, though I can't say I've ever
eaten it on a lady's bed."

"I can't say I've ever offered the privilege to any
other gentleman, either." She laughed, low and husky,
as she watched him crouch down to unlace his moccasins. He might approve of her silk and lace, but being

near him had given her a well-founded appreciation for how the narrow buckskin trousers clung to his thighs and buttocks, outlining every muscle and sinew.

"I should hope you haven't," said Jamie, glancing up to grin at her in a way that made her feel very wicked indeed. "I plan to keep you too occupied myself to squander invitations on all these other gentlemen."

Instead of coming to the side of the bed, he went to the end of it. He stood there framed by the curtains on either side as he looked imperiously down upon her, his eyes shadowed and that same lazy grin on his face. He rested his hands lightly on his hips, drawing her own gaze downward. Without the belt for his knife and tomahawk around his waist, the breeches seemed to be riding lower on his hipbones, and hastily she raised her gaze again, her cheeks pink, when she realized what she'd be admiring next. Inwardly she winced, remembering how first William and then Alec had taunted her about her unladylike desires.

"Go ahead and look, Rachel," he said, amused and unaware of her doubts. "Lord only knows I've been ogling you since I walked through that door."

That was precisely what she'd intended Jamie to do, but hearing it spelled out quite so baldly took her aback, and she sank, shamefaced, a little farther into the pillows, the spoon still in her hand.

"You must think I'm the boldest baggage you've ever met," she said, her cheeks hot but her green eyes not quite as contrite as they should have been. Unlike William, Jamie didn't seem to mind her interest at all, and her anticipation grew. "And here all I meant to do was persuade you to stay."

"That's all?" He drew his shirt up over his head and tossed it on the floor behind him, and nothing now could stop Rachel from unabashedly admiring him. Two months of her cooking combined with the heavy work of shoveling snow and splitting firewood had filled out his chest and shoulders even further, the dark chestnut hair glinting in the firelight. "What about my cherry conserve?"

She touched the spoon to her lips again, licking the last bit of sweetness from the polished pewter as her eyes glittered impishly. "You'll just have to come claim it, Jamie Ryder."

"Aye." He sighed dramatically. "I suppose I will."

He climbed onto the foot of the bed, the mattress shaking and shifting beneath his weight, and crawled on all fours toward her like some great animal until he was kneeling over her. He reached for the far edge of the coverlet and slowly drew it back from her body to gaze at her. Almost hypnotized by the raw hunger she saw in his eyes, she didn't move. She wasn't sure she could, even if she'd wanted to.

Hidden away as Rachel usually was beneath layers of petticoats and skirts, Jamie had only guessed at what she'd be like without them, and for once his imagination hadn't approached the reality. The coral silk draped over her hips and legs as if it had been poured over her, the dull sheen of the fabric emphasizing the rich curves of her body.

He reached out and tugged the ribbon from her hair the way he'd been itching to do since he'd first seen it, and the thick black waves tumbled freely over her pale shoulders. He'd never be able to look at her in those prim little white caps again, not after seeing her hair so gloriously free.

"Is it me, Rachel," he said slowly, "or does it seem that this cabin's warmed considerably since I left you before?"

She laughed softly, shaking her hair back from her face. "Of course it's you, Jamie," she said, the sensuous feel of the silk on her bare skin combined with the look in his eyes making her feel daringly wanton. "You know how to lay a most excellent fire."

"Do I, now?" His voice was lower, rougher, his broad chest rising and falling more swiftly now as the pace of his breathing increased. "Then you won't grow too chill if I help you from this. I've a mind to see what lies beneath."

Her gaze never left his face as she felt his fingers hook into the top bow of her dressing gown and pull it open. She saw how his blue eyes had clouded with concentration and need, how he swallowed hard as he undid the next bow and then the next.

Without looking she felt his fingers growing clumsier and more impatient with each bow, just as she felt her own heart racing as at last he pushed the dressing gown to either side to reveal the gown beneath. The gown, and her in it, for with its narrow straps and gossamer-light silk, the gown was more shameless than if she'd been naked. She heard how Jamie sucked in his breath and swore to himself.

"Damnation, Rachel," he said, his voice oddly strangled. "Do you have any idea what you're doing to me?"

From the tight set of his features, she had a very good idea indeed, so good that her mouth went dry and the pleasure ache low in her belly grew more insistent and she couldn't think of a single sensible way to reply.

"The cherries," she said foolishly, realizing that she still held the spoon in her fingers. "What about your cherries, Jamie?"

"Aye, lass, I want them still," he said as he plucked the spoon from her fingers and tossed it across the floor. "But I'd rather taste them on you."

He tangled his fingers in her hair and drew her mouth to his, and startled her with the searing intensity of his kiss. It wasn't the taste of cherries he wanted, it was her, and she eagerly opened herself to him, answering his fierce, devouring need with a longing that rivaled his.

She had thought after being married to William that she knew what to expect from a man, and from herself. She wasn't a green girl.

But with that first kiss, Jamie showed her exactly how wrong she was.

With his lips and mouth and tongue he was scorching her, marking her as his in a way she would never forget, and she reveled in his possession, seeking to brand him with the same searing passion. She had no words for what he was doing to her, all of it reduced to a single, breathless sigh of purest pleasure that vibrated deep between them.

She reached for his shoulders for support, clinging to the smooth, firm muscles as he pressed her back against the pillows. She felt his hands impatiently pushing aside the dressing gown, and one by one she lifted her arms only long enough to shrug them free of the sleeves, and with a *shush* of ruffled silk she heard it slide from the bed to the floor.

The second gown was no barrier at all. His hand sought and covered her breast, her nipple rising hard through the thin silk, and she gasped against his shoulder as his mouth caressed her next, teasing her aching flesh through the thin, wet silk. She arched against him, and felt one slender strap give way as he pulled the neckline lower, baring her breasts to his mouth. With a little moan she threaded her fingers through his hair, cradling his head against her breast, unwilling to lose the pleasure of it.

"You are so sweet, Rachel," he rasped as he pressed his face against her breast, the roughness of his cheek teasing her sensitive peak further. "So warm and sweet and beautiful, and you are mine."

She felt his hand on her calf, her knee, her thigh, as he shoved the thin silk upward and out of his way. She trembled when his hand reached her hip, following the swelling curve around to her belly, and she moved beneath him, instinctively guiding his hand lower, to the secret place that ached the most for his touch. When his fingers found her, she cried out, twisting into the blistering torment. Her skin burned with a fever hotter than when she'd been ill, and she reveled in it, wanting more, wanting him, desperate to reach that last tantalizing peak that she'd never found with William.

He pulled her higher against the pillows, her gown now no more than a tangled band of bright silk around her waist, and separated her thighs with his knees. He tore at the buttons of his trousers and she reached to help, her fingers shaking as they pulled away the buckskin, velvety and warm from his own fevered flesh.

She was more than ready, her whole body crying out for him, yet still she gasped when he entered her, shuddering with the intense sensation of him so deep within her. Instinctively she curled her legs over his hips, rocking to meet the rhythm of his thrusts.

"Oh, Rachel," he groaned, his fingers digging deep into the soft flesh of her hips as he pulled her closer. "Rachel, love, you are so—oh, Rachel!"

But her own world was beyond words, the wild, delirious joy building so fast that she could do nothing but feel it and ride it hard and fast until the pleasure burst within her, so sharp and sweet that she didn't realize that her wild, keening cry of release was his name.

Afterward they lay together, their limbs still intimately tangled, with the coverlet haphazardly drawn over them, and drowsily watched the orange ball of the winter sun sink behind the sun-covered hillside beyond their window.

Rachel smiled to herself and listened to the steady rhythm of Jamie's heart beneath her ear. How odd to think that the rest of the world would be going about its business as usual, tending to whatever needed tending on this late afternoon while she and Jamie—ah, she and Jamie had found paradise.

"Shall I tell you again, Jamie, how much I love you?" she murmured, indolently tracing her fingers through the whorls of hair on his chest. "I do, you know, and I don't think I'll ever tire of saying it."

"I trust you won't tire of me, either," he said as he smoothed her hair. "Otherwise you might begin to find me something of a nuisance."

"Oh, stop it!" she scolded, thumping his chest with her fist. She propped herself up on her hands to look at him. "I love you far too much to ever regard you as a nuisance, even if you deserve it for speaking such foolishness."

"If you say so." He smiled, and pulled her higher onto his chest so he could kiss her again. "Ah, Rachel, what did I ever do to earn you as my reward?"

She could only smile and shake her head, her heart too close to overflowing to be able to answer.

Gently he held her face toward his, stroking her cheeks with his thumbs as his smile faded. "You are my love and my life, Rachel," he said softly. "Would you honor me by becoming my wife, as well?"

She didn't hesitate, not even a moment, her eyes brimming with tears of joy. "Yes, Jamie," she whispered. "Yes, yes, yes."

A week later, with Mary and Ethan and Billy—and Blackie and Whitie, too—to act as witnesses, Rachel and Jamie stood before the fireplace with their hands clasped, prepared to say their vows.

Behind them still hung the white cutwork chains that Rachel had made for Christmas, now used as the only decorations for their wedding. Rachel's wedding gown, too, had seen service before, a pale pink lutestring sprigged with blue flowers that she hadn't quite been able to steam free of wrinkles after a year and a half in a trunk. There was no Mama or Father to send her off with tearful joy, no flowers, rum punch or fiddlers or bowls of oranges as there had been at her first wedding. There wasn't even a minister. But this time there was Jamie, and this time, she knew her groom loved her beyond everything else, just as, this time, she loved the man who would be her husband for the rest of her life.

"Are you certain this is quite proper, Jamie?" asked Ethan uncertainly, he and Mary both still stunned to find themselves in the middle of a wedding. "I'm happy enough that you two wish to wed, but shouldn't you wait until you can find a minister or preacher who can say the right words over you?"

"Among Friends, this is more than enough," said Jamie firmly. "Marriage is too serious a matter to be solemnized by man alone, nor is there any scripture that would make me love Rachel any more or better."

"It's what I want, too, Ethan," said Rachel shyly, her arm twined around Jamie's. "If I cannot trust Jamie's word and he mine, then we've no business marrying at all."

"An' I want Jamie for my father!" declared Billy, his initial surprise at Rachel's announcement swiftly forgotten.

Ethan sighed, resigned. "Very well, then. I don't see how I can argue. But come spring, when the roads are clear, I'll expect you two to go to the magistrate and make certain all the proper papers are signed."

"Oh, Ethan," began Rachel, but Jamie shushed her.

"No fussing, love, not today," he said gently, "and not now. Are you ready, Rachel?"

Solemnly he stood before her, her right hand in his and his eyes full of love and tenderness. "In the presence of the Lord and of this assembly," he said, "I take thee, Rachel Anne Sparhawk Lindsey, to be my wife, promising with divine assistance to be unto thee a loving and faithful husband until death shall separate us."

"Oh, Jamie," whispered Rachel, her hands fluttering up to her mouth as belatedly she realized it was her turn now. She loved him so much, oh, how she loved him!

"In the presence of the Lord and of this assembly," she said softly, "I take thee, James Owen Ryder, to be my husband, promising with divine assistance to be unto thee a loving and faithful wife until death shall separate us."

For a long moment she stared up into his eyes, unable to believe how happy she could be and yet feel so perilously close to tears.

"Well, amen to that," said Mary soundly. "Aren't you at least entitled to kiss the bride, Jamie?"

"Aye," said Jamie as he smiled slowly, with the special wickedness that made Rachel's pulse race with anticipation. "That, I believe, and a good deal more."

And he swept her back into his arms, their kiss sealing another promise of their love that words alone could never express.

"I've never seen Rachel look happier, or more beautiful," said Mary with satisfaction as she and Ethan began the long ride back to their home. "Jamie is the best man she could ever have for a husband."

"That he is," agreed Ethan gruffly. "You couldn't have chosen a better man for the lass."

"Oh, quit your grumbling, husband," said Mary. "They were already settled upon each other before I had anything to do with it. Have you ever seen two people more in love?"

"No, I haven't," said Ethan with a sigh, "and maybe that's why there's two little doubts niggling at my conscience."

Mary scowled. "Doubts? Pray, what doubts could you possibly have?"

"Things that Jamie told me when we went to fetch the horses. First off, he told me that there's been three men prowling around their land when they were away. Nothing touched, mind, but a worry in these times nonetheless. From the tracks he said it looked like an Englishman with a horse and a pair of Senecas."

Mary's scowl deepened into a frown of concern. "Didn't you hear that Alec Lindsey had taken up with two Indians? What did Rachel have to say about it?"

Ethan ducked beneath a low branch. "That's my doubt, wife. Jamie decided not to tell her."

"But it's her land!"

"Not any longer, Mary." He smiled wryly. "Now that Jamie's her husband, it all belongs to him, just as by rights it's up to him to decide what's best for her. Not that I've had much success with minding you over the years, have I?"

Impatiently she tossed her braids back over her shoulder. "You've had nothing to complain about, Ethan, as well you know."

"Not until now, anyway." His brows drew sternly together. "Jamie told me another peculiar thing, Mary. He told me I'd sent some special messengers clear to

Canada to find out for certain that William Lindsey was dead. Jamie thanked me, too, since he was sure Rachel wouldn't have given up on William until she had such proof. Now tell me, wife. Do you have any notion of how Jamie could have come to hear such a tale?''

Mary didn't deny it. "You've said yourself that William must be dead, that there were no prisoners," she said indignantly. "And Jamie's right. Rachel would have gone on clinging to the memory of that worthless husband forever unless she had good reason to believe he was gone."

"But to bend the truth like that—I don't like it, indeed I don't." He shook his head unhappily. "You'd best pray William's truly dead, Mary. And pray for the rest of us if he's not."

Chapter Fourteen

"So you've lost your sister-in-law, have you, Lindsey?" called Nate Wye as he came into the front room at Volk's. His snow-covered coat steaming in the relative warmth of the room, Nate bent before the fire to warm his hands. He looked over his shoulder at Alec Lindsey, eager to see what the other man's reaction to the news would be.

But Alec remained sprawled in his chair, his legs stretched before him, a glass in one hand and a pipe in the other, much the same as he had for the past six weeks. It would take considerably more to rouse him than some tattle from a low creature like Nate Wye. Hell, he hadn't heard anything truly valuable here in ages, yet still he stayed, unable to rouse himself to go elsewhere, even if there was an elsewhere.

Soon after Christmas, after the first heavy storm had trapped him at his own house for a week and he'd been forced to keep no other company than his own, he had as much as moved in under Volk's roof, gambling and smoking and drinking Volk's liquor and amusing himself with the Indian women. Whenever Volk rumbled ominously about bills and a tab grown far too long, Alec would feed him a few more coins and languidly promise once again to settle in the spring.

"So you say I've lost my dear shrewish bitch-in-law," he drawled. "I take it, then, that no one's gone to the trouble of seeking her in the snow where she fell?"

None of the others laughed, and Alec didn't care. His wit was always lost on these clodpates, especially where Rachel was concerned. Ever since she'd been taken up by that meddlesome blanket-trader Bowman and his wife, there seemed to be more and more who sided with her against him and William. More fools they, thought Alec sourly. He was growing powerfully tired of his brother's wife, and soon, once the snow was gone, he meant to be done with her for good.

He took another long swallow of the whiskey, considering. Perhaps he'd sell her as a slave to the Iroquois. That would take the stiff-backed pride out of her soon enough, and he'd get a good price for her and the boy together—more than they'd ever been worth to William.

"I said, Lindsey, she's not lost to the world, only to you," repeated Wye, more loudly this time, as if Alec had lost his hearing or his wits. "She's done with you Lindseys once and for all, and I say good luck to her."

Alec frowned through the haze of tobacco smoke. He couldn't imagine that Rachel would try to flee at this time of the year, but if she had, he'd send Manapog and Chepatachet after her. She wasn't going to escape that easily. "You're making no sense, Wye, not that you ever have."

Wye's teeth showed yellow through his beard, gleefully aware that he had the ear of every man in the room. "What I'm sayin', Lindsey, is that your brother's widow's gone and found herself a new husband. Right after Twelfth Night, it was. I heard it from Ethan Bowman hisself, and he was one of the witnesses at the wedding."

"Don't be ridiculous," snapped Alec angrily. "How can she remarry when she's already married to my brother?"

There was a shuffling of chairs from the corner as another man stood up to be better heard. "Your brother's not coming back, Lindsey," he said heavily. "My sister lost her boy Daniel at Oriskany, too, and you know as well as any of us the beating Captain Walker took at the hands of those savages, God rest the captain's brave soul."

A murmur of agreement rolled through the room. In this small community nearly every man there had lost a brother or son, cousin or friend, in the disastrous ambush at Oriskany, and Alec's insistence on his brother's survival when so many others had perished was viewed as one more example of the Lindseys' arrogance.

Wye nodded, his beard bobbing up and down. "True enough, Henry, true enough. Just as it be true enough that that pretty little Rachel's remarried."

Alec glared at Wye. He didn't like this and he didn't believe it. At least, he didn't want to believe it. "Who the devil would have the foul-tempered bitch, anyway?"

Wye turned around, flipping his coattails up before the fire's warmth before he told the best part of his story. "That be the real beauty of it, Alec. She wed that Tory deserter you were so eager to find afore Christmas, and now it looks like the pair of them are both well beyond your reach."

Though Alec's fingers tightened on his glass, he purposely kept his face impassive. These buffoons wished to see him squirm and, damn their eyes, he wasn't about to give them their foolish pleasure by doing it.

Yet he remembered all too well how he'd taunted Rachel about taking the deserter as her lover, and now, it seemed, she'd made him look the fool by publicly setting up housekeeping with the man. But now, with the heavy snows, most of the British and their Mohawk allies had retreated north to their bases, leaving the deserter safely beyond their reach. By the spring, if and when the British returned, the reward offered for his capture would have been forgotten; that was what Wye and the others believed, and were gloating over now at his expense.

But what if this deserter walked straight into their hands? What if he was led there by the woman who had sheltered him all these months? And what if Alec could come back to them with the final, unimpeachable proof that his brother was still alive, all at the same time?

"She's married, true enough," said Wye one more time with smug relish. "So, do you be ready to drink a toast to the happy couple, Lindsey?"

Alec downed the last of his whiskey and smiled, the plans already forming in his head. "I'll do better than that, Wye," he said. "I do believe I'll go call on the happy bride to wish her well myself."

Rachel stirred the wooden spoon one more time through the custard in the pot and sighed impatiently. The mixture was steaming, dangerously close to simmering, yet still it wouldn't coat the back of her spoon, let alone thicken enough to make a palatable dessert. She'd really hoped that the four eggs from this morning would be enough, a hope, she saw now, based more on her wishes than on culinary reality. Perhaps by now one of the hens had laid another, though this late in the winter, almost March, more eggs, too, could be another empty hope.

With both hands she carefully shifted the little iron pot from the coals and reached for her cloak.

"I'm going to the barn to hunt for one more egg," she said as she swung the cloak over her shoulders. "I'll be gone only a moment or two."

Jamie looked up from the tower of blocks he was building with Billy. "Must you go now, sweetheart? It's nearly milking time."

"The custard can't wait," she said, pulling on her mittens. "I told you, I won't be long."

Immediately Jamie was on his feet. "Then we're coming with you."

"No, Papa, not now!" wailed Billy, distraught at seeing his block tower abandoned before they'd used every last one of the blocks. "Don't go now!"

"Listen to Billy, Jamie. Stay here and finish that tower or you'll never hear the end of it until bedtime. Maybe even afterward." She stood beside him, her hands on his shoulders, and gently pushed him back down onto the floor beside Billy. Then she bent to kiss him quickly, though her lips lingered longer than she'd intended, the way it happened so often with Jamie. "I'll be fine, I swear it."

He reached up and touched her face, his expression serious. "Take one of the muskets. And be careful, love."

She grinned, but his concern touched her nonetheless. Though the winter snows had isolated them for weeks, he still watched over her and Billy with a fierce protectiveness that made her feel both safe and cherished. She understood that on some level his protectiveness had grown from the tragedies in his past, that first losing his own family and then being a witness to the brutal massacre of others had made him determined to protect his new wife and son. She understood, and loved him all the more for it.

"I will, Jamie." She kissed him again and then the top of Billy's head, took one of the muskets from the wall and hurried out the door.

With the musket resting on her shoulder she pulled her cloak more tightly around her against the cold. The days were longer now, the red sun just beginning to set through the trees on the hill. Though the snow still lay thick on the ground, the biting sting of winter had softened, and the air seemed somehow more gentle with the promise of spring to come.

Rachel smiled happily to herself, thinking of spring and of the fresh return of life to the trees and forest around her. Tentatively she touched a hand to her own belly. Though it was still early to be sure, she sensed the beginning of a new life within her, too, and she wondered if Jamie had noticed the ways her body was already changing. Perhaps tonight she would tell him, after Billy was asleep, and her smile widened as she imagined his ecstatic response. Though, if Jamie was protective now, what would he be like when she was with child?

She slipped inside the barn and rested the musket against the wall of Juno's stall before she crouched down and reached into the hen's roosts, shoving the indignant hens aside as she felt in the straw beneath them for that single elusive egg she needed for her custard.

"My, my, so this is what my brother couldn't give you?" asked Alec from the doorway. "The chance to root among filthy chickens for your supper?"

In an instant she was on her feet, lunging for the musket that Alec now held tantalizingly out of reach.

"You don't think I'd make that same mistake again, do you, Rachel?" he asked, smiling at her angry frustration. He had grown heavier, his once handsome face fleshier and more mottled from drinking. "You'll recall the last time I visited you, your welcome was less than hospitable."

"And it will be again, if I have anything to say about it!" cried Rachel furiously. "Get out, Alec. I have nothing more to say to you, and I never want to see you here on my land again!"

He swung her musket up onto his shoulder, reminding her again with infuriating ease of how careless she'd been. "Not quite yet, Rachel. Not until I've had the chance to congratulate you on your sham of a marriage to a man who's a deserter, murderer and coward, all in one neat package.''

"Jamie is my *husband*, Alec,'' she said hotly, ''and a better man than you can ever dream of being. You can't do anything to hurt us now. Butler's Rangers are long gone back to Canada, with the Americans chasing after them, and now you'll never have the chance to collect your blessed reward. And no magistrate would dream of taking Billy from two loving, *married* parents to put him with a reprobate uncle whose entire life is spent within a tavern!''

"Perhaps not, if it were true,'' he agreed. "But what if this loving mother you imagine married her second husband while the first one still lived?''

"That's ridiculous, Alec,'' she snapped. "William is dead. Ethan Bowman has the proof.''

Abruptly hatred mottled Alec's face. "The hell with Bowman's proof. I have proof of my own that William is still alive.''

"That's another lie, Alec, and you know it,'' said Rachel, too angry to even consider that what he said might be true. "And I'm not going to stand here listening to your rubbish any longer.''

She began to push past him, and he roughly shoved her back. "I'll decide when it's time for you to go, Rachel.''

"Jamie will kill you if he finds you here,'' she said wildly, already expecting to see him through the doorway, striding across the snow to find out why she'd been detained. "He'll kill you, Alec, I swear!''

"Only if Manapog doesn't kill him first,'' said Alec, sneering at the sudden fear that filled her eyes. "If your dear *husband* so much as opens the door, Manapog will shoot him dead. He's not a patient man, even among the Senecas.''

"Dear God, no, not Jamie!" Desperately she lunged forward again, but this time Alec caught her shoulder hard with the butt of her own musket, throwing her back into the straw with a yelp of pain. He yanked the door shut and came to stand over her, his legs wide-spread and the musket held ready to strike her again if she tried to flee.

"Listen to me, Rachel, because I'll only say it once," he said roughly. He was breathing hard, not from exertion so much as a kind of crude pleasure at seeing her humiliated like this. "There is a tavern—David Dancer's the keep—to the north of here that remains friendly to the king and his soldiers. If you begin at a decent hour, you can make the journey in less than a day by horse. I shall give you a small packet for a gentleman there, Lieutenant Rearden, and he will give you a packet for me in return. And if you do as I say, you shall also see William.''

She shook her head wildly, denying it all. "I'm not going to do it, Alec! William is dead. He died at Oriskany with the others. If he was alive, why would he have stayed away so long?''

Alec smiled bitterly. "Have you forgotten, Rachel, how much reason you gave him to leave, and how little you offered for him to return?''

Her conscience stabbed at her, remembering all that was her fault in their marriage and forgetting what was William's. "He can't be alive," she said miserably. "He *can't.*''

"Believe what you wish, Rachel," said Alec. "But if you don't believe me, then perhaps your new husband will. What would a man as honorable as you claim Ryder is make of a woman who willfully pretended her first husband was dead so she could entice another to her bed?"

Rachel gasped, her head spinning. William alive: she would be forced to live with him again as his wife, to watch him callously neglect Billy, to know that the child she carried now would be branded a bastard and loathed as such by William.

And as for Jamie—dear Lord, it would destroy Jamie, and destroy, too, the love that had made her life an endless joy.

"It's your choice, Rachel," continued Alec relentlessly. "Either you do this small errand for me and see for yourself if I'm lying about William, or I tell everything to Ryder. What will become of him, I wonder, if he presents himself in a tavern filled with British soldiers? Surely they would be tempted by the reward that the men in this valley are too squeamish to touch?"

She pressed her hand over her mouth, knowing what he said was horribly, dreadfully true. Jamie would be unable to resist going in search of William, even at the certain risk to his own life.

Again she had no power to refuse Alec, and despair and fear swept over her. Once again he had left her no choice but to do as he wished.

Alec tossed a small canvas packet onto the straw beside her. "You'll find the directions you'll need in there, plus a sealed letter that you'd be well advised not to read. And I wouldn't postpone your journey too long,

Rachel. There's no telling when William—if, that is, you believe he didn't die—might take it into his empty head to come home after all.''

Her fingers were on the packet when the barn door flew open. Alec reeled back, struggling to bring the musket to bear as he turned on his heel.

"Drop it, Lindsey," ordered Jamie from behind his rifle. "Drop it now."

"You wouldn't do it, not in front of Rachel," said Alec scornfully, stalling, the musket frozen halfway to his shoulder. "You won't shoot."

"Test me if it pleases you," said Jamie, as unmoving as a statue. "I know what a rifle can do at this range, and I'd be glad to show you, too."

But the musket still remained in Alec's hands. "Cowardly bastard," he snarled. "Why don't you—"

"I told you to drop the gun, Lindsey," said Jamie again, his voice as unyielding as his rifle. "And if your chattering is meant to keep me waiting until your Seneca friend comes to help, then you'll have a great deal more chattering to do. He's trussed up tight, behind the house where I left him."

"Alive?"

"For now, aye," said Jamie evenly. "Though I'd say his chances are better than yours at present."

"Worthless savage," muttered Alec as he let the gun drop to the barn floor, where Rachel swiftly retrieved it and hurried to Jamie's side.

"Are you all right, love?" he asked, lowering the rifle but not looking away from Alec. "He didn't hurt you, did he?"

"No, no, of course not," she said, even though she was trembling and light-headed from everything she'd seen and heard. Maybe Alec didn't believe that Jamie would have fired. She knew better; she'd seen Gelrichs's body outside this same barn. She slipped her arm around Jamie's waist, praying she wasn't going to faint. "Where's Billy? Is he all right?"

"He's well enough," said Jamie. "I left him feeding sweet biscuits to Blackie and Whitie."

The contrast between Jamie's deadly efficiency with his rifle and the image of Billy with his toy horses was almost unbearable to Rachel. She wanted her life and her family to stay as it was, blissfully happy and full of love, untouched by the violence of the outside world. She drew closer to Jamie, and felt Alec's packet rustle in her pocket, a grim reminder that she herself was no better than Jamie and his rifle, and likely much worse.

Lord, why did her happiness have to come at such an appallingly high price?

"You'll leave now, Lindsey, you and your friend," Jamie was saying, "and neither of you will ever come back to our home again. If you do, I'll shoot you dead. Can you understand that?"

Our home. Oh, she understood, thought Rachel miserably. She had offered Jamie her home as a haven for his battered soul, and she had given him not only her heart but also the unconditional love of the child who called him Papa.

And now, if William was alive, Jamie would be left with nothing.

Alec was watching her, smirking as if he could read her thoughts, and most likely he could. "I won't be back, Ryder, you can be sure of that," he said. "I've no reason in the world to return."

Rachel decided to go in three days.

On the second night, it seemed to her that Jamie made love to her with a special tenderness, almost as if he knew, and afterward she wept silently into her pillow to keep her tears, and their reason, a secret from him. He trusted her, and she would deceive him, and the cold certainty of it ate at her soul.

And she decided not to tell him about the baby, not until she returned.

On the third night she mixed a few drops of the laudanum that Mary had once given her into Jamie's chocolate to make him sleep more soundly. She lay awake beside him until it was close enough to dawn that she could dress and leave. Through it all he did not stir, not even when she kissed his forehead farewell.

The note she left, propped between the candlesticks on the chimneypiece, was simple enough.

Dearest Jamie, There is someplace I must go this Day. God willing I shall be back for supper so please do not worry, I shall be fine. Kiss Billy for me. I love you Forever,

Your devoted Wife & Love, R.

She rode Proudfoot with the musket across her saddle, and she carried a sack with bread and cheese and a wooden canteen for water. In her pocket was Alec's letter and his directions, as well as a small mariner's compass she'd had since Newport, and around her neck she wore the little carved heart that Jamie had given her for Christmas.

Though Alec had said she could make the journey in a single day, because of the snow on the ground she didn't reach David Dancer's tavern until well past noon. She wasn't surprised that Alec had neglected to tell her that the reason Mr. Dancer favored British officers was that his tavern was just outside a small fortified garrison, and the colors on the flagpole before it were those of King George. The messages he'd made her carry last winter had gone to other places like this, and she tried not to think how once again she was behind the lines of the enemy, a spy and a traitor. At least this time Billy wasn't with her.

She was all too aware of the men in red uniforms clustered before the tavern, smoking and talking among themselves, just as they in turn were all too aware of her. She was a young woman, she was white, she carried a musket and she was alone, and any of those singly would have been reason enough for them to look. As she slid down from Proudfoot's back, a young corporal came forward to greet her.

"Good day to you, ma'am," he said as he touched the front of his hat. "Corporal Denis Moore, ma'am, your servant."

"Good day to you, Corporal." She forced herself to smile as brightly as she could. "Perhaps you could be so good as to take me to Lieutenant Rearden? I was told he would be here at this tavern."

The young corporal's face fell. "Aye, ma'am, I can take you to him. You'll have to leave the gun with the keep, though. We all do. No firearms permitted." He beckoned to a boy to take Proudfoot. "Come with me."

She followed him through the crowd of officers—parting for her, she thought, like another Red Sea—into the tavern and to a small room in the back. Four men, all in officer's uniforms with gold braid to brighten the red wool, sat at a card table. All four looked up with interest and stood as Moore announced her, but only one came forward.

"I am Lieutenant Rearden, ma'am," he said, his manner chilly and his bow only barely perceptible. "And you are exactly whom?"

Rachel raised her chin. Bright smiles weren't going to work with this man. "I have business with you, sir," she said with as much well-bred authority as she could muster. "A message from a friend we have in common that should best be relayed in private."

Rearden looked at her sharply, clearly trying to reconcile her speech and manner with her plain woolen clothing. He glanced back at the other three men.

"If you gentlemen would be so good as to excuse me and this lady," he began, and that alone was enough for the others to leave the room.

"You say we have a mutual acquaintance, ma'am?" he asked skeptically. He didn't ask her name again, for which Rachel was grateful, but he didn't offer her a chair, either, for which she wasn't. After traveling since dawn, she was exhausted, but she wasn't going to beg this man for anything.

"We do, Lieutenant." She reached into her pocket and handed him Alec's letter. "He asked me to give you this."

His face emotionless, Rearden cracked the seals with his thumb and read the letter.

"Interesting," he murmured, and glanced back at Rachel. "Did our...*friend* confide the contents to you, ma'am?"

Rachel shook her head. "He did not, nor did I wish to know them."

"Most wise." He walked to a leather satchel on a chair near the table and drew out a large bag of coins. He counted out a stack on the table, knotted them into a napkin and handed the bundle back to her. "You may tell your friend—our friend—that the king is most grateful for his services."

He turned away, obviously dismissing her.

"Another moment, sir, if you please," said Rachel, her throat dry. "I am also here seeking another man. His name is William Lindsey."

"The turncoat." Rearden's lip curled with disdain. "You shall find him in the front room, ma'am. You shall *always* find him in the front room. I wouldn't dare to ask, ma'am, what business any lady would have with the likes of him."

"No business, Lieutenant," said Rachel as she opened the door. "He's my husband."

Her heart pounding with dread, she made her way back to stand uncertainly in the door of the front room. Here there were no officers, only common soldiers mixed in with the usual farmers, traders and trappers. She looked around in vain for the keep, hoping to find someone who could fetch William from the crowd of men for her. It wouldn't be the first time she'd had to go into a taproom after William, but that didn't make it any more agreeable. With her lips pressed tightly together she slipped among the clusters of laughing, boisterous men, dodging their invitations and their hands as she searched their faces.

And finally, near the window, she found the one she sought. He looked much older than she remembered, his face lined in ways it hadn't been before, his once golden hair now dull. He sat with his right leg stretched out before him, and he wore nearly the same clothes he'd worn that day, the coat now threadbare and missing buttons, the shirt grimy and frayed. He needed to shave, and more, he needed a bath.

He was complaining over some injustice to the man who sat beside him, his voice thick and fretful from whatever was in the tankard in his hand. His companion noticed Rachel first. He jabbed William in the arm and jerked his head in her direction. Irritably William turned, and swore.

"By all that's holy," he sputtered. "It's Rachel."

"It is," she said with a bitterness she didn't try to hide. "And damn you, William, you're alive."

Chapter Fifteen

"**Y**ou don't know what it's been like for me, Rachel," said William petulantly. "I've been to hell and back, and that's the truth."

"Have you, indeed?" said Rachel. They stood beneath a leafless tree in the yard behind the tavern, far enough from the others that their conversation wouldn't be overheard. There had been no question of a private room, not when the second sentence from William's mouth had been to ask Rachel for money. "I suppose the devil doesn't supply water for washing and shaving?"

"Rachel, look at me!" He held his arms outstretched and hobbled dramatically for two steps before he fell against the tree's trunk again for support. "I'm a prisoner of war, pitiful and friendless! I was most grievously wounded while defending my country!"

"Lieutenant Rearden called you a turncoat, William, and forgive me if I'm inclined to believe him more than you." She sighed, folding her arms across her chest. "Were you still with Captain Walker and the others when they were ambushed at Oriskany?"

He rested his hand over his heart and groaned. "What a terrible day that was, Rachel, what a black day for the American cause!"

"Answer me, William," she said. "Were you there?"

"I was," he declared. "I was there, marching with the rest of the company. But directly before the savages fell upon us, my horse took a stone and tossed me right off the moment he went lame. That's when I wrenched my leg, you see, and it's never been the same since. So there I was, left behind, while the others went ahead to their glorious deaths."

Rachel's eyes narrowed. "There is nothing glorious about death, William," she said sharply, contrasting William's empty histrionics with the hideous memories that would haunt Jamie for the rest of his life. "But I thought the Tories took no prisoners."

"The savages didn't, that's a fact," admitted William reluctantly. "But to the rear, keeping themselves clear of the bloodletting, were a couple of the finest British gentlemen officers you could ever hope to meet. I threw myself on their mercy, and they treated me as handsome as you please, especially after I mentioned that Father had been friends with the old governor in Albany."

Rachel stared at him, incredulous. "William, I cannot believe that you—even *you!*—would do such a thing! Other men were *dying* in horrible agony for what they believed in, and you, *you*, surrendered to the British without even a sputter for the sake of old times in Albany!"

"And who's alive and who ain't, Rachel, did you ever think of that?" he asked belligerently. He took off his hat and bowed his head, tugging on his hair. "See that, darling? It's all still there, which is more than can be said of the others. Better a live coward than a dead hero, eh?"

"No," she said coldly. "No, I don't believe it is."

"Don't be cruel, Rachel, please," he said, wounded, as he settled his hat back on his head. "There was a time, and not so long ago, either, when you said I had the most beautiful hair you'd ever seen on a man. Remember that, dearest? You called me your Phoebus Apollo. Swore you'd call me that right up there before the minister, too. 'I take thee, Phoebus Apollo, for my lawful husband.' Remember? You said it so many times in jest that I feared you'd actually do it."

She looked at him, really looked at him, dirty and shabby and completely without scruples or honor or courage, and wondered how she'd ever been so blind. He'd never be mistaken for a god now, not even by a spoiled, lovesick girl wild to be married.

And by every law of God and man, he was still her husband.

"That was a long time ago, William," she said unhappily. "Many things have changed since then."

"But not you, Rachel." He smiled and reached for her hand. "You were the loveliest young lady in the colonies when I married you, and you still are."

She pulled her hand away, not wanting to be touched by him ever again. "Are you going to ask after Billy?"

For a moment that stretched far too long he looked blank. "Oh, you mean little William," he said, smiling with obvious relief when he finally remembered. "How is he?"

"Quite well," said Rachel, her fury and despair increasing by the moment. She thought of how much Jamie loved Billy, and how Billy adored Jamie as the only father he'd ever known, and yet this man who could forget he even had a son was the one the world would call his father.

William sidled closer, trying to slip his arm around her shoulder. "You could stay here with me tonight, Rachel," he said suggestively. "Old Dancer would let us have a room on the cheap if I explained the circumstances. Surely you've a bit of brass to spare for a bed for two lovebirds? Wouldn't that be a grand way to celebrate, darling?"

"There is nothing at all to celebrate," she said, practically spitting the words as she pulled away from his embrace. "All I want to know is if you're coming back, William."

He let his arms drop to his sides. "I can't, Rachel. I've given my parole, you know, my word as a gentleman. I have to stay until they release me."

"Oh, aye, as a gentleman," she repeated bitterly. "But if it weren't for that, would you return?"

He scratched the back of his neck. "Alec says I should, if I want to keep the land in my name, and if I want a crack at your father's estate, too. Alec says it could get sticky if the courts think I abandoned you."

"And that's the only reason, isn't it, William?" she said, tears smarting behind her eyes. Everything about it was unfair: grossly, hideously unfair, yet there was nothing she could do to change it.

He smiled, meaning to charm, and instead she saw how his back teeth were beginning to rot. "We could try again, Rachel," he said as his gaze wandered lower, from her face to her body. "Hell, but I'd forgotten what a delicious creature you are."

"I wish that you had," she said. "Goodbye, William."

She turned on her heel and ran to the stable for Proudfoot. She held back her tears as she paid the ostler, and gave the boy another penny to retrieve her musket from the keep. Her eyes were dry and her back straight as she rode from the yard. But as soon as she was out of sight of the tavern and the garrison, she let the tears come, hot tears full of shame and grief that burned her skin as they slipped down her cheeks.

From the window of the card room Lieutenant Rearden watched her leave. He smiled to himself as he beckoned to the two other men, dressed inconspicuously like woodsmen, to join him.

"There she is at last," he said. "The note said she'd lead you straight to Ryder. But take care to bring them both back alive. It's been far too long since we've had any traitors for a decent hanging."

The shadows of the tall trees around her were too long already, dark stripes against the white snow. She wasn't even halfway home, yet the sun would set and daylight be gone before another hour had passed. She was close to exhaustion, her fingers stiff on the reins and her back aching, but still she urged Proudfoot onward, trying hard not to think of the wolves and mountain cats and Indians, Lord help her, that would prowl these woods at night.

She heard a rustle in the snow behind her, and spun around with the musket in her hands. Swiftly she scanned the stark landscape behind her for any movement, her heart pounding. Only a squirrel, she thought uneasily, a squirrel or an owl knocking loose a branch. But Proudfoot had heard it, too, and he nickered uneasily, his ears swiveling back to listen as he stopped.

"Don't mind me, big boy," she said firmly as she patted the horse's neck to reassure him. "Just because I'm frightened of my own shadow doesn't mean you must be, too."

Again the horse nickered, but at least he began walking again. Rachel cradled her musket in her arms and held her little compass up to the fading light. It was going to be bad enough to be traveling by dark, and the last thing she needed was to be lost, as well.

The trail grew steeper, rising past a huge outcropping of granite, when she heard the noise again. But even as she turned she heard the gunshot, close enough that she could smell the powder. Proudfoot heard it, too, and rose squealing with alarm. Caught off-balance, Rachel slid from the saddle into the snow, her musket landing far to her right.

Though the snow had broken her fall, she still had dropped hard enough to knock the wind from her chest, and she gasped painfully as she struggled for air. She tried to push herself up at least to her knees. The black-and-white world around her spun crazily, and she clutched her stomach, rolling back to the snow with her eyes squeezed shut.

Not the baby, she thought wildly. *Please, God, please, don't let me lose Jamie's baby now!*

She heard something thumping, and thought it was her heart. No, that couldn't be, for there was a rasping, rhythmic breathing with it, coming closer each second to where she lay. She forced herself to open her eyes, just in time to see a bearded man in dirty buckskins drop down over her.

She screamed, and the man's arm curled tight around her waist. He rolled back to his feet, dragging her upright with him. She couldn't see his face, could only feel the arm binding her too tightly around her waist and the prickle of his beard against her neck, and the dizziness made her stagger against him.

"Hold still, you foolish bitch, and quit your thrashing," he rasped into her ear. "Do you want him to kill us both?"

"Who?" she gasped, struggling to find her footing. *"Who?"*

"Who'd you think, you—"

The dry sound of the second shot echoed against the granite. The man's words changed into an odd grunt as his chest jerked hard against hers. Then they were both in the snow again, his body heavy and lifeless as granite on top of hers. Sobbing with fear and panic, she fought to crawl free of him, her skirts tangled between her legs.

"Rachel!"

And then Jamie was there, pulling the dead man from her and taking her into his arms, holding her close and kissing her forehead and making her forget her fear in the sanctuary of his arms.

"Are you unhurt, lass?" he demanded, turning her tearstreaked face up toward his. "The fall from the horse—does anything hurt?"

She shook her head, her breath still too tight in her chest. "I—I don't think so. Oh, Jamie, I—" She broke off abruptly, pressing her hand gingerly over her belly, and the tears welled up again. "Oh, Jamie, I'm going to have a baby, your baby, and if anything's happened . . ."

"I know you are, love," he said softly, and pulled her back against his chest. "I've been waiting for you to tell me."

Bewildered, she pushed back to see his face. "But how could you know?"

"The same ways you do, Rachel," he said, but then his face darkened and she dreaded what was coming. "And if anything happens to this baby, it's your fault and no one else's. What the hell have you been doing out here today, anyway?"

She swallowed hard, not wanting to explain. "Where's Billy?"

"With the Bowmans. Don't try to distract me. Now, where were you, Rachel?"

"I left the note," she said haltingly. "I told you. I had someplace I had to go."

"I know, and I wasn't to worry," he said, his blue eyes as threatening as storm clouds. "What kind of secret is this that you can't tell me?"

"Jamie, I—"

"And what the hell kind of *secret* is it that takes you by yourself clear into British territory?"

She gasped as she suddenly understood. "You followed me, didn't you? You couldn't trust me enough to let me go alone, and so you followed me this whole day!"

"Not into the garrison I didn't, but be glad I was there waiting when you came out." He yanked the dead man over onto his back so she could see his face. "Did you know he and the other had been close on your heels the entire way?"

She shook her head. Now she remembered the rustling sounds behind her, Proudfoot's frightened nickers, the two rifle shots—

"You killed them, didn't you?" she asked, stunned. She scrambled free of him, her hands bunched in fists before her as she struggled to control her fear now that she realized what had happened.

"It was an easy shot," he said behind her. "I wouldn't have done it otherwise. Rachel, the man had a knife, and he would have used it on you if I'd given him the chance. Damnation, I did it to *save* you!"

"But I didn't know that!" she cried as she spun to face him, and stopped short at the bleak, desperate look on his face that she remembered from when he'd told her about his family and what had happened at Cherry Valley.

"Rachel, I didn't want to do it," he said, pleading with her in a harsh, rough whisper. "I don't want to kill anymore. But when it was you who was in danger, I had to do it. I didn't want to, but I did it to save you."

Her anger melted away, leaving nothing but the core of sorrow in her heart.

"Jamie, my love," she began, taking a step toward him. She lifted her arms out to him, and as she did the knotted napkin with Alec's reward fell from her pocket and into the snow at her feet.

To her horror he bent and plucked it up before she could. Frowning, he undid the knots until the linen cloth fell open and the small pile of silver reflected the last of the setting sun. For a long time he stared down at it while Rachel's heart sank lower and lower.

"Oh, Rachel," he said softly. "And you said the gold didn't matter."

She rushed forward, grabbing his arm, wanting to make him understand and make the awful, frozen look disappear from his face. "You don't understand, Jamie, it's not mine, it's Alec's, and I—"

"I understand, Rachel," he said quietly as retied the napkin and placed it back in her hand. "I understand everything."

"Let me lift that for you, Rachel," said Jamie, taking the heavy kettle from her hand. "I don't want you injuring yourself or the child."

"Thank you, Jamie," she said shyly, stepping back from the hearth. "I appreciate it."

But though she smiled warmly he avoided meeting her eyes, hooking the kettle in place and returning to cleaning his rifle instead. Her smile crumpled away, rejected the same way he'd rejected every overture she'd made in the week since they'd returned. He wasn't mean tempered or sarcastic, the way William would have been, and he never openly accused her of anything. Each night when he climbed into the big curtained bed beside her, he would kiss her on the forehead and solemnly bid her good-night, and then turn away, offering nothing but his broad back for comfort.

He was kind and endlessly patient with Billy, and he continued to do his share and more of the work on the farm. When the Bowmans came to visit, he'd accepted their good-natured gibes about impending fatherhood with the bashful laughter that was expected, and he continued to be so solicitous of Rachel's condition that Mary took Rachel aside to tell her again what a prize her new husband was.

A prize to everyone but her, she thought as she fought back the tears yet again. No matter what she did, he was making the gap between them wider and wider until there would be nothing to bridge the polite, yawning emptiness. In her darkest hours she wondered if somehow Jamie already knew about William, and that this was his way of dealing with it. She hadn't begun to do that herself.

All she knew for certain was that she was more lonely now than she'd ever been before he'd come into her life, and that if she didn't try to do something, anything, now, she'd go mad from it.

She pulled off her apron and sat in the chair opposite his, keeping her hands in her lap so he wouldn't see how they shook.

"Jamie, talk to me," she begged, no pride left. "Please, just—just talk to me."

He looked up at her without lifting his chin, the firelight picking out the red in his hair. "We talk all the time, Rachel," he said evenly. "Is there something particular you wish to discuss?"

"But it isn't like it was between us, Jamie," she said forlornly. "We used to talk on and on, and you'd tease me and I would laugh and—and it was very nice. I wish we could do that again."

His gaze dropped back down to the rifle. "I'm not stopping you."

"Jamie, please, you've never given me a chance to explain!" she cried wildly, then dropped her voice as she remembered Billy sleeping in his trundle. "I went to that garrison because of Alec! He sells the gossip he overhears in the taverns to the British, but he doesn't dare go himself and so he forces me to go instead, since he says no one will suspect a woman!"

He sighed, and set the rag down on the edge of the table. "Rachel, that is the most ridiculous tale I have ever heard. How can Alec force you to do anything as reckless as trading secrets with your enemy? Do you know the penalty if you'd been caught?"

"They'd hang me," she said, eager to continue now that he was actually listening. "Alec doesn't leave me a choice, Jamie. He blackmails me. Last year he wouldn't give me food or grain unless I did it."

"Ethan told me he helped you out last winter. He never mentioned anything about Alec blackmailing you."

Rachel leaned forward. "That's because I didn't tell him. I was too ashamed of what I'd done, and frightened that I'd be caught."

Jamie waited, unconvinced, and desperately she plunged ahead. "I swore I'd never do it again, but this time he told me first he'd take Billy from me, and then that he'd betray you to the British. I had to do it, Jamie. I couldn't let him harm you. That money is his, not mine. I never intended to squander it on fancy stockings or whatever else you think I was going to use it for."

"Then why is the money still in our house?"

She looked up at the bundled coins where they'd sat all this week on the chimneypiece, a silent testimony to her guilt. But at least he'd said *our* house; that was a good sign. "I keep hoping Alec will come for it, and then he can explain it all to you. You'll see then that I'm telling the truth."

"You want me to trust the word of the man who blackmailed you?" he asked slowly. "You want me to believe him when he vouches for my *wife?*"

She winced, since that was precisely what she wanted him to do. "All Alec wants is the money."

Jamie rose to take the knot of coins from the chimneypiece, and tossed it on the table before Rachel. "Did you count them?"

"No," she said warily. "Why should I? I told you, it's not my money."

"It's not mine, either, but I counted it. There are twenty coins in there, Rachel. Twenty dollars. Did you have any notion of what little secret you were selling to the British this time?"

She felt the blood drain from her cheeks. "It can't be," she murmured. "Not even Alec would have sent me to do that."

Yet it was exactly what Alec would have done, and she knew it. To earn the reward he'd always wanted, to remove the rival from his brother's bed, to teach her an unforgettable lesson: all of it bore Alec's stamp. The two men from the garrison that Jamie had killed had only been following her so she could lead them to Jamie.

She bowed her head, appalled by the depth of her own dangerous ignorance. "Forgive me, Jamie," she whispered wretchedly. "I've no right even to ask, but I swear I didn't know, else I would have killed myself first. Oh, merciful heaven, how can you bear to stay with me?"

"Because you are my wife, and I love you beyond all else," he said heavily. "When we wedded, I promised before God that I would be a loving and faithful husband to you. But you're making it hard, Rachel, damned hard. You've lied to me, and betrayed me, and kept your troubles and secrets to yourself instead of sharing them with me so we can solve them together."

He reached down over her bent head and gently smoothed her hair back from her ear. "If you can't bring yourself to trust me, sweetheart, then all the laughter and teasing and silk dressing gowns in the world aren't going to save us."

"I love you, Jamie," she whispered without looking up. "You have to believe that much of me. I love you so much!"

He sighed, and she felt his lips warm on the back of her neck. "And I love you, too, Rachel. But no more lies, and no more secrets. Is that too much to ask?"

Yet even as she shook her head, she felt the blackest despair sweep over her. She loved Jamie more than she'd ever love any other man, and she desperately wanted to be the wife he deserved. But how could she ever find the words to confess that the marriage she cherished so dearly had been a lie from the start?

Chapter Sixteen

With his feet braced on the first rail he'd repaired this morning, Jamie dragged the top rail of the fence into place and stood back to admire his work. He wiped his sleeve across his brow and took a long drink of the spring water in the jug. It was warm for April, warm enough that for the first time in months he was working outdoors without a coat, and the cool breeze on his bare forearms and throat felt good. The snow was finally beginning to melt, with patches of brown soil visible at last here and there over the hillside. Icicles long enough to nearly reach the ground hung from every rafter, or at least they did until Billy smashed them off to use as wet, brittle swords.

"Can I try th' fence now, Papa?" begged Billy. "Please?"

"If you must," said Jamie. "Just be sure to hold on tight, or this horse will toss you for certain."

He lifted the boy up to straddle the top rail. The newly split wood was still flexible, and as Billy swung his legs the rail bounced up and down beneath him like a spring. Billy giggled, swinging his legs faster as his blond curls tossed, and behind him Jamie surreptitiously added a bit more bounce with his hand, grinning himself at the delight the boy found in such a simple game.

"Shall we show Mama how well you can ride now?" asked Jamie, and Billy nodded vigorously.

"Ma-ma!" he roared with all the strength of his three-year-old lungs until Jamie clapped his hand firmly over his mouth.

"Not like that, you loudmouthed little rogue," scolded Jamie benignly as Billy giggled against his hand. "I want you to fetch your mama here so she can see the progress we've made on the fence today, not stand here and bellow like the village bull. Now go on, ask her nicely."

Fondly Jamie watched the boy run down the hillside, stumbling only twice before he reached the stone wall where Rachel sat with her mending in her lap, or at least where her lap used to be. Jamie's smile grew tight as he thought of how much happier things had been between him and Rachel when that child had been conceived, and as he waited for her and Billy to walk slowly up to him, he prayed they'd be happier again by the time the baby was born.

He held his hand out to draw her up the last few steps, and she smiled at him, that bright, green-eyed smile that could so effortlessly stop his heart. Impulsively he leaned across the fence and kissed her, delighting in how she fluttered with surprise in his arms before she settled, her lips eagerly parting for him. Perhaps, he thought with fresh hope, things weren't quite as bad as he'd feared.

"I thought you wished me here to view your fence," she said breathlessly, her cheeks pink.

"I did," he said softly, "but then you looked so much lovelier than the fence, I decided to kiss you instead."

She laughed, a sound he hadn't heard nearly enough. "At least you won't get splinters from me," she teased. "But as for lovely—Lord, I'm looking more and more like a pumpkin every day."

He dared to rest his hand on the soft swell of her belly. "A very lovely pumpkin, love," he said tenderly. "Especially since you're mine."

He saw it then again, the flicker of panic in her eyes that came and went so fast he wanted to believe he'd imagined it. "Oh, Jamie, I do love you," she said with a desperate edge to her voice that made no sense. "Whatever else may happen to us, I want you to know that."

"Of course I know it," he said, bewildered. Mary had warned him that pregnancy could make Rachel moody or intemperate; perhaps this was what she'd meant. "Just as I hope you know how much I love you."

She smiled again, but the joy had left her face as she helped Billy climb to the top rail to show off his riding skills. But he'd barely settled on his steed when he suddenly clambered off again, rushing to cling to Jamie's legs.

"What is it, lamb?" asked Rachel with concern, bending down to the boy's level.

But Jamie already knew. Four men were coming up the hillside toward them, two white men on horseback and two Indians, Senecas, following on foot. The first man was Alec Lindsey, and immediately Jamie's rifle was in his hand, until Rachel's hand on his arm stopped him. Without turning from the men, she shook her head in an unspoken plea, and grudgingly Jamie let it slip to the ground by the fence.

The second man's face was hidden in the shadow of his hat, but there was something disconcertingly familiar about how he sat on his horse. To his surprise Rachel stepped forward to greet them, though her back was ramrod straight and her hands were clasped tightly over her apron.

Alec swept off his hat with a gallant flourish and, not to be outdone, the second man did, as well. At last the sun caught him full in the face, and Jamie's world shattered into a thousand irreparable pieces.

"Come along, Rachel, no kiss for your prodigal husband?" said William as he swung himself down from his horse. He was older and shabbier than Jamie had imagined him, not nearly the match that Rachel deserved. "You've Alec to thank, too, for springing me so convenient. He said after seeing me at Dancer's, you couldn't bear to be apart from me another day. Now tell me it's so, Rachel, and welcome me home proper."

She's seen him before, when she went to the British, thought Jamie wildly. *She's known William was alive at least since then. But did she know sooner than that? A week, a month, a year? Did she know when she agreed to the sham of their wedding?*

"Tell me you missed me yourself, Rachel," ordered William, moving to slip his arm around her shoulders. "Welcome me home proper, eh, wife?"

Lord help him, she wasn't his wife. She wasn't his, and never had been.

"No, William, not now," said Rachel, her whole body turning as stiff as if she'd been carved from wood. "Please not now."

Alec had dismounted, too, and was staring pointedly at her apron. "I'd say we didn't get you home quite soon enough, William," he said cynically. "Your loving wife seems to have given you a splendid new rack of antlers and plumped her belly with a bastard, too."

It isn't a bastard. It was his child, his son or daughter, his and Rachel's.

Rachel's face was deathly pale, her hands spread over her belly to shield the child within from Alec's crudeness.

Stunned, William now stared at her, too. "Now this was deuced unkind of you, Rachel," he said, grabbing her arm. "Who's the father, eh? Or do you even know?"

"Leave Mama alone!" shrieked Billy, and before Jamie could stop him he had hurled himself at William's leg, flailing away with both fists and his teeth for good measure.

With a yowl of pain, William released Rachel, and Rachel grabbed Billy and held him tight in her arms. With a sobbing sniff Billy snuggled close.

Rubbing his shin, William leaned warily closer to peer at Billy. "Strong-willed little devil, ain't he?" he said sternly. "Don't look at me like that, boy. I'm your papa, and you'd best learn to obey me now."

"No!" wailed Billy, shrinking away from him and farther into Rachel's arms. "You're not my papa!"

But he was. The resemblance was as strong as any father's and son's could be. No one could doubt that they were bound by blood, bound together in a way Jamie would never be.

The woman he'd thought was his wife belonged to another man, the son he'd loved as his own would never call him Papa again, the unborn child he'd longed to hold in his arms was branded an unwanted bastard, even the home he'd thought was his was gone....

In the space of three minutes he had lost everything that mattered, and he couldn't bear to stay here and watch the man who'd taken it all away. Without a word Jamie turned and left, walking, almost running, up the hill and toward the woods and away from the heartache that was destroying him.

"Papa!" screamed Billy desperately. "Papa, don't leave!"

"Jamie, come back!" cried Rachel. "Jamie!"

Alec sniffed with contempt. "I'd say the brat's fingered the culprit, William," he said. "At least he's saving you the trouble of running him off your place."

Rachel wheeled around to face him, her eyes on fire. "How could you be so heartless?" she demanded. "I always knew you were a low, vile man, Alec Lindsey, but I never dreamed you'd do *this!*"

As she spoke Billy wriggled free, determined to run after Jamie. He'd taken only three short steps before William grabbed him. "Come here, little William, and mind your manners with your papa."

"You're not my papa," sobbed the boy as he fought to free himself. "Jamie's my papa, not you! I hate you! *Mama!*"

But Rachel was already running after Jamie herself. Her side hurt and her breath was short, but still she ran harder than she'd ever run. If she didn't catch Jamie now, she might lose him forever. Finally she reached him, at the top of the hill where the fields ended and the forest began, and where he'd stopped for one final look at the family he'd lost.

"Jamie, oh, my poor love!" she gasped as she threw her arms around his waist. "I'd no idea William would dare come back like this!"

Roughly Jamie tried to push her away. "Go back to him, Rachel. He's your husband, not me."

"Not in the ways that matter!" she cried. "Jamie, please, don't turn me away!"

"Did you know he lived when I asked you to be my wife?"

"No!" She shook her head, desperate to convince him. "I swear to it, Jamie, by all that's holy that I didn't! It wasn't until later, much later, that—"

"Then why in God's name didn't you tell me?"

"Because I loved you too much to lose you!" she cried wildly. "Oh, Jamie, I knew you would leave if you knew the truth, and I—"

They both heard the scream at the same moment, the high-pitched scream of a terrified child, both jerking around to look back to where they'd left Billy.

And like a nightmare that is done in an instant, what happened next was something that Rachel would always remember. The two Indians, forgotten before, suddenly came forward to where William was trying to hang on to Billy. With a lethal, fluid grace, the taller Seneca swung his tomahawk through the air and struck

William in the back of the head. William slumped forward to his knees as the Seneca grabbed Billy from his hands. Alec struggled to draw the pistol from his belt, but the second, larger Indian had already struck him, too, though with the flat of his belt ax and not the edge. Effortlessly he hauled Alec's limp body over the neck of his frightened horse and clambered into the saddle himself. He reached down and took Billy from the first man, who then knelt beside William's body and with his knife deftly cut away his scalp.

"No!" gasped Rachel in horror as she tried to run back to save Billy. "Dear God, *no!*"

Swiftly Jamie clapped his hand across her mouth, dragging her back. "Stay, lass, and be quiet," he said urgently. "Let them forget we're here. We'll be no use if they take us, too."

With William's bloody scalp hanging from his hand, the second Seneca swung himself onto the other horse and pulled Billy onto his lap. The two sent their war cries echoing across the empty field, then dug their heels into the horses' sides and thundered away.

"They have Billy," sobbed Rachel as soon as Jamie uncovered her mouth. She sagged against him, overcome with grief and the horror of what she'd just witnessed. "Oh, Jamie, why couldn't we have stopped them?"

And as Jamie held her, the answer was appallingly obvious. There, leaning against the new section of the new fence, only a few feet away from William's body, was his rifle, the brasses winking in the sun. For the first time since the war had begun he had left the gun behind, and here, now, was the grim consequence.

"We'll get Billy back, Rachel," promised Jamie, and he'd never meant anything more in his life. "We'll get him back."

Rachel insisted on coming with him, though he told her he'd be faster without her. She told him he was wrong, that with Billy's life at stake he'd be the one who'd have to keep up with her. He reminded her of the risk to their unborn child, and she swore she wouldn't abandon her first child for the sake of the second.

And when he climbed onto Proudfoot's back, she was there with him.

In the snow the tracks of the two horses were easy to follow, and Jamie and Rachel rode after them until it was nearly dusk. Then, abruptly, the horseshoe tracks stopped, and soon after they found the horses themselves, both blown from exhaustion and abandoned to stand shivering in the snow.

"We'll have them now, lass," said Jamie, crouching down to study the fresh moccasin tracks in the snow. "Alec must be conscious enough to be able to walk by now, but I'll warrant he'll still hold them back."

"Maybe they'll leave him behind, too," said Rachel, still on Proudfoot. "Like they did the horses."

Jamie shook his head. "If they did, then he's dead."

Rachel said nothing, too clearly remembering William's mutilated body.

Jamie patted her knee. "Remember that they don't know they're being followed," he said. "They're not in any hurry, and we are. We're bound to catch them soon."

Rachel nodded, and with all her soul prayed that Jamie was right.

"You filthy savages," croaked Alec as soon as Manapog yanked the gag from his mouth. "So this is how you repay your masters, eh?"

"Drink," ordered Manapog, handing Alec a wooden flask. "Drink now."

"You like giving the orders for a change, don't you, you flea-bitten buggers," said Alec, struggling to hold the flask with his wrists bound. "Cut these ties, damn you!"

The look Manapog exchanged with Chepatachet spoke volumes. They left Alec's wrists bound, Manapog in particular enjoying the sight of Alec's struggles.

They'd made a small fire, here in the shelter of a stone wall, and Chepatachet roasted strips of meat from the rabbit they'd killed earlier. He wanted the little boy to eat. He was too silent for a child, huddled in the blanket they'd given him, and Chepatachet feared he would weaken and die if he didn't eat. He'd wanted the boy from the moment he'd seen him with the woman at Volk's tavern, wanted him as a slave for his mother, who loved such English baubles.

All that Manapog wanted were the scalps of the two blond brothers who had seduced his younger sister for their pleasures, then let her sicken and die from their diseases. He turned William's scalp before the fire, the trophy already lashed inside a willow ring for safekeeping, and considered how long he'd torture the older brother before he took his scalp, too.

Rachel crawled along the rock beside Jamie. The Senecas had camped in the shelter of a hillside, surrounded by trees and rocks, and Rachel and Jamie were able to watch them from above. "You were right," she whispered excitedly. "Oh, there's Billy!"

Jamie laid his finger across her lips to silence her, and put his hand out to take her musket. They would have to count on surprise as their best bet. The two Senecas had rifles much like his, and he didn't doubt they knew how to use them. Once he fired, they'd know where he was, and by the time he'd reloaded, he and Rachel would be dead. Instead he would fire first the rifle, then Rachel's musket, and pray he made both shots count. Rachel would get Billy, and as for Alec, Jamie planned simply to leave him here, his wrists bound with rawhide and without a weapon, and let his fate fall to someone—or something—else.

"Are you ready, lass?" he whispered, and when she nodded, he kissed her quickly for luck. She grinned and eased herself off the rock and into the darkness to wait.

Manapog bent over the fire and turned the sticks with the rabbit pieces to cook more evenly.

Jamie steadied his rifle on the edge of the rock, and fired. Without even waiting to see if he'd hit the tall brave, he grabbed the musket, rolling to one side beyond the gunpowder smoke for a clearer shot, and fired again.

From the shadows of the trees Rachel heard the rifle's shot, and saw how the first Indian flew back off his feet from the impact, and then lay still, the skewered meat still clutched in his fingers. Immediately the second brave reached for his rifle and aimed at the place where the first shot had come from.

Rachel gasped, fighting back the urge to shout a warning to Jamie. What if he missed, she thought wildly, what if her musket misfired, what—

The second gunshot tore through the night, and the second Seneca spun and fell over his own rifle.

Immediately Rachel ran through the snow-covered brush to the clearing and to Billy, so small and frightened as he huddled in the dirty blanket.

But even as she saw his eyes light with recognition as she called his name, Alec staggered between them, reaching Billy before Rachel. Swiftly he looped his bound wrists over the little boy's head and jerked him back, the thongs biting into the child's pale throat.

"I know you mean to kill me next, Ryder!" rasped Alec, his gaze darting along the rocks where he knew Jamie must be. "But would you risk the brat's life to take mine?"

"Let him go, Alec," begged Rachel as she stepped into the glow of the firelight. "He's only a child. Hasn't he suffered enough this day? Please, please let him go!"

"Why should I, Rachel?" said Alec, his eyes wild as a madman's. "Why should I do anything to favor you? If you'd loved William like you should have, then he would still be alive now!"

Billy whimpered, clawing at the thong around his throat, and Alec pulled it sharply back.

High on the rocks in the shadows, Jamie hesitated. The shot was long, made more difficult by the uneven light and the way that Billy twisted and fought with Alec. Though he lay in the snow, he was sweating. Over and over again he saw the face of the boy he'd let die in Cherry Valley, his anguished eyes blending into Billy's.

He didn't want to fail again. *Lord, please, no more death, no more killing.*

Rachel edged closer. "Take me in his place, Alec. Let Billy go and take me instead. He won't dare shoot at me."

It happened too fast for her to react. Billy was scrambling across the ground, holding his throat and crying, and then Alec was jerking her back against him, lifting her off her feet so her own weight pulled the thong deeper into her neck. Her fingers scratched at the thong, but already she could feel it cutting off her air, her life, and that of her unborn child.

Why didn't Jamie help her? Why didn't he shoot?

With all her dwindling strength she shoved back against Alec, gulping for the air for a handful of words.

"Like...seeds...apple," she gasped, and then the shot came, and Alec swore, and she was falling forward, falling into nothingness, falling into Jamie's arms.

"You...did it," she gasped. "You did it."

He shook his head, holding her close. "No, love, I didn't," he said softly. "I couldn't."

And instead he pointed to the second Indian, his now-lifeless fingers still curled around the trigger of the smoking rifle.

Jamie lifted Billy into Rachel's arms, and as the little boy burrowed against her she rested her head wearily against Jamie's broad shoulder. "No more," she said. "It's finally done, isn't it, Jamie?"

"Aye, love," he said. "It is. Now let's go home."

Epilogue

Their daughter was born on the first of October, on a night with a full moon. She had a great deal of black hair and a most exuberant voice, and Jamie swore that already he could tell her eyes would be as green as her mother's.

Billy set Blackie and Whitie on the bed beside Rachel, and let them, too, inspect his new little sister.

"She's very beautiful, don't you think?" asked Jamie softly.

Billy rubbed his nose. "She's all wrinkly an' pink, an' she doesn't smell good."

"She'll improve," said Rachel, stroking her tiny daughter's cheek with her finger. "You certainly turned out well enough."

Billy nodded. "What's her name?"

"She doesn't have one yet," said Jamie. "Do you have any suggestions?"

Billy gently trotted his two horses a little closer along the coverlet. "I think Pinkie would be good, just like Blackie an' Whitie."

Somehow Rachel managed not to laugh as her gaze met Jamie's. "What was your mother's name?"

"Rebeckah."

She nodded. "And your sister's?"

"Sarajane."

"Then we'll name her Rebeckah Sarajane Ryder." Rachel's eyes filled with tears of joy as Jamie bent to kiss her.

"A fine name for a pretty little lass," he said softly. "Almost as pretty as her mother."

"How I love you, Jamie Ryder," she whispered. "How I love you!"

Billy sniffed. "I still like Pinkie better."

The tiny girl yawned and smiled and waved her little fists at her brother and the horses.

And Pinkie, to Billy's endless joy, was what they called her ever after.

* * * * *

Harlequin® Historical

From the Maggie Award-Winning Author of
FOOL'S PARADISE

Tori Phillips

comes the delightful tale of an ill-fated
noblewoman, and the would-be monk
who becomes her protector

SILENT KNIGHT

Don't miss this delightful Medieval, available in
November, wherever Harlequin Historicals are sold!

Look us up on-line at: http://www.romance.net

Merry Christmas, Baby!

A romantic collection filled with the magic
of Christmas and the joy of children.

SUSAN WIGGS, Karen Young and
Bobby Hutchinson bring you Christmas wishes,
weddings and romance, in a charming
trio of stories that will warm up your
holiday season.

MERRY CHRISTMAS, BABY! also contains
Harlequin's special gift to you—a set of
FREE GIFT TAGS included in every book.

Brighten up your holiday season with
MERRY CHRISTMAS, BABY!

Available in November at
your favorite retail store.

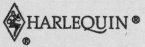

HARLEQUIN ®
®

Look us up on-line at: http://www.romance.net   MCB

HARLEQUIN ®

Scandals

A passionate story of romance, where bold, daring characters set out to defy their world of propriety and strict social codes.

"Scandals—a story that will make your heart race and your pulse pound. Spectacular!"
—Suzanne Forster

"Devon is daring, dangerous and altogether delicious."
—Amanda Quick

Don't miss this wonderful full-length novel from Regency favorite Georgina Devon.

Available in December, wherever Harlequin books are sold.

SCAN

Harlequin® Historical

In the spirit of the season,
Harlequin Historical brings you
two delightfully different holiday tales!

GIFT OF THE HEART

The new Sparhawk book from
award-winning author **Miranda Jarrett.**
The touching story of a wounded enemy
soldier who brings love and protection to an
abandoned woman and her young stepson.

BEAUTY AND THE BEAST

An enchanting new Regency tale
from **Taylor Ryan.** The unforgettable story
of a remarkable young woman who
teases, goads and inspires an injured
nobleman into regaining his health and
his will to live following a devastating fire.

Don't miss the chance to celebrate with
Harlequin Historical!

Look us up on-line at: http://www.romance.net

HHXMAS

The collection of the year!
NEW YORK TIMES BESTSELLING AUTHORS

Linda Lael Miller
Wild About Harry

Janet Dailey
Sweet Promise

Elizabeth Lowell
Reckless Love

Penny Jordan
Love's Choices

and featuring
Nora Roberts
The Calhoun Women

This special trade-size edition features four of the wildly
popular titles in the Calhoun miniseries together in
one volume—a true collector's item!

Pick up these great authors and a chance to win
a weekend for two in New York City at the
Marriott Marquis Hotel on Broadway! We'll pay
for your flight, your hotel—even a Broadway show!

Available in December at your favorite retail outlet.